DAYS

OF

LITTLE TEXAS

BY THE AUTHOR OF *TEACH ME*

R. A. Nelson

Alfred A. Knopf

NEW YORK

THIS IS A BORZOI BOOK PUBLISHED BY ALFRED A. KNOPF

Visit us on the Web! www.randomhouse.com/teens

Educators and librarians, for a variety of teaching tools, visit us at www.randomhouse.com/teachers

Library of Congress Cataloging-in-Publication Data

Nelson, R. A. (Russell A.)
Days of Little Texas / R. A. Nelson. — 1st ed.
        p. cm.
Summary: Sixteen-year-old Ronald Earl Pettway, who has been a charismatic evangelist since he was ten years old, is about to preach at a huge revival meeting on the grounds of an old plantation, where, with help from the ghost of a girl he could not heal, he becomes engaged in an epic battle between good and evil.
ISBN 978-0-375-85593-1 (trade) — ISBN 978-0-375-95593-8 (lib. bdg.)
ISBN 978-0-375-85361-6 (e-book)

[1. Evangelists—Fiction. 2. Ghosts—Fiction. 3. Christian life—Fiction. 4. Slavery—Fiction. 5. Good and evil—Fiction. 6. Supernatural—Fiction.] I. Title.
PZ7.N43586Day 2009
[Fic]—dc22
2008033855

The text of this book is set in 10-point Parable.

Printed in the United States of America
July 2009
10 9 8 7 6 5 4 3 2 1

First Edition

To Deborah Jean Nelson

≫ONE≪

There is this girl in my dream.

She has blond hair washing down her back, and eyes so blue it makes me want to pray. Only this isn't a praying dream.

I'm with the blond-headed girl in this big, empty farm-house. The rooms are large, and they go on and on.

"In my Father's house are many mansions."

The girl is covered with a bedsheet that billows and ripples. We walk around awhile till we come to a room painted all in white with a mattress on the floor. It puts me in mind of that story in the New Testament where Jesus tells the lame

1

man, "Take up thy bed and walk." We sit on the mattress together, and my heart puffs up like a maypop ready to pitch out all its seeds.

The blond-headed girl smiles the most beautiful smile I've ever seen. Then she drops the bedsheet, and she doesn't have any clothes on. Not one stitch. But—*oh Lord*—I'm buck naked, too.

I lay down alongside the naked girl, and we stretch out skin to skin. We look at each other a little while, not saying a word. Finally I have to reach over and *touch* her, and she feels so good and warm and soft, and I can't stop. Can't stop touching her. Then she touches *me.* Touches me in places nobody *ever* touched me before. Nobody. And the touching gets better and better till—

I wake up, and the devil is standing over me.

I nearly scream. But there is no devil; it's only one of Sugar Tom's suit coats hanging on the door. The real world floods back in—I'm in the motor home with him and Miss Wanda Joy. I look out my small window and see lights winking in the Alabama gloom.

I sneak to the other end of the motor home, heart near bursting from shame.

Do they know? Did they see? Hear anything?

But nobody else is awake. Thank the Lord it's still dark.

When I close my eyes again, all I can see is the lake of fire, big lumps of brimstone burning on its banks. And I feel like I'm dying.

≫TWO≪

Verbena, Alabama.

On the other side of the curtain, the crowd is rustling, murmuring in anticipation. I can hear them saying my name. But I'm not watching them. Through the saddle flap in the tent I can see fields of sorghum, heavy green in the June twilight. The air smells like something growing.

Sugar Tom grunts in his sleep. "Lord Jesus."

"Praise Him," I say.

Sugar Tom is eighty-seven years old today. When he's not preaching, he's liable to fall asleep anytime, anywhere. Tonight it's a rusty folding chair round back of the curtain, where the congregation can't see. His eyes are wriggling like mice under a bedsheet. His long legs are spraddled out in front of him, twitching like he's fixing to run right straight to glory.

I bet he's dreaming about South Dakota again.

See, Sugar Tom was a child evangelist just like me. He once shook hands with the great Billy Sunday. When he was my age, going on sixteen, he worked the revival circuit with Mordecai Ham all the way north to Sioux Falls and Rapid City. That's where he got his revival name, Sugar Tom Walker.

"'Cause all the gals thought my sermons were so sweet," he likes to say.

His hair looks like cuttings left on the barbershop floor. He has cornbread crumbs on his pants. That's what he asked for instead of a birthday cake. Sugar Tom believes South Dakota is heaven.

"Skies that reach right up to Canaan, Ronald Earl," he likes to tell me. "Grass like a woman's hair. Ponds blue as cornflowers. South Dakota is the place where the hand of the Almighty reached down to touch the world. It's where I'm going to die. Amen."

I inhale the outdoors one more time and feel for the knife in my pocket. I take it out and flick it open; the blade is cold on my fingers. I sit down next to Sugar Tom and whittle the chess piece I've been working on—a rook tall as my pinkie finger, carved out of white aspen. Whittling takes a lot of concentration. It generally helps me calm down before a service, but tonight my hands are shaking.

Because I'm a fraud.

I put the rook away but hang on to the knife, thinking how easy it would be to make a long cut in the canvas, slip off into the woods, and disappear. Forever.

But where would I go? How would I live? What would I do? Besides, Certain Certain is watching me. I can see him in the shadows over by the prayer box. His hair is speckled with dabs of white and shaped just like a halo. I put the knife away and watch him cross the pinewood stage.

"You need be thinking about the sermon," Certain Certain says, voice full of creek gravel.

"I know," I say.

But really I'm not. Witnessing for the Lord has always come natural to me. It has nothing to do with thinking.

"What's eatin' at you, boy?" he says.

"Nothing," I say.

This is the second time I've had that dream this week. Sooner or later somebody's going to find out how strange I am. Then it will all be over.

Certain Certain comes into the light of the drop cord and sinks down into a chair next to me.

Even after all this time, his mouth can still make me flinch. Part of his top lip was once blown off by a bullet, and it never healed up quite right. Underneath you can see the stumps of broken black teeth and gums red as death in the sunshine. Years ago Certain Certain was shot climbing out a woman's bedroom window in Corinth, Mississippi.

"I turned back to look at her," Certain Certain says, "like Lot's wife turned back to look at the destruction of Sodom. I didn't turn into no pillar of salt, but that gal's husband rained the fire of hell on me. And that's when I gave my life over to the Lord."

Certain Certain is the only name I've ever known him by. He's descended from South Carolina slaves and wears a brass slave tag round his neck to prove it. The tag is engraved PEMBROKE PLANTATION, SERVANT 653, 1851. Certain Certain says his great-great-great-granddaddy had to wear it whenever he went to town so he wouldn't get whipped or sold as a runaway.

Certain Certain is somewhere around sixty. Nearly twice the age our Lord and Savior was when they nailed Him to the cross. But he's still powerful strong. He grabs hold of my arm. His big hand is warm and moist, and his breath smells like the Crown Prince Kipper Snacks he always eats for lunch.

"I reckon I know what's bothering you," he says. "Every rooster ever lived thinks the whole world turns on them pretty little gals. Always have, always will. You think you the first boy ever discovered his ping-a-ling?" His laugh sounds like a bark.

I look away, face burning. "Turn me loose," I say.

He lets me go, still grinning.

"Let me tell you something, Lightning." Certain Certain

calls me Lightning on account of how I got the name Little Texas. "I know what you goin' through. Nothing to be ashamed of. Most natural thing in the world. That's your problem. Don't know nothing 'bout the real world even though you gettin' to be a man. And a man who don't know anything about women is useless as tits on a boar hog."

Sugar Tom snorts, but his eyes are still closed.

"'Abstain from fleshly lusts, which war against the soul,'" he mumbles.

I stand and brush wood shavings off my leg, feeling the blood come up in my face.

"You got to learn to *control* it," Certain Certain says. "That's all. When I was your age, I didn't have nothing like no control. Shoot. Every spare chance I got, there we'd go, back behind the woodshed—"

"Hey, I . . . I don't want to talk about it."

"Well. If you ever *do* want to talk about it, I'm right here."

I walk away from him and take a peek around the curtain at the congregation.

Lord.

They kill me. The shape of their legs in the white dresses. The way the material pushes away from their skin in places. The softness of their faces, eyes big as barn owls', hungry, wet. Bare toes in sandals. I notice how their bodies shift in their seats, how they whisper to the girl next to them. I feel it all like a burning cord running straight from their chests to my stomach.

CHAPTER

≫ THREE ≪

Miss Wanda Joy's standing in the back of the tent ushering in stragglers and handing out scripture. Miss Wanda Joy is a tall woman, big-boned and straight as a loblolly pine. Her hair is pulled way up and over the top of her head, then it waterfalls down her back, all the way to the green bow in her white dress.

Was she ever pretty? I don't imagine so. Still, you can't help but stare. Her eyes are like buckeyes, hard and black and shiny. Sugar Tom calls them "arresting."

Miss Wanda Joy is my "mother by deed, not by seed." That's how she puts it. She's really my great-aunt, and only by

8

marriage, but she's real proud when folks mistake her for the mother of Little Texas.

I reckon I love her. I know that sounds funny, but Miss Wanda Joy is a hard person to love. She only lets you go so far and no farther. But she took me in when nobody else would. I know she cares about me, but she always expects things to go her way, and when they don't, she can flare up hot as melted plastic.

Miss Wanda Joy's got me wearing Sugar Tom's pin-striped suit tonight. If I straighten my arms at my sides, my hands almost disappear up the sleeves. My pant legs are bunched on top of my shoes.

"People expect to see *Little* Texas," she says. "The preaching prodigy. You're growing too fast. If they stop coming, we stop eating. It's as simple as that."

Miss Wanda Joy always ties my tie too tight. I put a finger inside my collar and give it a tug, trying to give myself a little room to breathe.

Sugar Tom bolts upright in his chair.

"Where's the Book?"

He always wakes up raring to go. Certain Certain takes the Bible from the prayer box and hands it to me—a big old King James that Sugar Tom has had for fifty years. It hangs open across my hand like a bird with broken wings.

Sugar Tom coughs to wake up his big voice and says "Glory" into his hand a couple of times. He winks at me and slips out from behind the curtain. The people clap and holler;

they know what's coming. Sugar Tom pulls himself up to his full height in front of the pulpit. He never needs a microphone.

"Good evening, brothers and sisters, on this day the Lord hath made."

Sugar Tom starts his witnessing slow, quoting scripture, but pretty soon he does what the best of us evangelists do, lets it rip. Faster and faster, louder and louder. Before you know it, he's worked the congregation into a frenzy, roaring like a righteous hurricane.

"When the spirit of the Lord, *ah!* comes down to you, *ah!* I say, my brothers and sisters, *ah!* It's not a thing you can control, *ah!* It's like the ocean, *ah!* It's like the Bay of Fun-dy, *ah!* But you never can tell, *ah!* I say, you never can tell, *ah!* when or where the wave, *ah!* is going to hit, *ah!* You must ride it, *ah!* you must ride it, *ah!* when it comes, *ah!*"

You would think he was forty years younger. That's what happens when the Holy Spirit comes into me. Lifts me up till I'm strong as ten thousand Philistines.

Some are standing now, swaying next to their seats, arms in the air, shouting, "Yes, yes!" and "Amen!"

Sugar Tom finishes up.

"And now, *ah!* I want to bring one out to you, *ah!* One whom you all know, *ah!* One who has seen the glory of the judgment seat, *ah!* One who has witnessed the rebuilding of the Tabernacle, *ah!* One who has been sanctified by the blood of the Lamb, *ah!*"

Here we go.

"Little Texaaaaaasss!"

My knees feel like they are locking up, and my throat is closing off.

Too late to run. I gobble one last, shuddery breath, then step out from the curtain. Even after all this time, I am never quite ready for the screams.

"LITTLE TEXAS! LITTLE TEXAS! LITTLE TEXAS!"

A wind from the sorghum fields hits me, and the pages of Sugar Tom's Bible flap all the way from Leviticus to First Corinthians. And I begin.

CHAPTER

FOUR

I'm never sure what's going to come out of my mouth during a service. Tonight, to get my courage up, I start the easiest way I know how. At the beginning. My life before joining up with the Church of the Hand. First, to help the words come, I close my eyes and remember.

CHAPTER

 FIVE

Covington, Georgia.

We live in a trailer next door to the Oxnard Chemical Company. I can only remember the world ever smelling like one thing: Magic Markers. I don't know if I'm five or six years old.

"We don't keep up with birthdays much around here, little man," Daddy says.

He's big, always sweating, has hair the color of nighttime. "Half Cherokee," Daddy tells people.

Today we're working under the trailer. There's cobwebs and mud dauber nests and creepy places only a snake would like. Daddy is doing something with the long tubes of light that are shining under the bottom of the trailer.

"Walmart sunshine," he says, and laughs. "That's what makes the plants to grow."

Daddy's plants have pointed green leaves and are shaped like a hand with long fingers. "Don't ever tell anybody about these plants," he says, saying *shhhh* to his finger. "They're magic plants, Ronald Earl."

But I know he's told some folks about the magic plants. I've seen them come at night to buy them. Men with cuts on their faces. Laughing boys with tattoos on their big arms. Skinny, quiet girls. Daddy keeps me in the trailer when he's doing business. But I watch from the windows. I'm always watching.

Momma is short and heavy with skin the color of cracker crumbs and hair that blows in the breeze like feathers. She mostly sleeps a lot and listens to country music.

Momma calls me "my little accident." Like I'm a car wreck. I don't have any brothers or sisters, and there is nobody else to play with. I can't wait to start going to school, on account of watching the school bus go by. All those kids inside. I think it will be fun.

Sometimes my great-aunt, Miss Wanda Joy King, comes around.

"Women would kill for your complexion," she always says to me. "It's your father's Indian mixed with your mother's Swedish. Your mother is Swedish. Did you know that, Ronald Earl?"

"Church Lady!" Daddy calls her when she leaves. He won't let Miss Wanda Joy take us to services. "More hair than brains," he says.

After we're done under the trailer, Daddy pushes me in my swing in the yard.

"Don't be a pussy, Ronald Earl," he says. I know being a pussy is not a good thing, on account of the look on his face. "All you have to do is let go of the chains, and you will fly. You'll like it." He pushes me higher and higher, but I can't never let go. I start crying. Daddy cusses, calls me a pussy again, and stops pushing.

Our yard is nearly high as me in weeds. You never can tell what you might find. Pieces of cars, a Coca-Cola sign, cinder blocks, a sling blade. One morning there is a fat man with a beard lying in throw-up right next to my seesaw.

Our dog, Rusty, will just as soon bite your hand off as lick it, Daddy says. Sometimes men fight in the middle of the night in the gravel drive. Rusty barks and barks.

Tonight we drive the truck to another man's place where Daddy says the man is clearing land for a footer. I don't know what a footer is. There is hickory firewood stacked between two trees in the headlights. The ends of the logs are all in circles. Daddy says to hurry before anybody sees. I tote as much as I can carry, and we pitch it in till the truck is full.

Another night I wake up, and a red light is moving on the walls. I get up to look out the window, and Daddy is there. A man even bigger than Daddy and wearing a uniform is pushing

Daddy's head into the sheriff's car. Another man with a long pole puts something on Rusty's neck and hauls him away. I go outside and see that the secret door to Daddy's magic plants is open. His plants have all been cut down.

Daddy is gone a long time, and finally he's just *gone.*

Miss Wanda Joy comes around. I'm sitting on the floor in the living room eating the marshmallow parts of the Lucky Charms straight out of the box.

"Where is your mother?" Miss Wanda Joy says.

I take her big hand and we head to the back, and I show her Momma laying in bed in her pink nightgown. Miss Wanda Joy jerks her up and calls her things and tells her Bible things. Momma goes back to sleeping, and Miss Wanda Joy goes away again.

A tall man comes to visit Momma. He stays awhile, laughing in her room. More men come. Not all of them laugh, but they keep coming.

Momma sleeps with the radio on. One day when I wake up, I don't hear music coming out of her room. I open the door and she's not there. I eat two bananas and a spotty apple clean to the core. The Lucky Charms box is full of camel flies.

It's so quiet everywhere.

I watch for Momma. I walk up and down the trailer, looking out all the windows. I don't like going in the bathroom anymore, the way it is now. I go in the bushes instead. Miss Wanda Joy catches me and tells me she's going to jerk a knot in my tail. But she doesn't after she takes me inside and sees.

16

Then she calls the sheriff. He comes over, and she tells him some things. They're sitting in the living room talking quiet. But I can hear what they're saying.

"But where *is* she?" Miss Wanda Joy says over and over. "His father's in prison. I'm his only other living relative. How could she have just gone away?"

Miss Wanda Joy stays the night. The next morning she cleans and cleans, and I help.

The next day the sheriff comes again.

"They found her ten miles from here, Miss King," he says. "With a man in his house."

"A man?"

"Old boy was running a meth lab," the sheriff says. "I don't think your niece intended to abandon the child. There was a fire. . . ."

"What are you saying?" Miss Wanda Joy says.

"I'm saying . . . there was a fire. And no one got out."

Miss Wanda Joy beats her fist on the kitchen table. She beats it so hard, the legs are jumping. "That little *fool*. The stupid little fool."

The sheriff says he's sorry and leaves.

Miss Wanda Joy gets up from the table. "Get your things, Ronald Earl," she says.

"Where's Momma?" I say.

"You're coming to live with me," Miss Wanda Joy says.

She gets my clothes and lets me bring some of my other things in a box she gives me. It's a box that some shoes came in.

CHAPTER

 SIX

I know without even looking, most of the women in the congregation are already crying. Now it's time to tell them. Tell
them about the day of my anointing.

The day I found my name.

⇒ SEVEN ⇐

San Angelo, Texas.

Now I'm ten years old, sitting at a picnic table with Sugar Tom and Certain Certain.

I can see a sun-blinded lake, bass boats racing by a gray wooden dock. We're here to bring the gospel of our Lord Jesus Christ to the World-Famous Lake Nasworthy Lamblast and Chili Cook-off.

I've spent the morning earning my keep, helping Certain Certain, running errands, setting up folding chairs, hauling water. This is the first chance I've had to sit down all day.

"You know why Lake Nasworthy is world famous?" Sugar

Tom is saying. He taps a skinny paperback book laying on the table with a bony finger. "I've read about it right here in *Stories of the Strange.* In the 1960s a boy jumped off that very dock and came up covered in water moccasins."

A chill runs all through me.

"Sounds like a damn fool," Certain Certain says. "Jump in Lake Nastywater. You ever seen water so brown?"

"Matthew, chapter five, verse twenty-two," Sugar Tom says. He's talking about the verse in the Bible that says you will go to hell for calling someone a fool. He takes a mouthful of chili. "*Lord,* that is good. But I swan it's incinerating my gullet!"

"Exodus, chapter twenty, verse seven," Certain Certain says. " 'Thou shalt not take the name of the Lord thy God in vain.' "

These two have done this long as I can remember— battled back and forth with holy scripture.

Sugar Tom gulps sweet tea. A mariachi band is booming over the loudspeakers. There's hot food, folks are dancing, and even the air smells like something you want to bite.

But later in the evening when Sugar Tom begins his sermon, a huge storm comes up. Long thunder bumpers roll in off the lake, one after another. Even Miss Wanda Joy's hair can't stand up to the squall.

Right in the middle of the sermon, one of the tent poles comes loose, and me and Certain Certain rush over to fix it. We struggle with the pole while the canvas flaps around our ears, making a snapping sound. I'm too little to do much of anything but hang on tight and watch the sky flash. That's when I see the boy.

He's a couple years older than me, standing a few yards away. His long hair is sticking straight up all over his head, like seeds on a dandelion. It's the strangest sight I've ever seen.

The boy is grinning, saying over and over, "Look at this! Look at this!"

But everybody is paying too much attention to Sugar Tom and the storm. It's like that boy is there just for *me.* My skin prickles all over watching his crazy smile and floating hair. I can feel it; something awful is about to happen.

My whole world goes white. A white so pure it's what I figure it would be like staring into the face of the Lord. My eyes are knocked clean back in my head. The same instant there comes an almighty *boom,* and everything disappears.

When I come back into myself, my ears are clapping like bells and I'm not in the tent anymore. I'm sitting outside in the rain feeling cold, muddy water leaking into my pants. The colors of the trees on the shore look *reversed.*

Sugar Tom has stopped speaking—everything stands still for a heartbeat or two, then somebody screams.

But where is Certain Certain? I can't see him anywhere. Then I see his legs wrapped in a piece of tent. I crawl over and pull the canvas loose.

Certain Certain is sprawled facedown in a mud puddle. I

tug hard and roll him over. His hair is stained with red clay. His eyes are closed, and his chest isn't rising.

People are hollering and praying all over. They push up a circle around me, almost like they are too scared to touch him.

I start to cry.

I go down on my knees next to Certain Certain and lay my hands on his chest. Instantly his whole body jumps. It's not really much more than a twitch, but to me it feels like he hopped six inches off the ground.

"Oh, my sweet Jesus," a woman says behind me.

"Praise the Lord!" somebody else hollers.

"It's a miracle," a man says. "Blessed, merciful Lord."

Certain Certain shakes all over and starts to sit up. His eyeballs flutter, then he tries getting to his feet. Some of the men catch him up under his arms when he falls.

"Somebody call an ambulance!" a man hollers out.

"Already on the way from Fort Sam," somebody else answers.

"He *died*," a woman says. "That man was stone dead. I *seen* it. This boy"—she points at me—"he laid *hands* on him and brought him back. I seen it, plain as day." She jerks my arm up so hard, the rest of me follows. "You *healed* him," the woman says. "You *resurrected* him."

"I saw it, too!" somebody else yells.

"That's the gospel truth."

People are talking all over. There's little moans here and

22

there, and some of the folks begin weeping outright, praising Jesus or kneeling in prayer, right there in the mud.

What happens next is like a dream. There I am, wet to the skin, muddy, scared to pieces, and everybody is clapping me on the back like I'm a hero. They tug me up to the front, where Sugar Tom is standing.

"Pastor Tom!" one of the men hollers. "This boy has performed a *miracle.*"

A bunch of other folks yell "Yes" and "Amen." Next thing I know, I feel hands all over me, rubbing my wet hair, patting my back, hoisting me up on the stage.

I look at Sugar Tom, with my eyes saying, *What am I supposed to do?* There's a microphone on the pulpit. Sugar Tom turns it on and sticks it in my hand. He smiles at me, saying, "Just open your heart, son."

The congregation claps and hollers for me to speak. I can see Miss Wanda Joy standing in the corner, eyes digging holes in my face.

I look out across the crowd and see Certain Certain sitting on a folding chair. I lock eyes with him. And he smiles. Then he nods and says something that looks like *"Yes."*

That's all I need.

Ten years old, and the Holy Ghost comes up inside me for the very first time. I can feel it burning the soles of my feet, plowing its way up and filling every empty space. At first the feeling is frightening, and I'm light-headed, like I'm leaving my body behind.

I don't remember one single solitary word of what I say. But they are still clapping and hollering an hour later.

Little Ronald Earl Pettway, of Covington, Georgia. Born in Texas.

Little Texas.

⇒EIGHT⇐

After I get done telling about the day of my anointing, the Holy Spirit comes up in me so strong, it's like somebody opened the top of my head and poured in liquid fire. I am wide open, taking it in. The Spirit is the only thing protecting me now.

Then I'm not even here anymore. I am not anywhere but inside their eyes, the girls' eyes, and it all begins again. I put my mouth against the microphone. It tastes like a metal flower.

"The Lord is a-coming, *ah!*" I say, but it's not really me saying it.

Something has me by the shoulders, lifting me clean off the earth.

"He's a house afire, *ah!* He's a freight train, *ah!* He's a wrecking ball, *ah!* He is eternal, *ah!* Watchful over the sanctified, *ah!* He's driving the tides of resurrection in your souls, *ah!*"

I don't know where the words come from. They aren't mine. On and on, gushing from my mouth like a raging flood. At the same time this big, blistering whiteness fills my stomach, rushes up my throat plumb to my eyeballs. Begins to carry me off.

"I say now, put your hand in the hand of Jesus, *ah!* Make yourself ready, *ah!* Because in my Father's house there are many mansions, *ah!* He prepareth a place for the bridegroom to take your hand in marriage, *ah!* In the final days the clouds will roll back, *ah!* with a blasting of trumpets, *ah!* and the graves of the righteous will burst open, *ah!* and those who believeth on His name, *ah!* The dead in Christ shall rise, *ah!* Take His hand, *ah!* No man knoweth when his time cometh, *ah!* I say *no man* knoweth, *ah!* And those who do not repent, *ah!* shall be cast into the lake of everlasting fire, *ah!*"

My eyes roll back and flutter. I can't feel the Bible in my hands anymore. The Holy Spirit is lifting me up, floating me away; everything is floating, someone is screaming, then ten thousand voices are screaming, and my soul comes flooding out my temples, pouring down the sides of my head like molten light.

It's like I've swallowed the world.

But somehow I'm weightless. There is no roof to the tent anymore; I'm moving into the open sky. I can see myself down there, no bigger than a hickory nut.

I've left my body behind. I'm outside. Outside with her.

The girl from my dreams.

CHAPTER

⇒NINE⇐

When I'm done testifying, the spirit that has toted me up to heaven slowly hauls me back down from the clouds. I become aware of things around me again—people standing, screaming, waving, clapping their hands. The girls, especially the girls.

They are reaching their arms out like they could touch me from twenty feet away. Some of them are weeping.

Sugar Tom's Bible is heavy on my wrist now. I hand it to him. He takes it with both hands, saying "Amen," and I watch Certain Certain put it back in the prayer box.

I turn my eyes from the congregation to look for Miss Wanda Joy. Her black eyes push their way into my head. She raises her arms and says the same thing she says after every sermon.

"If you believe in the Resurrection of our Lord and Savior Jesus Christ, if you are ready to offer up your soul in hope of eternal salvation through the blood of the Lamb, come forward. Come kneel at the Calvary Rail."

The Calvary Rail runs along the edge of the stage. It's nearly twenty foot long, made of heavy white oak varnished dark brown. The idea is, there's room for all the Apostles.

But far more than twelve people come forward. Those that can, squeeze in, with the rest of them left standing. Miss Wanda Joy directs them to kneel, their fingers twined, heads bowed.

Miss Wanda Joy keeps her fingernails short for a reason; she goes down the line tapping each person on the head, repeating words I know by heart in one long string:

"AreyoureadytoacceptJesusChristasyourLordandpersonal-Savior?"

Each sinner nods, and Miss Wanda Joy goes to work, praying over them. Some of them shout. Some raise their hands as if drawn up by a heavenly magnet.

A woman with a purple shawl starts speaking in tongues, saying something like "Radda daddaa tat a ta!" and flops on the floor like a catfish. She lays there kicking and hollering awhile, then a couple of men get her up and help her back to her seat. Gradually the rest of the kneelers stand up and go sit back down again.

I turn my attention to a line of folks that has formed up beside the stage. Certain Certain is waiting with the first woman. She comes forward careful, like she's scared her legs are going to fold up under her. Certain Certain takes her by the elbow, holding her arm so ginger, you'd think the woman was made of spun sugar.

"It's my hip, praise Jesus," she says. "But I just know you can help me, Little Texas."

She starts to pull up her white dress, lifting it up to show her veiny blue leg, but Certain Certain puts his hand on top of her hand, saying, "That's all right, sister, that's all right. We understand."

"The doctor tells me I need hip replacement surgery," the woman says, voice cracking. She looks at me. "And I'm so afraid. Praise Jesus, I am *afraid*."

"Bring the sister forward," I say to Certain Certain.

As Certain Certain guides her closer, I catch the cloggy scent of some fancy perfume. I take her hand; her skin is loose, cold, and her jowls are saggy. But that's the outside. Sugar Tom always says for a healing to do its business, it's more important what's on the *inside*.

"Welcome, sister," I say. "Now, tell me. Just how long have you been burdened with this affliction?"

She gives a sad little smile, and her eyes nearly disappear in wrinkles.

"Well, it started after my husband—his name was James—after he passed on. Four years ago this March. James was a big man. He helped me so much. There are just so many things a small woman can't do for herself—"

"And have you been to many doctors to help you with your pain?"

"Oh yes, Little Texas." She brings up her tiny hands. "Nashville, Atlanta, Birmingham. All over. They all tell me the same thing. What I've got—it's degenerative. They can't fix me without putting in a replacement hip. I'm so afraid." She turns to face the congregation like she is speaking to them now. "I don't like hospitals. I don't even like visiting people in hospitals."

"I understand," I say. "Now, would you like to have this burden lifted from you today? This very minute?"

"I would! I would!"

"And do you declare Jesus Christ to be your personal Savior and Redeemer?"

"I do! Praise Jesus, I love Him so much, of course I do!"

"Well then. Do you believe He can heal you, sister?"

"Oh yes. All things and more He can do. I believe that, Little Texas. With all my heart."

"And can you feel the power of your belief deep down in your soul?" I say, readying my other hand.

"Why, yes, I do!"

Her eyes get wider and wider—she has a look I've come to know so well. Sugar Tom calls it the "house afire look." Eyes wild, staring. Just about crazy with hope. But mostly the look says this: *Deliverance.*

"We are *delivering* them from their sickness, their burdens," Sugar Tom says.

The time is right. I snap my hand out and holler, *"Praise Jesus!"* At the same time popping the heel of my palm against the woman's forehead, *hard.*

There is a moment, an instant truly, where I feel something like a heat hot as orange coals in my hand, and the fire rams the woman straight upside the head, and she tumbles over backward into Certain Certain's big hands—I hear a *whoosh* come out of her. Then she's soft as tallow dripping down a candle and flops over into his arms.

The healed woman's eyes are closed, and she is *smiling.* Smiling all over, as if Jesus Himself had just laid hands on her. Certain Certain gently drags her to the other end of the stage—one of her flat little shoes comes off, and Miss Wanda Joy picks it up and hands it into the congregation.

Then the next one comes, and the next and the next and the next. And each time there is that feeling of the fire leaping, something jumping from me to them, and that smile. That everlasting smile.

Healing all these folks, it's like—it's like passing into a cloud, one of those kinds that goes straight up like a triple-scoop ice cream cone. Coming out the other side, full of mist and sunshine.

I think maybe it's like love.

Like love is coming out the tips of my fingers and straight into their bodies. The love runs back and forth between us. Everything else falls away. When I'm in it, there is nothing else for me.

And I'm okay again. I'm all right for a little while. Till the fear starts all over again.

CHAPTER

⇒ TEN ⇐

Sometimes I'm so drained after a service, I can sleep ten hours. Tonight I wish I could jump down from the stage and run straight to the motor home to my bed. But there are always people wanting to talk about the sermon, needing a prayer, or just wanting to touch me, shake my hand.

Miss Wanda Joy says meeting folks after a service is the second-most-important part of a ministry. Certain Certain calls it "ginning up repeat business." I'm so used to it, I almost don't have to listen.

"Lord bless you, Little Texas!"

"Praise Jesus for bringing you to us!"

"I was hoping you could pray for my boy overseas in Iraq. . . ."

Tugging my arms, pulling at my suit coat, touching my face. I move through them quick as I can, but it feels like walking through a car wash without the car.

I'm not who they think I am. I'm not who they think I am. I'm not . . .

Finally the last of them go, and the road leading back to the highway looks like a ribbon of red taillights. I can already taste supper without even knowing what it's going to be.

Then, as I'm about to leave, a small woman comes rushing up out of the shadows and grabs my hand. Her light, curly hair is a wreck, and her eyes are shiny with tears.

"It's my daughter," she says, blowing it all out in one terrified breath.

A tall man comes hustling up behind her carrying a girl. *Oh Lord.* This girl is blond-headed and wearing a blue dress that comes about to her knees. Her skinny arms and legs are dangling, head lolling. Her mouth is open and her eyes are closed.

"My *baby girl* . . . ," the man says, so choked up the words come out in pieces. "We've been—everything was fine—she was *fine*—Lucy—please, please, Little Texas. Help her. *Please.*"

The man goes to lay the girl flat on the stage, but Certain Certain brings some blankets to make a pallet. I look at the girl. Her face is red, skin wet, soft pink lips turning bluish.

"What is it?" I say, mouth going dry.

"She got—we were on vacation—she got sick coming up from Pell City," the man says. He is crying now. His wife is clutching his hand so tight, the blood is draining out of it.

"Anything, we'll give you anything, just help my baby girl. . . ." His voice chokes off again.

"I—I don't know," I say. "This looks to be an emergency. Regular doctors might could handle it better. . . ."

The woman's eyes cut me off. *Pleading.* She turns the man loose and clutches my arm.

"Please."

I look at Certain Certain; he raises his shoulders. Miss Wanda Joy comes over, her mouth set in a tight line.

I kneel beside the girl. My heart is in my neck. "I'll do—I'll do what I can."

She looks to be about my age. Thin and small with curly blond hair. Her face is wet, wet as if somebody just splashed her. I bend over her.

"Y'all step back, give her some air."

The top of Lucy's dress is open a little bit. Her skin is smooth and perfect.

I have absolutely no idea what I am doing.

I don't feel ready. Everything is wrong. When the Spirit comes over me, when I'm full of the Holy Ghost, I can move mountains. I *know* I can. But everything strong has already rushed out of me tonight. I am empty. Tiny. *Weak.* This is just

Ronald Earl Pettway kneeling here, not Little Texas. *Pray,* I think. *Pray to heaven. . . .*

I close my eyes and clasp my hands together in the air over Lucy's chest.

"*Dear blessed heavenly Father.* Please guide my hands and bring about a healing to this girl's—to *Lucy's*—spirit, her soul, and her body."

I open my eyes. Her father is hovering over my shoulder, her mother at my elbow. I put my ear close to Lucy's mouth. She is breathing, but it sounds shallow, rough.

Then Lucy's eyes flick open and lock on mine for just a second. She moans, face twisting in pain. Her hands clutch at her stomach, fingers digging in. She starts tearing at her dress, pulling so hard the buttons are about to tear loose.

"Get her hands!" I say to her father, and he and Certain Certain bend low to pull them back.

Lucy screams and bucks forward, then flops back, limp. I lean over and put my hands over her. I've never been so close to a girl like this. She's everything I've ever been afraid of, all of it, in one soul, one body, taunting me.

I glance at Miss Wanda Joy. She makes a face like she disapproves. But I've got to do something. *Anything.*

"*Please,*" Lucy's mother says.

My hands start to shake. I don't know how to make them stop. I drop them down to the only place it feels safe to touch, the place between Lucy's chest and belly—so warm!—

the material of her dress is so thin, I can feel her hot skin. Her bosom is small—that's what Sugar Tom says to call it, a bosom.

"Lift her up," Miss Wanda Joy says.

"But . . . ," I say.

Certain Certain has already got Lucy under her arms and is standing her. She doubles up in pain again and slumps toward me. Her father helps Certain Certain prop her up.

"Now," Miss Wanda Joy says, looking at me. "Do it now."

"Hurry," Lucy's father says again. "Look at her, look at what she . . ."

Her lips are turning bluer. Is she even breathing? *Lord help me, help me, please.* Then her eyes pop open and she is staring right straight into my eyes, pleading for something:

Take the pain away, take me away, save me, save me, save . . .

A single tear burns down her face.

I clap my eyes tight, force myself to clear my mind. *Think. Something clean. Something pure. Remember. Remember.* And I do remember. Mark, chapter nine, verse three: "And His raiment became shining, exceeding white as snow."

Shining white as snow, shining white as snow, shining white as snow.

I say it to myself over and over—till it seems like I've said it a thousand times. And at last the whiteness, the goodness, the *clean* fills up my head. It's all I can see, even when I open my eyes. Now, thank the Lord, I can feel His power flood into my fingers, boiling straight up to the tips. My voice comes out hoarse.

"Are you ready to be sanctified by our Lord and Savior Jesus Christ?" I say.

Lucy's answer is barely a whisper, more lips than throat.

"Yes."

I slam my hand into her forehead, not the heel this time, but laying my whole fingers up into her wet hair—

A sound comes up in my ears, a sound like I've never heard. Like something *moving,* something tearing apart. I don't even know if it's anywhere besides my head.

Lucy howls and bows her shoulders. I open my eyes—I can see again. Then Lucy goes slack and drops straight into Certain Certain's arms. He lays her back on the blankets. I look down. Lucy is smiling.

A smile that only comes from a deep inside healing.

CHAPTER

⇒ELEVEN⇐

Lucy's body is limp. Certain Certain wraps her in one of the blankets, and her father picks her up again.

"Little gal gonna be just fine now," Certain Certain says, patting her yellow hair.

"Thank you, thank you so much," Lucy's mother says, hugging me tight and kissing my cheek. She stuffs something in my coat pocket.

"God bless you, Little Texas," her father says, tears rolling down his face. He works a hand free to shake. "I can't tell you how much this means to us."

Lucy's eyes are closed, but there's still a little half smile on her mouth like she's out of pain, at least. As her parents leave the tent, I can see her legs dangling out of the blanket. Her mother is walking alongside her father, holding one of Lucy's feet. For the first time I notice she's wearing little white basketball shoes. High-tops. It's the last thing I see of her as they round the corner.

Something about those shoes . . . or maybe it's just how frail she looks, how slack her legs are hanging. . . .

I sit down hard on the stage, head spinning.

"You all right, doctor?" Certain Certain says, touching my arm.

"I'm—I'm a little dizzy," I say.

"You need some supper, that's all. Sit still a spell, and we'll all of us go get something to eat. Ain't never been prouder of you, boy."

He claps me on the back and walks over to the volunteers to get them started breaking down the tent. But it feels like something is breaking inside me. Miss Wanda Joy comes bustling over.

"Little Texas. Did they—I saw her put something in your pocket. . . ."

I pull the crumpled twenty-dollar bill out and push it into her hand. Jump down from the stage and start running. I rush out of the tent, see a big motor home perched alongside the sorghum field with the words *Gulf Breeze* painted on it.

Miss Wanda Joy has always warned me not to hang around with the folks I heal.

"People can be . . . unpredictable," she says.

The taillights flash, and the big motor home is rolling, making the long, slow curve back toward the main road.

Take me with you!

I pull up, breathing hard, sweaty in Sugar Tom's suit. I take the suit coat off and loosen my tie and yank it off, too.

Then there is nothing but crickets in the sorghum and stars covering the sky in tiny fires a million miles away.

CHAPTER

⟫ TWELVE ⟪

I never knew my great-uncle, a man Miss Wanda Joy calls Daddy King. Certain Certain says Daddy King brought a truckload of souls to the Lord.

"Then one night in Galveston, he was hollering about 'smiting the idolaters' and keeled over from a brain aneurism."

Daddy King was twenty-five years older than Miss Wanda Joy when they got married. She carries a picture of him wherever she goes. He's got a big, wide face, an old-timey mustache, and slicked-back hair. Eyes that follow you.

I try to think about what that must have been like, falling in love with a man so old. But maybe a woman like Miss

Wanda Joy doesn't really fall in love in a romantic way? She's always so practical. She would think about things from every angle, then choose the best one.

I admit I can't picture any man sniffing around her these days. She has got to be close to fifty or more. But Certain Certain says it's the way she looks at the world that has hardened her up the most.

Miss Wanda Joy keeps a ledger detailing every place we've gone. It shows how much of a love offering they gave in such and such a town, going back years. She always says things are getting tougher every year.

"Folks just don't believe like they once did," Certain Certain says under his breath so she can't hear. "Rather sit at home, watch some fool on TV, pay by credit card. 'Pray for my soul, Pastor, I can't go to the baffroom by myself no more.' Hallelujahjesus.com."

We're sitting in the IHOP waiting on our food. Miss Wanda Joy's sitting by herself in a booth, counting the collection. She rolls all the bills in rubber bands. Certain Certain claims all that twanging and popping is the most irritating sound in the world.

She must be home by now, right?

Lucy's family. Probably they live in a two-story house with a yard and a dog. Somebody comes by every day and throws them a newspaper. They keep their grass cut. Ride the bus to school. Sing songs at Christmastime around a big old tree.

"I didn't even get her last name," I say, almost not realizing I'm talking out loud.

"That sick little gal?" Certain Certain says. "She in no mood to fool with you, boy. Besides, what you gonna do, chase them all the way to Mobile?"

I feel a tickle of excitement in my stomach. "Mobile? Is that where they're from?"

Certain Certain reaches across the table and smacks the side of my head.

"How would I know? Alabama tags, all I saw. What you wanna go mess with her for? Little thing is too narrow in the hips."

"Hey."

"Am I lying?"

"She's not a horse."

Certain Certain laughs. "I could eat me one right about now."

I sigh. But it feels good to be back in my jeans. Not many folks in the restaurant this late; most of the other customers have tattoos and motorcycle head rags. All the waiters are very polite, with thick black mustaches, black hair, and accents. Our server says his name is Azeem.

"It means 'defender,'" Azeem says. "It is one of the ninety-nine qualities of God."

"That a fact," Sugar Tom says. I stop his arm from dragging through the boysenberry.

Azeem smiles. I have never seen teeth so pure beautiful.

"I am from Kandahar." He makes his hands like he's holding a rifle. *"Bang!"*

"May I have more orange juice?" Miss Wanda Joy says from her booth, scowling.

"That's what you think, is it not?" Azeem says. "When I say Kandahar. *Bang.* CNN." He points up in the air as if there is an invisible TV there. "But it is a very important city. Founded by Alexander the Great. You do not know this, I think."

I have barely touched my Colorado omelet. *How far away is Lucy right now? Is she sleeping at home in her own bed?*

"You know they put pancake batter in that, don't you, Lightning?" Certain Certain says to me.

"Orange juice?" Miss Wanda Joy says, coming over and sitting down with the prayer box tucked under her arm.

"Ninety-nine qualities of God," Sugar Tom says. He shakes out his pack of Marlboros. The front of the package always reminds me of chess, on account of the two horses that look like knights leaning against the king's crown.

"No smoking, please," Azeem says, wagging his finger.

"Everything is no smoking these days," Sugar Tom says, frowning so hard his eyeballs are near lost in his eyebrows. He glares at Azeem. "Do you believe Christ the Lord is your personal Savior, young man? Have you been born again?"

"Sugar Tom," Certain Certain says, touching his arm.

"Who is this Born Again?" Azeem says. "Once is enough, I think."

46

Miss Wanda Joy clonks her glass on the table, making everybody jump.

"Orange juice. *Please.*"

Azeem looks her square in the eyes and gets the full jolt. He scoots off and doesn't say another word the whole rest of our meal.

Certain Certain drives the motor home back to the camp. When we stop for gas, Miss Wanda Joy fishes out a couple of bills so Sugar Tom can buy the latest copy of the *Star.* He holds it open so I can see it, too. There's a story about a man who lived forty days in the Australian desert with nothing but a Bible. He ate the pages.

"Made it all the way to Galatians," Sugar Tom says. "And look here. Astronaut James Irwin has finally discovered Noah's ark on Mount Ararat. I swannee."

"That man is dead as my grandma Florala," Certain Certain says. "He was a Christian. They had a write-up about it in the *Christian Examiner* years ago. How can a dead man be discovering anything?"

"It's all right here in black and white," Sugar Tom says.

"So maybe old James is a holy *ghost,*" Certain Certain says. "Maybe Noah give him some instructions up in heaven on where to find it." He laughs.

"Keep it up, make all the fun you want," Sugar Tom says. " 'Let those be stricken with terror, that come against thy holy people to blaspheme.' One thing I have learned is every story of the strange has a mustard seed of truth."

"So you think he is a haint?" Certain Certain says. "Come back down to Earth till his mission is complete?"

"Better reread your scripture," Miss Wanda Joy says, biting a link sausage in half. I can tell by the way she's sitting, she's got the prayer box settled across her lap. "Ecclesiastes, chapter nine, verses five through six: 'The dead know nothing; they have no more reward, and even the memory of them is lost. Their love and their hate and their envy have already perished; never again will they have any share in all that happens under the sun.'"

Worst thing about being on a revival tour? Sooner or later all the talk doubles back to the Bible. Like that man lost in the Australian desert makes me think of Deuteronomy: "Man doth not live by bread alone, but by every word which proceedeth out of the mouth of God."

I take that to mean all kinds of things. I need more than just bread to live. More than just old folks and their Words. I need someone who—

"What you thinking 'bout, Lightning?" Certain Certain says.

"Nothing."

"That little gal in the blue dress?"

I look out at the dark. There's a picture of a pancake with a blond-headed girl on it. She's looking right straight at me.

"Can we go?" I say.

CHAPTER

⟫THIRTEEN⟪

Back in camp Certain Certain climbs inside the truck. I see the dome light flick on, and he is already in his undershirt. The light flicks off again. Certain Certain sleeps up in that little space above the cab. I've always liked small, secret places like that.

Sugar Tom has settled into bed, but he wants the light on so he can finish reading his magazine. I step outside to stretch my legs. The tent is packed away, and all the volunteers are gone, but I can still see the tire marks where Lucy's motor home was sitting.

"Little Texas."

I jerk around, and Miss Wanda Joy is standing behind me.

"I'm going to take a little walk before turning in," she says. "Would you like to come along?"

I know better than to say no. She heads straight across the sorghum field, with me dragging along behind. I can barely see to keep from stepping on the plants. Miss Wanda Joy stops close to the gurgling sound of a little brook.

"Are you all right?" she asks.

"I'm okay. A little tired, I guess."

She circles around me, getting between me and the motor home. I can see little pieces of light in each of her eyes and not much else.

"What happened tonight with the healing?" she says, voice tight.

"What? I thought it went pretty well—"

"You know what I mean. The little girl in the blue dress. Do I need to worry about you?"

"No, ma'am. I'm okay."

"Are we doing too much? Too many services?"

"I don't think so. It's just . . ."

How can I tell somebody like her what's bothering me? I'd sooner run naked down Bourbon Street with my hair on fire.

"Just what?" she says, waiting.

"Nothing. It's just . . . I didn't know . . . I didn't know what to do for her. She was so hot—I mean, her *skin.* She was so *sick.* I was scared I maybe couldn't help her."

Even in this light I can see Miss Wanda Joy's hands go to her hips.

"Well, of *course* she was sick. They are *all* sick."

"Well, ma'am, some of them . . ."

"What are you saying?"

"Well, most of them . . . they aren't so hard to heal. You know what I mean?"

"No, I do not. Please explain it to me."

My mind jumps to the little old woman in the flat shoes. "Like that woman with a hip problem. I knew—I *knew* I could help her. Most of them are like that. They are so . . . so *ready.* She believed so hard, Certain Certain could have healed her. It's like Jesus says—"

"And what does He say?"

I swallow. "Well . . . that *anybody* can do a miracle. It's the believing that does it. Jesus just said a thing and it just *was.* It was already there. Because they *believed* so hard. But this girl, she wasn't even completely *awake. . . .*"

Miss Wanda Joy puts her hands on my arms, squeezing hard.

"Do you *presume* to know what was in our Lord and Savior's mind when He performed His great works?"

"No, ma'am, it's just that—"

"If just *anybody* could perform a healing, if just *anybody* could do *miracles,* then why don't they?" She lets me go.

"Because they—um, maybe on account of they don't *know* they can—"

"Let me tell you something, Little Texas. This whole ministry was founded by my grandfather on one very sacred element—the absolute *uniqueness* of the anointed. Do you understand what I'm saying to you?"

"Yes'm, I think so."

"The Church of the Hand. That is *your* hand it's referring to. *Your* anointing."

I feel her straighten, and her breathing eases up a little. "People come to see *you,* Little Texas. *A uniquely anointed servant of God.* That is the wheel that makes everything turn. If you cease to be *uniquely anointed* in their eyes, everything—all our work, our ministry—all falls to naught."

"But what . . . what if it's something I can't help?"

"Are you saying your *belief* is failing?"

I think very carefully about what I say next. "No, ma'am. No. It just . . . it was *hard,* that's all. I was afraid—afraid of what might happen. That girl—Lucy—she might have *died.*"

And it would have been my fault.

"How could that have been your fault?" Miss Wanda Joy says, just like she can hear my thoughts. "Did *you* bring the sickness on that child?"

"No, ma'am."

"Did *you* make the decision to bring her to a spiritual healer?"

"No, ma'am."

"Well, then. But she didn't die, did she? That's what's important. Come on, let's get to bed."

And she walks away, leaving me standing inside the sound of the water I can't see.

CHAPTER

⇒ FOURTEEN ⇐

The next morning I'm riding in the truck cab with Certain Certain. We head out of Verbena and pass a bunch of small towns that all look alike: tractor parts stores, old brick schools, squashy frame houses, gas stations.

Tell you the truth, I'm sick to death of little towns. But Miss Wanda Joy says big cities like Nashville and Memphis and Birmingham are all wanting to charge you for a space to put up the tent or even park the motor home.

"Let them burn in their iniquity," she likes to say.

But whenever I see those big lights creeping past the

windows, I feel this yearning spread through my whole body, like my soul is pushing at the seams.

Today I'm drifting in and out of my memories of that girl in the blue dress. The way her golden hair hung on her shoulders. How hot her skin was. *What it felt like to put my hand on her face.*

Certain Certain fiddles with the radio. Don't strike me down, Lord, but country music reminds me too much of being stuck inside a trailer next door to the chemical factory. My original momma was always listening to one sad song after another, till it got to feeling like torture, trapped in somebody else's messed-up life.

Last fall I heard a car pumping music out of these big, booming speakers that was so wild, loose, *hungry*—I couldn't understand the words, but I could understand the *feeling.* The kids in that car are probably going straight to hell. But here's my awful secret: I would've followed them right out of the fairgrounds if I could. Just to keep listening.

We pull off at a rest stop and get out to stretch our legs. Miss Wanda Joy always makes us park far away from everybody else. Older men sit at tables and watch the girls. *Girls.* A couple of kids are throwing a Frisbee around. What would it be like to have a brother or a sister? What would they think of me?

Inside, the air-conditioning feels good. There are computers where you can touch the screen and find out information about the Smoky Mountains, the Gulf, New Orleans, caves, state parks. This is my dream, to see each and every one of these places. Not like a tourist, but to find the one that's right for me. Get a claim to a piece of it and don't ever let it go. I believe I could sit still in the same house forever. Living on the road will do that to you.

Coming out of the welcome center with my hands full of brochures, I run into a group of kids ganged up around the entrance. There are at least nine of them, all wearing black and yellow T-shirts that say CONOVER HIGH YELLOW JACKETS. A couple of the bigger boys step in my way.

"Hey, can you tell us where the bathroom is?" one of them says. "I need to go *real bad.*"

"It's right in there," I say, feeling squirmy. Some of the girls start giggling. The two big boys are still blocking my way.

"You have to drop a deuce?" the second one says to me. A big, barrel-chested boy maybe a couple of years older than me, with ham-bone fists.

"Excuse me?" I say.

A bunch of them bust out laughing, braying like mules.

"Excuse me!" the first boy says, trying to imitate my voice and nearly choking on himself. "Did you really just say that?"

The other one, the one with the fists, turns to the girls. "Hey, this guy just polluted the whole place. I think I can smell it." He sniffs the air and wrinkles his face up, cussing. "Didn't you flush? It's that little silver handle."

"Maybe they don't have indoor plumbing in Jesus Land," the first one says.

I start forward again, but they push together in front of me.

"Look at that hair," a girl says, laughing. I feel my face go hot. "He's got *preacher hair*." She takes out something small and black, flips it open. It's a cell phone. She holds it up between the heads of the tall boys and aims it at me. "I've got to get a picture of this."

"Wait a minute," the first kid says. He has a big potato face. "Don't take it yet. Hey, Preacher Hair, your shirt's tucked in. You want me to help you with that?"

He grabs at my shirt and starts to jerk it out. I knock at his hands and drop all my brochures. They scatter all over the sidewalk, some of them laying open: Clingman's Dome, Tuckaleechee Caverns, Rock City, Port Saint Joe. I bend down to pick them up, but the kids are stepping on them, kicking them around. I get the ones I can.

"Will you move, please?" I say, trying to get at the other ones. Nobody moves. Finally I just give up and straighten back up.

"How old are you, boy?" the first kid says.

"Sixteen. Nearly."

"You're one of them hard-core Baptists, aren't you? Can't dance, can't chew gum, got to hold it with rubber gloves to take a leak."

"Naw, he can't be Baptist," the second boy says. "My cousin's a Baptist. They're not *that* weird. Church of Christ maybe."

"Church of God?" somebody says in the back.

"Nope. None of them are *this* strange," Ham-Fist says. "He's *Penicoastal.* Yeah, baby. That's where you whip out your *Peni* and take it *coastal.*"

"Fundamentalist," somebody says. "Emphasis on the *mental.*"

"Oh, you guys are so *mean,*" another girl says. But she's grinning when she says it. "Leave him alone, Brett. Let him go."

"What's your problem?" I say to the one she called Brett.

"That your bus over there?" he says.

I don't look, but I know where he's pointing.

"That's it, isn't it?" he says. "Bet it's full of damn snakes. I heard y'all milk 'em and wave them around in church. I saw it on the Discovery Channel. No, Animal Planet." He laughs.

I start walking again; he steps in the way.

"Let me go," I say, baring my teeth a little.

"I bet that bus stinks like a mofo, doesn't it? All those snakes crawling around in there." He turns to the girl with the cell phone. "You know what snakes smell like, don't you, Genna?"

"Hell no," the girl says.

"Like two people doing it."

"How would *you* know?"

"I'll show you sometime."

"So that's your *momma* sitting over there?" Ham-Fist says, pointing at the stone picnic table where Miss Wanda Joy is sitting with Sugar Tom and Certain Certain.

"No—" I start, but he cuts me off.

"Your momma *and* your daddy. No wonder you're messed up. She's one of those bitches never washes her hair, right? Keeps it blowed up like a football on top of her head, except for the part in back where it's running down to her ass. Hasn't cut that tail since she was *born,* right? Otherwise she goes straight to hell, doesn't she?"

"Shut your mouth," I say, feeling my jaw tighten.

"Ooh, I'm pissing my pants, Preacher Hair."

"Let him alone, Tommy. Let him go. That's enough." It's the same girl as before, the one in the back. She's not smiling now.

"Aw, we're just messing with you, right?" Brett says. "He knows we're just messing with him, don't you?"

I feel every muscle in my body tightening now, feel a white-hot rage building up behind my eyes. What Sugar Tom calls a "righteous fire."

"Look out now, Brett," Tommy Ham-Fist says. "Watch those eyes. He's fixing to kick your ass."

"You want to kick my ass, don't you, Preacher Hair?" Brett says. "You believe I'm going to hell, don't you? Look, you got me all scared and everything. You really do. So I tell you what I'm gonna do. I'm gonna make it up to you. Isn't that right, Genna?"

The girl with the cell phone clicks it shut and drops it into her pocket. "What?"

"Make it up to him," Brett says. "That's what we should do."

He smiles at the girl, Genna. She doesn't seem to know what he wants. Then her mouth falls open, and you can see something change in her eyes. She grins at Brett.

"You sure?" He nods and lets her come forward. "Okay," Genna says.

She stands facing me and grabs the edge of her shirt, hauls it up to her chin. I can see them for just the tiniest little split second. Her *bosoms.* She's *showing* them to me. Genna yanks her shirt back down.

It happens so fast, I don't know if the other kids can even see, the way Tommy and Brett are bunched up around her. Then the whole gang laughs like crazy and pushes past me into the welcome center. I'm standing there holding my breath and my brochures like a broken dog.

"Have a deviled egg," Sugar Tom says when I get back to the picnic table.

I push the plate away. "No thanks. I'm not hungry."

I lay my brochures out and start pretending to go through them. I feel my mouth bunching, tears coming, and my jaw clenching. *They are evil. Evil.*

"What did they say to you?" Miss Wanda Joy asks. Those eyes don't miss a thing. "Did they say something profane?"

"No, ma'am," I say. "Not so much."

The Conover High kids are coming back out now. Miss Wanda Joy gets up, pulling her dress from between her legs. "Well, maybe I'll just go have a talk with them and find out for myself."

"*No.*" I say it so sharp, it surprises even me. "*Please.* Let's just leave."

But she is already on her way over there, long skirts dragging the grass. My face is burning. I glance at her, and she is standing in the group of Conover kids, looking like a person out of the pioneer days. She is taller than any of them, except Tommy and Brett. I can tell by the way they are slouching, they want to get smart with her. But they don't dare; who could, staring into those blazing eyes?

What could she be saying to them?

"Second Samuel, chapter thirteen, verse thirteen," Sugar Tom says, croaking a little. "'Whither shall I cause my shame to go?'"

I look at my hands. Does it show that much?

The Conover kids seem kind of subdued after Miss Wanda Joy leaves. But the minute we climb into the motor home, I can hear them out the open window.

"Little *Texasssssss,* Little *Texassssssss,* Little *Texasssssssssssssss!*"

Hissing like serpents.

CHAPTER

⟫FIFTEEN⟪

We're back on the interstate. I'm wondering, *What would it be like to* touch *that Genna girl there? Soft? Warm?*

Forgive me, Lord.

"Your face is red as a prickly pear," Certain Certain says. "Them boys mess with you?"

"Yes, sir. And she just *had* to make it worse," I say.

Certain Certain downshifts, making the gears grind. "Don't let 'em get to you, boy," he says. "Proverbs, chapter one, verse twenty-two. 'Scorners delight in their scorning, and fools hate knowledge.' "

I turn my head to the window and close my eyes. *She*

didn't even have any underclothes on, I think. *Nothing but pure skin. Soft, pale, round, and pinkish.*

My fingers tremble, so I pick up the map to give them something to do. Why would somebody show something so mysterious and secret and sweet, for all the world to see? What kind of person would do that to her soul?

And how do you get to know a girl like that?

The feeling I had in that dream is coming back. Like whatever is *me,* the *inside* me, is all of a sudden collecting right in the middle. Everything below my belt buckle seems like it's tightening and lifting, drawing every ounce of heat in my body.

I unfold the map and lay it across my legs. *Snakes. Hellfire. Damnation. Heaven. Soft. Lucy.* Lucy. I press down on the map and talk to Certain Certain without looking at him.

"Did you . . . did you ever have . . . I mean, did you have a girlfriend when you were my age?"

He chuckles. "Be more accurate to ask, was there ever a time I *didn't* have me a girlfriend? How far we talking 'bout going back into prehistory, Lightning?"

"You don't have a girlfriend now."

"I've sowed all the wild oats I'll ever need to sow."

"But what if everybody did that?"

"Did what?"

"You know. Did what we're always telling them in services. Stopped . . . *lusting.* There wouldn't be any babies. The human race would die out."

Certain Certain scratches his chin. I can see the slave tag flash in the sun. "You don't have to worry about that anytime soon, *believe* me."

"But what if . . . what if you were my age and somebody . . . they showed you their . . ."

"What?"

"I can't say it."

"Titties? That the word you hunting for?"

My hands keep pressing the map.

"Let me tell you something," Certain Certain says. "You think the world just woke up and happened yesterday, don't you?"

"No I don't."

"Yes you do. Young people . . . y'all think you invented everything. Everything new to y'all is new to anybody who ever lived." He spits out his window. "Think I didn't never slip around behind my daddy's corncrib with some pretty little gal now and again? Shoot. Some of them little gals 'bout near tore me *up.*"

"But . . . didn't you ever think they were crazy when they did that?"

"Mo' crazy the better."

"No, so crazy they would . . . wreck your whole life?"

"Shoot, boy. Don't take a crazy gal to do that. Sane as Jane will do. You ask anybody."

"Do you ever wish . . . do you ever think about how maybe things could've turned out different?"

"Different don't matter," Certain Certain says. "What matters is, did they turn out for the *best*? For me they did. I know what you worried about. You worried are you going to be stuck in the ministry business your whole life? Is that all you ever going to know? All you ever *supposed* to know? Isn't that right?"

"Yes, sir."

"I knew it. Here's the thing I learned. There's my plan, there's your plan, there's *His* plan. His plan is the one that counts. His plan is the one workin' in our lives every second of every day, whether we know it or not. Sometimes it seems like the worst thing in the world, way things work out for you in life. But it's all part of His plan, and when you look back on things, you see it more clear. Fifteen, shoot. Everything's in front of you, boy. Plenty of time for His plan to unfold in your life. Let go and let God."

I've been saying the same thing to congregations for years. "I was hoping for something a little more specific," I say.

"Lord ain't into specifics," Certain Certain says. "That's your part. Lord is into *faith*."

I turn back to the window and watch the world pass by, wondering what goes on inside all those houses. Is there a kid right now, right there, in *that* little blue house—somebody my age? Does he have a girlfriend?

Or maybe it's a girl. Is she like that Genna girl? Ready to lift her shirt up and laugh? Or Lucy . . . could Lucy ever be that way? No. I don't believe it. Lucy wouldn't do that. Would she?

➤SIXTEEN➤

Cobbville, Mississippi.

The Burger King is fringed with Queen Anne's lace and thorny purple bull thistles. Sugar Tom sits at one of the outside tables trailing blue cigarette smoke.

"I'll never forget the first time it hit home with me," he says. "I was twelve, thirteen years old. I remember exactly where I was standing—next to the only lamppost that survived the burning of Atlanta in the Civil War. Corner of Whitehall and Alabama.

"Well, out of the clear blue this skinny gal with Shirley Temple hair came up and dang near took my arm off, she shook it so hard. 'It's *you*,' she kept saying. 'It's *you*.' Like I was some kind of wonder. I didn't know her from Adam's house cat. She drug me into a little diner and forced me to eat a patty melt while she sat there smiling like a simpleton and telling me how amazing I was. I'm telling you, Ronald Earl, it was downright *disturbing*."

Certain Certain shows up holding two vanilla shakes for him and Sugar Tom and a strawberry one for me. Miss Wanda Joy is waiting in the motor home. She doesn't believe in sweets.

"You know what you are to them, Ronald Earl?" Sugar Tom goes on, his cheeks caving in from sucking. "*Show people.* That's what it comes down to. And you can't change that once it gets fixed in folks' heads."

"But what if . . . what if I just want to *meet* somebody?" I say. "Someone who doesn't care about all that stuff? Somebody who just wants to know me for *me*?"

Sugar Tom coughs into his hand, nearly touching his eyeball with the cigarette ash.

"You get a dog," he says.

"Saddle up," Certain Certain says.

Turns out the only setup spot is another cow pasture. Miss Wanda Joy is not one tiny bit pleased. She has to make some quick changes to the poster, and we have to rush around town making copies at the Kinkos and covering up the old ones.

CHURCH OF THE HAND

Come see the legendary evangelist

~Little Texas~

as we share with you

the glory of our Lord

and His promise of

everlasting redemption.

The Faith Tabernacle Revival Meeting

will be held in the Wilbanks pasture

on Leadmine Road

tomorrow night,

June 13, six o'clock.

Be there and Be Saved!

You ever try to shoot a staple gun into a telephone pole?

With all the extra work, it's dark by the time we get the tent set up. Certain Certain aims the truck lights across the pasture, showing humps of grass and staring red eyes. Cows are funny. It's like they have just one brain amongst them, and all of them have to share it.

"Mind the coyotes," Mr. Wilbanks says, and waddles off without smiling.

"Getting too old for this," Certain Certain says. He settles into a folding chair behind the stage. "My momma didn't raise no circus roustabout."

"What would you do if you didn't do this?" I say.

He reaches into the neck of his shirt and handles the slave tag, thinking about it awhile. "There's someplace I sure would like to see before the day I die," he says.

"Whereabouts?"

He blows out a long breath. "Place called Ouidah on the west coast of Africa. Gate of No Return. That's a spot on the beach where over three million folks left on slave ships. Ouidah was the center for the slave trade. I want to stand at that gate, walk through it. Walk around the Tree of Forgetfulness, too."

"What's that?" I say.

"Tree they forced them slaves to walk around. Men had to walk around it nine times, women seven. It was a ritual . . . so the souls of the slaves would forget where they come from and never return to Africa to haunt the kings that sold them."

Certain Certain never made it past the eighth grade, but he has read books thicker than my arm. Everything from the Civil War to the Louisiana Purchase and folks like de Soto and Frederick Douglass.

"I didn't know there was an actual place where you can still go and see things about slavery," I say. "I mean *over there.* Why don't you go do it, then? Go see it?"

"I might. I might. Take you with me."

"Why me?"

"You involved, Lightning, whether you know it or not. We *all* involved. Ghosts of slavery still with us today."

"But—"

"You think on account of Michael Jordan selling his drawers all over TV, everything is hunky-dory? No, sir. Still got a good ways to go. Something like that done to a whole race of people—*millions* of them—it echoes a good long while. Hundred years, *two hundred,* that's an eye blink—walk a mile in a black man's shoes, tell me we ain't still feeling it, black and white both."

"But *I* didn't do it. I wasn't even alive back then. Besides, I'm part Cherokee."

He gives a little snort. "Good for you, *Tonto.* So you tell yourself, 'This ain't my fight. My people were doing just fine and dandy till these white and black folks showed up and all hell broke loose.' "

He rubs his eyes and lets out a big yawn.

"It's what we all owe, Lightning. You know what I'm sayin'? Ain't enough just to say, 'Wasn't me, wasn't you.' And I ain't letting my own people off the hook, neither. Them African kings sold they own down the river, right? Can't forget that."

"But it doesn't seem like doing much," I say, thinking about Ouidah again, "just to visit a place."

"Yeah, you right. But I'll tell you one thing: it's a *start.* Least we can do is pay our respects. Help spread some *awareness* about what happened. Tell other people about it."

The volunteers straggle by. We sit there listening to their engines rumble away across the pasture, till they've left us in darkness.

"What do you ... what do you think would have happened?" I say. "You know, if slavery had never happened? What would Africa be like now?"

"Huh. You askin' the wrong man that question, doctor. Too many ifs. Too much water under the gate. Who can say? Maybe the flag of free Nairobi be planted on the moon today, all we know."

Certain Certain stands and stretches so hard, I can hear his bones cracking.

"I'm tired like to death." He says good night and climbs into the truck.

When I crawl into bed, it's hard to shut off my mind. I have a thing I do when it gets like this. Miss Wanda Joy taught me to pray for all the sinners and whoremongers and alcoholics and a whole long list of folks trapped in a living hell on Earth. So I lay there in my bunk praying for their deliverance from the bondage of evil, eyes clamped shut, where I can see nothing but black in front of me.

Before I know it, it's like I'm inside the blackness with them. I can feel their presence there, held in slavery to Satan. I go forward and touch the blackness. I push against it, and a hole shaped like an *X* tears through. I poke my fingers through the *X,* peeling the darkness back. There's light on the other side.

That is the light of our Great Redeemer, Jesus Christ. All the trapped people, they are attracted to the hole I've made. They come over, all of them, tearing through that hole. Through the light of His love, I have set them *free.*

Later in the night I jerk up in my bunk, thinking I'm still inside my dream; something heavy is moving around outside, tromping the ground close to the motor home. My heart sets to hammering.

The sound is so close, it's like it's trying to bust its way through the door. I can hear creakings and groanings and smell dirt through my little side window.

I listen for Sugar Tom or Miss Wanda Joy, but they're not stirring. I think about calling out, but something tells me, *No, sit still, don't let* it *know you are here.* I feel the motor home begin to shake; the steps get heavier and heavier. Praise Jesus, how many of them are out there? *What* is out there?

Then I remember: we are parked next to a whole herd of cows. I feel pretty silly, even laugh at my fear. I listen awhile longer as everything begins to settle down. Then I lay back down, and in a wink it's morning.

I ask Sugar Tom and Miss Wanda Joy what did they think about the hullabaloo? They didn't hear a thing. I step outside the motor home and walk around blinking in the sun, feeling a chill crawl all over my back.

Nothing. No hoofprints.

Not a single one.

CHAPTER

⇛SEVENTEEN⇚

The congregation is a little better at the Cobbville service.

I handle thirteen folks, all told. Everything from TMJ to shingles to back troubles caused on account of one leg being longer than the other. By the end of the night, Certain Certain is flat exhausted just from catching them as they fall.

"Twenty-three new souls dedicated themselves to walking with the Lord," Miss Wanda Joy says. I catch a crooked little smile as she jots down the total in her big green ledger. Sugar Tom calls my healings "the crowning moment of the service."

Now they're passing the collection plates, and Sugar Tom

is drowsing behind the curtain while I watch the night through the saddle flap.

This is the first time since Verbena that I've felt halfway comfortable with the way things are going. Maybe I'm being ungrateful? Is this the life I need to be in? Maybe I haven't truly understood the whole importance of my mission up till now. Maybe—

It's her—a flash of blue at the rear of the tent, mixed in with the back of the congregation. That same shade of blue . . .

Lucy!

What in the world is she doing here? What should I say? What should I do? I scramble to straighten my shirt, smooth my hair.

Should I go straight to her, ask her if she's all right? But she must be, elsewise why would she be here?

She wants to thank me. Thank me for saving her life.

I stand frozen and slack-jawed watching her. She's staring straight ahead, not speaking to anybody else. How long has she been there like that? The whole service? What is she waiting for?

She's waiting for me.

The congregation is starting to break up. I look around quick, scanning the faces. No sign of her parents. I haul back the saddle flap and look outside: no Gulf Breeze motor home. Maybe she rode over with a friend? *To see me.*

Okay, Ronald Earl. Just go talk to her. Do it now.

I hop down from the stage and make a beeline for the center aisle, keeping my eyes straight ahead so they will let me through. I can see folks swirling past Lucy. I feel like there's a big silver hook in my side yanking me toward her.

"Little Texas," Miss Wanda Joy calls, but I pretend I didn't hear.

Lucy. The inside of my head is on fire. She's starting to move away now, skirting the last row of chairs. There's something odd and jerky about the way she is walking, like her leg is hurt or something.

I spy a blue flick of Lucy's dress as she turns the corner of the tent. *What do I say? Ask her about her school? Her folks? Her town? Anything but the healing. Let her bring that up.*

I run to the back entrance and race around the corner. I jerk my head right and left; I see people streaming across the lumpy grass. A scattering of cloudy stars. The Wilbankses' little frame house glowing yellow. The line of a fence, cars, a dog nosing around a tractor tire.

And nothing else.

➤ EIGHTEEN ➤

"So how'd we do?" Sugar Tom says.

"The Church of the Hand won't starve . . . yet," Miss Wanda Joy says, clutching the prayer box to her lap.

"Speaking of which," Certain Certain says, "I could eat the hind end of a mule. Without the sauce."

We pile into the motor home and head out to Shoney's. Everybody else is keyed up from the service, saying it was our best in weeks. They all chatter away, Sugar Tom having fun with a cute little waitress. But I was that close to talking to Lucy. *That close.* I am pure heartsick.

"You were quiet tonight at supper," Miss Wanda Joy says when we get back.

"Yes'm."

She shakes the box in her lap, letting me hear the coins bounce. "It was a good service. Nothing to worry about."

"I know."

"Our next stop is Clampton. They were good to us last time."

"I don't remember."

"Well. Sleep."

She moves away from my end of the motor home, skirts swishing and leaving behind a cloud of lavender.

Laying down in my bunk, I feel like a car is squatting on my chest. *Why is she so important to me? Why do I feel like I've lost something I never had to begin with?*

I fall into a ragged sleep and keep waking up with pieces of dreams on the edges of my mind. Each scrap of dream has something blue in it, hanging just out of reach.

The next morning the sun comes up like three-day-old orange juice. I rub my stinging face and stare out at the dark green of the trees against the horizon.

YOU ARE NOW ENTERING CLAMPTON, MISSISSIPPI, a little sign tells us. The town looks to be a little bigger than Cobbville, but every bit as run-down—a gang of saggy old homes ranging around a town square, and brick stores with messages painted on them advertising stuff nobody has bought for probably fifty years.

"I suspect the national pastime around here is sitting on your ass shelling purple hull peas," Certain Certain says.

We have a lot of volunteers in Clampton, so Sugar Tom and me spend the hours reading and playing chess while Certain Certain supervises. Sugar Tom likes to call the chess men things like Hittites, Amalekites, and Jebusites. I have never beaten him.

"'I will bring you up out of the affliction of Egypt,'" Sugar Tom says. "Checkmate."

"Huh?"

"Some days the Spirit is close, Ronald Earl, others it's far away."

When it's time for the service, I sit peeking through the saddle flap. No Lucy, only the same kinds of faces I always see. I know what they're expecting. I just don't know how much of it I want to give.

"Game time," Certain Certain says.

After Sugar Tom introduces me, I stand there in the lights and the screaming, and that's all I do. I'm not smiling, I'm not doing anything. I let it soak into me, not thinking about the whiteness, not thinking that I need to get started. Just *feeling*. I let them settle down. Then I let them *more* than settle down. They go so ghostly quiet, you would think I was all alone.

My head is hanging a little, eyes down. Then I begin to hear them whisper, wondering if something is wrong. Maybe I won't do it this time. Maybe this is the time I just walk off and keep going. Quiet. Quiet. And then I see it. The chess-board still sitting there over behind the curtain, the game pieces still laid out. I raise my head and say this:

"Have you ever played chess, brothers and sisters? A chess-board has pieces on it. Pawns. Bishops. Knights. Rooks. A king and a queen. One player takes black, one takes white. If you corner the other player's king, you win. Simple as that."

Even I'm not sure where this is going.

"Are we the Lord's chess pieces, my brethren?" I say. "Is that what we are here for, for Him to play games with us? Do we even have any say in where we end up on the chessboard of *life*?"

Miss Wanda Joy looks like she just swallowed a broom-stick sideways. She makes motions with her hand, cutting it across her neck: *Cut it off.*

But I can't.

"Maybe one side of the board belongs to Jesus, the other to Satan. Which side do you pick? And what piece? Are you a bishop, thinking you can sneak catty-corner past the devil? Or maybe you're a knight, hopping out of trouble? A pawn, where you can only march straight ahead, Satan's sacrifice? A rook, plowing straight in a line, no matter what? Or maybe you're a queen. You can go anywhere, do anything you want. All the power is in *you*. But maybe, my brethren, just maybe, you are a *king.* You spend your time hiding from life, letting others fight your battles. The most powerless player on the board."

A smattering of voices holler out, "Amen."

I sneak a glance at Miss Wanda Joy. She's not slashing her throat anymore. I feel my voice rising, the whiteness coming up behind my eyelids, climbing my throat. I close my eyes and raise my arms.

"This is what I'm here to tell you, brothers and sisters, *ah!* It doesn't matter *what* piece you are in this game, *ah!* Because a great reckoning is coming, *ah!* The arm of Christ Jesus, *ah!* is coming to sweep aside every piece on the chessboard, *ah!* Each and every one of us, *ah!* Queen to pawn, *ah!* The Lord's side, *ah!* Satan's side, *ah!* *All* will fall like wheat to the thresher, *ah!* For the Great Harvester, *ah!* He is coming to take His accounting, *ah!* at the End of Days, *ah!* when the dead in Christ, *ah!* I say the *dead* in Christ, *ah!* shall rise like a great anointing, *ah!* and 'they that sow in tears shall reap in joy,' *ah!*"

Now they're on their feet, waving their hands in the air, swaying back and forth, yelling out "Amen" and "Praise His name!" It goes on and on, the praising and the hollering, my arms up in the air, and I remember again why I'm standing here, why I'm talking. It's not me. It's not me, it's something *using* me, something bigger and brighter and cleaner than I could ever be.

Hallelujah!

⇒NINETEEN⇐

"As there is no sanitary hookup here," Miss Wanda Joy says, all grim, "we will be staying in a motel tonight."

What she's really saying is the place where we've parked the motor home, sidled up against a used-car lot, isn't somewhere we can just let our toilet hosepipe dump on the ground, like we're used to out in the country. Folks would talk.

"The devil's playground," Miss Wanda Joy says when she signs for the rooms.

The man behind the counter just smiles; he doesn't have tooth one, and his skin looks like a field that's been left fallow, all sunken and punched with holes and stubble.

The rooms are small and damp, but it feels good to get a shower in a tub where your elbows aren't knocking the walls. Me and Certain Certain bunk in together, and Sugar Tom and Miss Wanda Joy take the room next door. I figure they spend most of the evening reading, holy scripture for her, stories about things like a girl from Russia with X-ray vision for him.

Miss Wanda Joy generally doesn't like us watching much TV, but the first thing Certain Certain does is grab the remote and flip it on, keeping the volume low, on account of the thin walls.

He skims down to his drawers and socks. Certain Certain's legs look like they haven't seen the sun since birth. The slave tag is a hot little square of brownish gold on his chest. He pretty much never takes it off, like it's some kind of protection for him.

We watch a show where a man gets to pick from twelve different sinful women to marry. He gets to kiss them *all,* sometimes even with the other women looking. They squabble and cuss each other something fierce. Miss Wanda Joy would have an aneurism.

"Not worth spit," Certain Certain says. "He might as well throw darts. Not one of them gals got the brains the good Lord gave a turnip."

But I can sure stand looking at them.

We watch a bunch of other stuff we shouldn't be watching, too. This is how we keep up with things in the outside world. Certain Certain laughs at a cell phone commercial.

"Day is coming, Lightning, people will always know where they are. Satellites, navigators, tracking each and every one of us. But don't let folks kid you . . . they lost the true path a *long* time ago. Ain't no GPS indicator goin' locate their tails for them."

Last thing I remember is Arnold Schwarzenegger toting a casket full of weapons on his shoulder while the army tries to blow him up. Then somewhere Certain Certain must've cut out the light, on account of I wake up hours later with a big old blob of moonlight on my belly, coming through a gap in the curtains.

I've always liked watching the moon, so I slip out of bed and yank the curtains back—and holler the worst cuss word I've ever said.

By the time Certain Certain gets the light switch, I'm scrabbled up against the door, trying to find the knob.

"What is it, boy? What's got you spooked?" he says, scratchy and fuddle-headed.

"Out there!" I say, shaking my finger at the window. "She—she's *looking* at us!"

Certain Certain goes over and hauls the drapes all the way open. "Can't see a damn thing," he says. "Too bright in here. Cut the lights out."

I flip the switch on the lamp. "Ain't nothing," he says. I dare to look—an empty sidewalk running in both directions and the shiny parking lot, all lit up by a big fat spring moon.

"She was there!" I say, starting to feel a little ridiculous. "I saw her. Her face was pushed up against the glass, looking straight at me, when I opened the curtains. . . ."

I could see her hair brushing her shoulders, her wet eyes, not much more. The thing is, she didn't move one bit when she saw me—just kept staring straight into our room, giving me the awful feeling she had been standing right there for hours, knowing I would have to take a look outside sooner or later. Waiting all night, just hoping to catch a glimpse of me. Stare straight into my eyes.

Somebody's beating the door down. We cut the lights back on and drag on our pants. Miss Wanda Joy hurries in wearing a purple bathrobe with a gold cross crocheted on the pocket. Her hair is done up all over with bobby pins, with one or two wispy pieces trailing down her back. Her eyes look like two fried eggs.

"Just what is going on over here?" she barks.

"Night terrors," Certain Certain says, grinning and putting his elbow into my side, making my face go hot. "Ronald Earl thought a burglar was trying to bust in."

"A burglar?"

"Well, let's make that a burgla*rette,*" Certain Certain says. "Some little gal peeking in the windows."

"She wasn't peeking, she was *staring,*" I say. "Did you see anybody coming up the sidewalk?"

Miss Wanda Joy pinches her lips together. "There's no one out there, Little Texas."

But just in case, we pile out on the sidewalk to peek. The air smells of French fries.

"She must've run off the other direction," I say.

Close by there's a set of busted concrete stairs and a Dr Pepper machine. It's dark up under the stairs, making a little chill go through me. She could be hiding right there, all I know.

"Where's Sugar Tom?" Certain Certain says.

"Asleep," Miss Wanda Joy says. "As should we all be. It would take the final trumpet to wake that man."

We crawl back into bed, but I can't sleep. Is she still out there lurking in the shadows, just waiting for our lights to go out so she can come back?

The next day my head feels sour and my eyes are burning. We eat a quick breakfast and head over to the car dealership to break down the tent.

"Oh my sweet Jesus," Certain Certain says when we pull into the vacant lot. My mouth falls open, but I can't find words to speak.

"'And he said unto them, I beheld Satan as lightning fall from Heaven,'" Sugar Tom says.

There are long, jaggedy tears in the canvas side of the tabernacle. The pulpit has been tumped over and smashed.

But the worst part is this: some of the folding chairs are hanging thirty feet up in the trees.

⇒ TWENTY ⇐

The sheriff of Neshoba County is named Mr. Jimbo Martee. He wears a ring big as a gold lug nut and nearly breaks my hand shaking it.

"So, regarding the contents of your—um—*tent,* you've said that the only thing damaged—"

"We've been all over that," Miss Wanda Joy says, rolling her shoulders. She is every bit as tall as Sheriff Martee and twice as motivated. "I want something *done,* and I want it done *now.*"

Sheriff Martee grunts and honks his squashed-up nose into a handkerchief.

"And you're certain, ma'am, that there wasn't nobody—*anybody*—suspicious hanging around after the service? Anybody that bothered y'all around town?"

"No—if you would try listening this time—this is obviously a deliberate, malicious act against our *ministry*. You have to find these people and find them *now*."

Sheriff Martee takes off his ventilated cowboy hat and wipes his brow on his shirtsleeve.

"Well, Miss . . ." He studies his pad. "Miss *King*. Tell you the truth, ma'am, being how they didn't leave any messages behind, nothing to go on, there is nothing that makes me think your . . . *ministry* was being targeted in particular. So I figure it was just some kids that done this, out having fun."

"Fun?"

And off she goes, and I can't stand to listen to another word. I head over to where Certain Certain is surveying the damage.

"A man is bringing a thirty-foot double-cleat ladder for the folding chairs," Certain Certain says, looking up at the trees. "Rest is rigging a new pulpit and patching them tears."

He makes his hand like a claw, shows us how something ripped at the canvas in three stripes, over and over again.

"You mean to tell me some kind of *animal* got hold of it?" Sugar Tom says. "What kind of animal hangs folding chairs in the trees like Christmas ornaments?"

"No animal I know of got three-toed claws that big,"

Certain Certain says. "Somebody using a three-prong hay fork, more like. Awful sharp one, too."

"You think it was those Conover High School guys we ran into at the rest stop the other day?" I say.

Certain Certain snickers. "Sure thing, Lightning. Them kids are following us all over creation, just itching for the chance to tear up our tabernacle."

"Well, they were pretty mean."

"Look at them cuts. This was done by something *power-ful*. Something slashing *hard*. Something *angry*. *Damn* angry."

Sugar Tom clears his throat and nods at me like my ears are being polluted.

"Wait a minute," I say, feeling cold. "You think it was that girl I saw at the motel?"

Certain Certain smiles. "You mean that little invisible gal nobody else saw but you? Naw, little invisible gals don't have it in 'em to do something like *this*. Even if they did, they don't have the strength, neither—"

"Can you mend it?" Sugar Tom says.

"Why, hell yes I can mend it, doctor. You fetch me a little industrial-strength thread and a needle big as a rug hook, we in bidness."

"Then what are we going to do?" I say.

"Pack," Certain Certain says.

CHAPTER

⋙ TWENTY-ONE ⋘

Meridian, Mississippi.

"They call this town the Queen City—you know that?" Certain Certain says, laughing a little. "Don't know why. Ain't no *royalty* round this locality. Used to be the largest city in the state. Set up on land borrowed from the Choctaw. Funny how sooner or later everything winds up getting owned by the white man."

He laughs and gives my head a rub. I push his big hand away.

"Cut it out. I hate it when you do that."

"Whew. Simmer down, boy. Things'll smooth out. Every

revival I've ever been on had its lumps and bumps 'long the way."

He punches on the radio, and I nod off for a while. When I wake up, he's gulping kipper snacks from a little red tin with a plastic fork, steering with his knees.

I sit up and rub my eyes. We're rumbling along a quiet road on the outskirts of town. Meridian looks like it has a lot of trains. Certain Certain is talking just like I never even went to sleep.

"Forty thousand folks. Ought to be our biggest crowd this season," he says. "Back in the Civil War, General Sherman burnt Meridian to the foundations. 'Meridian no longer exists.' That is a di-rect quote to General Grant. You can look it up."

I yawn. "How come you know so much about this town?"

"My Uncle Fish used to live here. Called him that on account of he had this sunk-in scar on his side from a accident with some ice tongs. Shaped just like a *fish*."

"Will he be at the service tonight?"

"Not unless they dig his raggedy tail up from the Rose Hill cemetery. Here we go."

Certain Certain turns the truck down a patchy paved road between a stand of hackberry trees and pulls to a stop. The setup place used to be a drive-in movie theater; now it's choked with milkweed and poke salad. You can see the paint peeling off the big white screen at the far end of the field, and metal posts stubbed up in rows.

"That's where they used to hang up the speaker boxes," Certain Certain says. "Used to come here with Uncle Fish a time or two myself. Bet you've never been to a drive-in picture show, have you, Lightning?"

"No, sir."

There's a train embankment on the far side of the theater lot, crawling in kudzu. A gang of men is already waiting. We get out and stretch, and Certain Certain gets the helpers started. The air is buzzing with katydids calling to each other.

I don't like the feel of this place, hemmed in by trees on one side, the steep hill on the other. Only one way in, one way out.

The cars start arriving early, engines growling. Some of them have signs taped to their windows saying things like WELCOME, LITTLE TEXAS or GOD BLESS CHURCH OF THE HAND.

Certain Certain was right. It *is* a big crowd, so many there's not enough seating. The latecomers stand in the back, shifting and restless, some of the younger ones picking at each other and laughing. I hear people asking about the claw marks in the canvas. It doesn't feel like a regular church crowd.

I wait, tugging at my tie and kicking at gravel behind the stage. Listening to the voices and wishing I could let go of her.

Sugar Tom stands and has his say, getting the crowd worked into a lather. But something feels wrong—the congregation is not just loud, it's *rowdy*. When I step up to the microphone, you would think they were trying to bring down the walls of Jericho.

It feels strange not having the pulpit to lean into or beat on. Things start to settle down a bit, but shouts and giggly squeals keep breaking out. People are turning and glaring at a gang of kids standing in the back.

Forget them.

I raise the Bible and close my eyes, trying to let the whiteness come. With so many people, it feels awful close in here. I need to get above the hot lights, need to step outside my body, outside the tent walls.

"Hey!" somebody hollers in the back. "I got something you can use to slick down that hair. Come around back, and I'll give you a squirt."

A rough laugh dances around the tent. My eyes wink open.

"You come to heal us?" a different boy says. "I got something needs healing. It's all *swole up*." Another burst of crazy giggling spills over us.

"*Little* Texas, huh." A *girl* this time. "Just *how* little we talking here?"

This really sets them off in the back, screaming and whooping.

Finally a barrel-chested man with a cowboy hat stands and faces the crowd.

"Excuse me," he says. "*Excuse me.* I don't know what some

of y'all's problem is, but we come to hear this boy speak. Now if y'all can't act civil and behave, you need to get on out of here. Otherwise you're going to have to answer to *me*." He sits down again and looks at me. "I'm sorry, please continue."

The kids in the back quiet down some, but I can still see them smirking, sticking their tongues out. Some of the girls are moving their bodies almost like they are dancing. Tank tops, belly buttons, sneers, those white iPod wires dangling from their heads.

A little bead of sweat comes sliding down my temple right into my ear.

I lift the Bible higher and stand there for maybe thirty seconds not saying a word, sweat pouring off my face. I can smell dust burning on the halogen bulbs. *Say something. Say anything.*

I pour every speck of concentration I have into the moment. My vision begins to blur, till I can see the congregation only as one big blaze of light and shapes.

It's working.

I close my eyes again, feeling the lightness coming into my feet, my legs, and I open my mouth—

A train smashes by on the hill, whistle shrieking through the kudzu.

I bring the Bible down, open my eyes. Now all the girls are laughing at me, even if I can't hear them over the screaming of the train. I can see it, see their scorn and disgust.

I walk over to Sugar Tom and hand him the Bible.

"I can't do this," I say.

"Ronald Earl?" he says. His eyes look smoke-colored and yellow.

I touch his spindly arm and put my mouth close to his ear. "I can't do this tonight. I'm sorry, Sugar Tom. I'm not—I'm not feeling right."

He stands there a couple seconds. Then he nods and goes out on the stage, but I can see they are not looking at him. All those heads are turned toward *me*.

Miss Wanda Joy's mouth is open, face froze halfway between horror and pure disbelief. I turn my head in the other direction, see Certain Certain waiting next to the Calvary Rail. He lifts his shoulders, his eyes making a question.

I step behind the curtain at the side of the stage. Pull off my suit coat and hang it over a chair. Sit down heavy as a stump.

Miss Wanda Joy comes huffing around the curtain, jerking it back. She fixes her eyes on me, and I can't help it; I have to look away. I can feel how mad she is just looking at her legs, the way she is standing, the way her arms hang. I have never let her down like this before. Not on stage. Not once.

"What is going on?" she says, teeth in her voice.

"I'm sorry, I just can't go on tonight," I say, looking down. "I'm just not feeling right. I—I can't do it. I'll be better at the next service."

She slaps a hot hand up against my forehead. "Are you ill?"

"No, ma'am."

She takes her hand away. "Then what is it? What could *possibly* cause you to leave the stage like that? You do realize this is our largest congregation of the season?"

"I know, I *know*. I'm sorry, but I don't know what to tell you."

"One last time—are you going to get up and speak or not?"

"No, ma'am. I'm not. I *can't*."

Miss Wanda Joy takes a long breath and lets it back out slow.

"I will never forget this."

She turns and leaves. I watch out the corner of my eye as she takes her place in the same chair as before. I hang my head and listen to Sugar Tom apologize to the congregation. Folks are starting to trickle off. Miss Wanda Joy turns her head sharply away from the people, refusing to watch them leave.

CHAPTER

➤ TWENTY-TWO ➤

"Reckon it's tuna and jerky for supper," Certain Certain says, his torn-up lip curling. He glances at Miss Wanda Joy. "I don't know what got into you, boy, but if you need to rent yourself a new backside after she gets done chewing on it, just call me. I got plenty extra."

I sit on the half-dark stage listening to people talk through the canvas as they head out to their cars.

"But he was so *good* last time."

"Wonder is he all right?"

No, I think. *He's not. He's all wrong, and I don't know if he'll ever be all right again.*

Sugar Tom vanishes into the motor home to smoke. The volunteers grumble and cuss breaking down the tent. Miss Wanda Joy circles like a turkey buzzard, waiting for them to leave.

When everything is packed away and the last car is gone, Certain Certain squeezes my shoulder.

"Good luck."

He leaves me sitting on an upturned trash barrel with the drop cord hanging from a speaker box post. The light doesn't help, just makes the dark closing in around me that much worse. At last Miss Wanda Joy comes in for a landing.

"I have *never* been so embarrassed in my *whole life,*" she says, face broiling red.

"Said I'm sorry."

"You are supposed to be a *professional.* How would you feel if you attended a music concert, and the band refused to play because they just didn't *feel* like it?"

That's different, I think. A band always has its instruments.

"But nobody pays to see me," I say.

Miss Wanda Joy pulls her fingers through her hair so hard, I'm afraid she's going to snatch herself bald-headed. She gets in my face.

"Pay you, *pay you!* They pay you when the show is *over*!"

Never mind that's not what I said. Her words bounce off the drive-in movie screen like the voice of God.

"They pay you when you are *worth* being paid! They pay

you when you give them what they have come to *expect.* They come expecting something *spectacular.* They come expecting *miracles.* Miracles performed by an anointed son of the *Lord.* That. Is. What. You. Give. Them." She jabs me in the chest on every word. "And. You. Let. Them. *Down.*"

Forgive me, Lord, but I want to hit her so bad. I do.

White foam has collected in the corners of her mouth. I have to wipe spit off my cheek. Miss Wanda Joy steps away from me, arms crossed, shaking her head. Her breathing sounds like she's been hoeing a garden. She breathes that way a little while, not looking at me.

Finally she turns to face me again and tucks some loose hair around an ear.

"That's all I have to say. Except this: you are not only a professional, Little Texas, you are also a *celebrity. More* than a celebrity. You are a *living representative of the One True God.* With that status comes a responsibility. You have to treat these people as your *fans,* as much as I despise that word. No matter how they behave. No matter what you feel like. *Do you understand me?*"

"Yes'm, I do. It won't happen again."

"It *can't* happen again. It *can't.* Our ministry *will not survive it.*"

She drops her hands, exhausted, and makes her way to the motor home, slamming the door behind her.

I wait a little while, then get up and walk away from the light, toward the railroad embankment.

I think for a long time, looking at the hillside, hands in my pockets. The hill is steep, but I could do it. Claw my way through the kudzu to the tracks at the top. Follow them wherever they go. There is a world out there.

After a little while I take my hands out of my pockets and start walking back across the parking lot. And I see a blue dress.

TWENTY-THREE

Lucy's standing in a puddle of yellow light, blond hair shining. Same blue dress. Same little white basketball sneakers. Same skinny arms hanging against her sides. She's looking right at me.

My chest starts to ache; finally I realize I've forgotten to breathe. I take a long inhale; I can smell honeysuckle on the air.

What's she doing here?

I guess I know the answer. *She's following me. Following me wherever I go.*

But why?

No car, nobody else in sight. She couldn't have just walked here, could she? Is she all right? Where are her parents? *Please, Lord*—she hasn't run away from home on account of me, has she?

A thought stabs me like an icicle.

What if—*what if there's something wrong with her?*

Standing so straight and still, she could almost be a wax figure in a museum. I take a couple of slow steps toward her, afraid I might spook her if I move too quick. Everything's so quiet; the only sound is my shoes on the gravel.

I'm closer now, so close she has to see me coming. If it's bothering her, she doesn't show it.

Fifty feet. Twenty. *Ten.*

"Hey—"

There's something different about her hair.

I stop walking.

I remember Lucy's hair being so thick, but now it's hanging flat against the sides of her face. And that one difference makes me start to see others. And then—

I'm afraid; all I can do is stand still and just watch her, waiting to see what she does.

I'm sure of it. I'm sure.

This is the girl I saw last night pressing her face against the motel window.

CHAPTER

⇒ TWENTY-FOUR ⇐

"You," I say. "It was you last night, wasn't it? At the motel?"

She doesn't change her look, doesn't even open her mouth to speak.

"Are you all right? Is there anything wrong? Do you—do you remember me from the healing? You're Lucy, right? Is something wrong, Lucy? Do you need help?"

I take a couple of steps, till I come all the way into her circle of light. I'm barely more than an arm's length away from her. . . .

Jesus Christ our Savior.

Her eyes . . .

The color of her eyes has changed.

The blue is still there, but only enough to remember that's what they used to be. Now they are cloudy as pond ice and all shot through with tiny, curling lines. She hasn't blinked. Not once.

She's still pure beautiful but seems even skinnier, and her dress is wrinkly and hanging lower on one shoulder than the other. The hem at the bottom is tattered and stained.

Before tonight I had dreamed of looking into her robin's-egg blue eyes and taking her for a walk. A walk where nobody could look at us, bother us, wonder what we're doing. As far away from the Faith Tabernacle as we could get.

But I know in a heartbeat I won't ever be able to talk to this being. Can't touch her hand. Can't go for a walk with whatever this is standing in front of me.

Still, Lucy's small mouth trembles like she is going to speak. My skin races all over with goose bumps.

This is all that's left of her.

This must be what men see on the battlefield. What policemen see on the highways. Doctors see it in hospitals. It's right here in front of me.

It's all that's left of her.

"Why?" I say.

Now she is reaching for me. But it looks so hard for her.

She lifts her arm higher and higher till it's level with the ground, then holds it there, her little hand in a fist. Her mouth opens. It opens wider and wider, showing nothing but black on the inside. She works her jaw slowly, slowly, no words coming out.

Turns her fist over, opens it, lets a little piece of paper fall.

She looks like . . . *oh no, please* . . . she is trying to smile. That's exactly what she's doing, the corners of her mouth lifting up slow and gradual, as if they were being tugged by a wire.

So . . . beautiful.

Even like this.

"Lightning!" Certain Certain calls. I snap my head toward the sound. When I turn back, she's gone.

⇒ TWENTY-FIVE ⇐

Something hurts. I've put a fist to my mouth, and I'm biting down on my knuckles. Harder and harder till I can near taste the blood. I can see the speaker box posts, the dead white movie screen, the hackberry woods. All solid and real.

She couldn't be gone that quick. The woods are too far away.

Somebody lays a hand on my shoulder; I feel my legs nearly go.

"Hey, boy," Certain Certain says. "You all right?"

I turn and look at him like I've never met him before in my life.

"What?" I say finally.

"You don't look so good. She take that big a plug out of your hind end?"

Did he see her?

"Miss Wanda Joy, she's just like that." Certain Certain starts to tug me toward the motor home. "Come on. Let's get some supper. That's right, she wants to head into town. Reckon Miss Wanda Joy feels a little guilty for chewing on you so hard."

I look at the woods again, working to haul my words up from so far away, I don't even recognize my own voice. "Did you—did you see her?"

"See which?"

"*Her.* That girl, Lucy. She was standing right here."

"All I saw was you. My Lord. Tell me you didn't really see somebody. *Tell me.*"

I pull away and take a step toward the drop cord.

"She left something! Help me look! It's got to be right here somewhere. . . ."

I get down on my knees in the gravel beside the drop cord, raking all over with my fingers.

"Here! Here it is. I found it!"

I rush to the light with the little piece of paper. It's a piece of an article torn out of a newspaper.

ARREST IN INMATE DEATH

THE ASSOCIATED PRESS
July 28, 2001

MIAMI — Two nurses at a juvenile jail were charged with murder and manslaughter Tuesday for allegedly failing to treat a 17-year-old male inmate who died of a burst appendix in June after three days in pain.

I grab at Certain Certain's shirtsleeve. "What does it *mean*? What do you think it means? Is she trying to tell me something?"

"I'll tell you what it means. Means you found some trash on the ground. Elsewise, Miss Wanda Joy's liable to sign you up for a rubber room over in Tuscaloosa. Nothing but Ritz crackers and green baloney from now on."

"But the article!"

"Hold your water. We'll talk about it."

I shove the scrap of paper in my pocket. "Please believe me. If you don't, nobody will."

"I believe *you* believe. You ain't never been one to lie. Probably some little old town girl fooling with you, same as them during the service."

I stand there, look at the woods one more time. It's too dark, too thick to see anything. Could he be right?

"But I know it was her. I *know* it."

Whoever I was before seeing her, I'm a different person now.

Lucy's dead.

That sweet, beautiful girl is *dead.*

I will wake up tomorrow, and it will still be true, and there will still be nothing I can do about it.

What is she? Where is she now?

A *ghost.* What does a ghost want with me?

For some crazy reason I recall the way they handled witches up in Massachusetts. They piled big stones on their chests, one stone at a time, till finally the witch was slowly crushed to death. I'm feeling the very first stone.

⟫ TWENTY-SIX ⟪

I have a handheld computer Sugar Tom gave me for Christmas that holds the entire King James Bible. The word *ghost* shows up a grand total of 112 times. Eighteen times in the book of Acts alone.

But it's not talking about ghosts like in the movies, the kind that walk through walls, rassle over your bed at night, and go "Boo!" It's talking about the *Holy Spirit*.

The dead are dead. They can't hear a thing, see a thing, speak, think, or turn up in your closet with bloody red eyes. They don't even go to heaven right off the bat; they hang around waiting on Jesus to wake them when the dead in Christ shall rise at the Final Judgment. Amen.

But seeing Lucy's face up close—if I can even call her Lucy anymore—even if my mind doesn't believe, my body is telling me the plain truth; every hair I ever owned is standing straight out like bluegill spines.

But could she be something else? Believe it or not, the word *demon* doesn't crop up in the Bible one single solitary time. I know it looks that way in the movies. People waving Bibles, shaking crosses, throwing holy water. But the Bible calls those creatures *devils. Devil* pops up 122 times altogether.

Devils have to be cast out.

⇒ TWENTY-SEVEN ⇐

"Navy beans," Sugar Tom says. "Mother made them in a huge pot with little dabs of chunk bacon cut in. She never sat down for supper, not once, she was so intent on serving everyone else. Oh my Lord, if I close my eyes, I can smell them."

All I can smell is Krystal hamburgers, the little square kinds with the steamy wet buns. The night is cloudy, and green mayflies are bumping the glass. The motor home and the truck take up half the parking lot. Certain Certain is working on a chili pup, and Miss Wanda Joy is sitting by herself outside.

"I know just what she doing," Certain Certain says. "Got

that prayer box in her lap, poppin' them rubber bands till her finger turns blue. You in the doghouse, Lightning. You shoulda played sick, maybe you would've made out all right."

"But I don't feel sick. I feel . . ."

The world is a different color. A different taste. Sound.

"I'll speak with her," Sugar Tom says. Mustard on his mouth, and he doesn't even know it.

"Clean yourself up there, doctor," Certain Certain says, handing him a napkin. "Daddy King was still here, we'd have us a buffer. He could handle her."

I'm glad we're eating here. This is the best kind of place to tell something like this.

"I saw what I saw," I say. "It was her, *Lucy.*"

Certain Certain takes a big bite, chews around his thoughts. "Just consider it was some little towheaded gal that favored her, and she just run off. You know how shy them little gals can be." He winks at Sugar Tom.

"But how could she have run away that fast? It's not possible . . . I would have seen her. . . ."

"I've known me some girls who could flat *get it,*" Certain Certain says. "Leave you chokin' in their dust. Maybe she's on the track team."

"But she wasn't—she wasn't all *there.*" I don't know what I'm trying to say. "It's like she was there, but she wasn't there, you know what I mean?"

"Nuh-uh."

"You had to see her up close to understand. She was

111

different. Different from a . . . regular girl. It was like she was . . . made of different *stuff* or something."

Certain Certain winks again. "I've run into a few of those myself."

"Ectoplasm," Sugar Tom says. "The stuff of spirits."

"Yes," I say. "That's what I'm saying, a ghost."

"An *apparition,*" Sugar Tom says.

"I won't say I don't believe you," Certain Certain says. He leans back in his seat. "I won't. On account of my grand-mammy saw a ghost one time. It was a pastor they used to have. Apparently, he was walking across a field of winter wheat. Hat on, same old jacket he always wore. She tried to call out from the buckboard, 'Hey, Pastor *James.*' The words just hung in her throat. See, that man'd been dead three weeks."

"What happened?" I say.

"*Whoom,* he was gone. Just like that. Like the earth opened up, plumb swallowed him whole." He takes a long pull on his drink. "That said, ain't never seen one myself. And I sure didn't see yours."

"But—she came to the motel, too. And what about Cobbville! How likely is that if she's some local girl?"

"Don't know. Only know most things, nine times out of ten—no, ninety-nine times out of a *hundred*—whatever makes the most sense, the easiest, simplest thing is the most likely. Been that way all my life."

"I need to show you my book on Borley Rectory," Sugar

Tom says. "Could change your tune a mite. The most haunted house in England. Ghosts of every shape and description. A phantom nun, a headless man, a minister who was hanged while his bride was bricked up alive in a wall—"

"So you believe in them?" I say to Sugar Tom.

He cuts his eyes in the direction of the motor home. "I won't say I don't believe in them," he says. "Won't say I do. But one thing's certain, they can't be ghosts of the dead. That goes against scripture. But I believe there is *something* out there."

"Are they evil?" I say. "Devils?"

"Quite possibly."

"What do they do?"

"At Borley Rectory? Bells rang by themselves, there were flapping noises. Objects moving in the night."

"But—do the—the ghosts—do they ever *hurt* anybody?"

Sugar Tom swallows his last bite of Krystal, making his goozle pipe jump.

"I recall there was a gal moved in there, named Miz Marianne Foyster, wife of the Reverend Lionel Foyster. The spirits took a special interest in her. She got thrown from her bed a lot in the middle of the night. Slapped by invisible hands. Struck by stones. Near smothered to death by a mattress. Her daughter, Adelaide, was attacked, husband took sick until they were driven from their home. Is that evil? I reckon it could be. . . . Anything that is not of the Lord is not of His kingdom. You know that, Ronald Earl."

"But are they people? What if they are people?"

"Devils. They have to be devils. Scripture says—"

"Yes, sir, I know what it says . . . but if you *saw* somebody . . . saw them *alive,* and then—then you saw them again, and they were *changed.* And you knew the person they were wasn't alive anymore, what would you think then?"

"Think you been watchin' too much trash on TV," Certain Certain says.

"But she gave me something." I take out the scrap of newspaper again and spread it open on the table.

Certain Certain pushes it away. "Trash on TV, trash on the ground, what's the difference, Lightning?"

"There *were* some messages," Sugar Tom says. "Written to Mrs. Foyster on a mirror."

I feel my heart ticking. "What did they say?"

"Mostly just calling out for help. Like that poor woman could do anything. When we all know the House of the Lord is the target for all such foul things."

"But . . . couldn't that have been a spirit trying to make contact? Not a devil, but somebody . . . a person who had really been alive. Supposing they really *were* desperate? Needing some help? You think maybe Lucy needs me? Needs my help . . ."

"Son, just pray on it," Sugar Tom says. "Where are my cigarettes? Have you seen my cigarettes?"

"You up past your bedtime, doctor," Certain Certain says. "Don't need to be doing any of that right now."

Sugar Tom checks his wristwatch. "Well, goodness. It's after nine. You are right. Good night, all."

He steps out to the parking lot and disappears inside the motor home. I stuff the clipping about the boy with the burst appendix back in my pocket, disappointed.

"Don't let on 'bout any of this to her," Certain Certain says when we get up to go. "You liable to end up stuck in that motor home praying on your knees, six hours straight."

I find Miss Wanda Joy waiting stiff-backed in the driver's seat, snapping those rubber bands. Her fingers are striped red. I start to make my way to the back.

"Wait." She taps the seat next to her. "Up here."

Uh-oh.

"I know what you're going to—" I start.

She holds up a hand to shoosh me and touches the photo of Daddy King when I sit down.

"You know, I've probably never told you this, but even Daddy King had his moments. Times when the challenges he faced in this ministry seemed *insurmountable.*"

I look at his picture on the dashboard; I swear I see his mustache twitch.

"Yes'm."

She takes my jaw in her big fingers, just the way she used to do when I was seven or eight. I watch her bosom rise and fall as she lets out a big, horsey sigh.

"Is there something you need to tell me?" she says, looking into my eyes.

I gulp hard, feeling it all the way to the pit of my stomach. "No, ma'am. I don't think so."

She lets my jaw go. "You don't think so?"

I take in a deep breath.

"I'm all right. Really. I think . . . I think I just need a change. I just really need to do something *different.* Something is happening. I can feel . . . the Lord . . . I can feel Him telling me to try something different. You think maybe . . . the things that have been happening lately . . . you think it's some kind of sign?"

"A sign of what?"

My eyes light on the picture of Daddy King. "Daddy King . . . didn't he always preach that we were to look for the signs? To try to see what the Holy Ghost is telling us, so that we can do His will?"

"He did indeed."

"I think these things—these *signs*—I think they are telling me something—telling me I'm not a kid anymore. I need some breathing space. Little Texas needs to grow some, you know what I mean? I'm so tired of people thinking of me like I'm still this little kid, like somebody in a freak show. I can't pretend to be Little Texas the whole rest of my life—"

"You will *always* be Little Texas," Miss Wanda Joy says, clicking her tongue.

"I know, I know, I didn't mean it that way. I meant, what is Little Texas going to be five years from now? Ten? I can't keep pretending like I'm never going to grow up. I can't. I don't know what is happening, I just know something bad is coming if I just keep doing the same thing. Don't you feel that?"

Miss Wanda Joy reaches over and smooths my hair. I get nervous when she acts this way; Certain Certain says it runs too much against her nature. I see little knots of muscle working on either side of her jaw.

"So. I can see your mind is set," she says. "You are getting older, turning into a young man. Wanting to make your own decisions. I have been slow to recognize this, perhaps. It is partly me to blame; I have been too easy. Daddy King always said this was my weakness, my flaw. Suffering the hearts of others."

I let out a long breath. "But—"

"If this is the way you want it, that is the way it has to be. I have been praying about this. More than you know. And I believe you are telling me it's time . . . time to climb another rung on Jacob's Ladder, praise His name. You need a new challenge, you are set on that?"

"Yes, ma'am."

"Vanderloo Plantation," she says, as if she has been thinking about it all along.

"Waterloo?"

"Vanderloo. An old family surname. It means 'Place of Wandering.' You recall the time our Lord spent in the wilderness?"

"Forty days and forty nights? When He was tempted by Satan?"

"That was the turning point in His ministry. When He was offered all the kingdoms of the earth to follow Satan and turned them down. I believe Vanderloo will be something like that for you. The crossroads in your personal growth as the spiritual leader of our church."

"So we're going to be up against something different, something bigger at this Vanderloo place?"

"I didn't say *we*."

≫ TWENTY-EIGHT ≪

It takes Miss Wanda Joy most of the next day to get things arranged. When we pull out, the sun is already going down.

"That woman," Certain Certain says. "I've been working with her thirty-five, no, thirty-*six* years now. Every time I get her figured out, she throws me a new one. Shoot."

"You know anything about it?" I say. "Vanderloo, I mean. What is it?"

"Big pre–Civil War cotton plantation. Used to be thousands and thousands of acres close by to Pickwick Landing."

"Is there something bad about the place?"

"How much she tell you?"

"Nothing, really. She was kind of mysterious about it. You ever been there?"

"Once. Long time ago. Didn't never want to go back."

"How come? You love all that history stuff."

Certain Certain scratches at his chest through his shirt a long time. The truck tires make a thrumming sound.

"Put it this way, Lightning," he says finally. "They bought and sold human beings at Vanderloo. Called 'em chattels, old-time word for property. Kept them penned in a shed where buyers could look at their teeth, pinch their arms. Make them bend over to check for ruptures, hidden wounds. But I've been to plenty of places even worse. Doesn't get any worse than the slave market at Charleston, South Carolina."

"So what's so bad about Vanderloo in particular?"

Certain Certain looks out the window, the muscles of his jaw working.

"Can't say, exactly. Just a reputation it has. Stories. Miss Wanda Joy needs to tell you about that. This is her plan, not mine."

"But what's up there?"

"Original plantation house burnt down. The new house is well over a hundred years old, what I recollect. As for the rest of it, it's most all sunk now."

"What do you mean, 'sunk'?"

"You'll see."

We leave the county highway and pick up a curvy two-lane road, nothing but black woods on either side. I can barely see Miss Wanda Joy ahead of us, practically putting the motor home on two wheels.

"Woman going to get us wrapped around a tree or throwed in jail if she don't slow down," Certain Certain says.

He squints hard at the road. His eyes aren't so good for night driving anymore. I'd help, but I don't even have my permit yet. We never seem to set still long enough for me to take the test.

"'Sides, Lightning," Certain Certain likes to say. "Takes a *man* to drive a big rig."

I am a man.

We head down a long slope, and when we bottom out, the moon breaks through the clouds, showing reedy, flat land. Soon there's open water glistening on one side of the road. I crank the window down and can hear bullfrogs plonking and smallmouths jumping. Certain Certain pushes back in his seat till his bones pop.

"Town of Vanderloo is out there," he says, pointing off to the west.

"But there's nothing but water," I say.

"Told you. The old town was drowned dead as a mud turtle seventy-some years ago when the Tennessee Valley Authority built the dam. *That's* what I meant by 'sunk.' Congress said bring power to the folks living out in the woods. Rural 'lectrification Act. So the town had to go when they dammed the river."

"The plantation was sunk, too?"

"Man who owned it, the first Vanderloo, I s'pose, picked the highest spot of ground along this stretch of the river. The site of the plantation home was too high to be flooded. When the waters come flushing through, there it stood, clean as a church, its own little island. Now they call it Devil Hill."

My throat catches a little. "Why'd they name it that?"

"They had their reasons. There's an old trestle left over from when the railroad ran to the landing. I wouldn't walk on it naked and barefoot. Only safe way to get to the island is by boat."

Finally we turn off and follow Miss Wanda Joy up a jouncy dirt drive. Lightning bugs are burbling through the woods. I can see the moon through a tangle of branches on top of a low hill, and there is a house there. It's a tall place built of stone and brick, with two chimbleys at either end and yellow squares of light marking the windows.

"This is the new house," Certain Certain says. "The other one is across the water."

"How'd the old house burn down?" I say.

"Some fool throwed a lit cigar on a pile of trash when they were renovating the third floor. Went up faster than a cotton bale soaked in grain alcohol."

Across the pasture I can see little dark rectangles that must be cows. The motor home swings to a stop in front. We pull up alongside and get out. The house is even larger than I figured, with pieces of stone at the corners big as feed troughs. The windows are deep-sunk, some of them taller than a man, others small and crisscrossed with slats of wood in shapes like diamonds and crosses.

"This is the Barlow estate," Miss Wanda Joy says, coming over with Sugar Tom. "Tee and Faye Barlow have owned it for the past twenty years or so. Tee Barlow is a very important admirer of Little Texas. Get your bags. This is where we will be sleeping for the next several nights."

"I haven't slept in a real house in a coon's age," Certain Certain says, nudging me. "And I've sure never slept in a real *mansion.*"

Miss Wanda Joy leads the way up to the plank front porch. A man is already standing there in a skinny piece of light spilling out the open front door. He looks to be maybe in his late fifties. Pretty old, anyhow. He has wavy gray hair with a bald spot, a big chest, and a frost-colored beard.

"Welcome, Church of the Hand! Little Texas, welcome," the man says, nearly wringing my arm loose when we shake. "Tee Barlow. We are so happy to have you here. Bless you in the name of the Lord."

"Psalm one twenty-nine, verse eight," Sugar Tom says.

"Praise His name," Tee Barlow says, winking at me. "It's a great honor for me and my wife to be able to share our home with you, Mr. Texas. We've been following your ministry a good while now. The miracles of healing you have performed, the souls brought to everlasting redemption. I can't tell you how much this means to us—especially my wife. . . ." He puts his fat hand next to his mouth, calling through the door, "Faye! Faye, honey. Come on out here and meet Little Texas."

"You can call me Ronald Earl," I say. "It's nice to meet—"

"We don't see a whole lot of folks up this way," Tee Barlow cuts in. "Faye had some last-minute things to take care of to make sure everything is perfect—you know how you women are." He nudges Miss Wanda Joy, who tries to smile. "A place for everything, and everything in its place."

We follow him into the first room.

"This is the entry hall."

There's a great big wooden wheel hanging from chains in the ceiling, all full of candles. But the only things lit are bulbs in little brass holders on the wall. Big frame timbers run across the ceiling, and a wide, curvy staircase loaded with spindles leads upstairs, just like something out of a movie. A big carved piece of scrollwork hangs above the staircase: LORD, BLESS THIS HOME. The room is *cold.*

"That a gen-u-ine Confederate battle flag?" Certain Certain says, squinting at a moldy-looking Stars and Bars in a glass frame on the wall.

"Yes, sir," Tee Barlow says, poking his chest out. "Battle of Chickamauga. The River of Blood. September twentieth, eighteen hundred and sixty-three. General Bushrod Johnson. That's from his personal standard, which they carried across Reed's Bridge."

"How'd you come by it?" Certain Certain says. "Your great-granddaddy fight in that battle?"

"Bought it on eBay," Tee Barlow says. "I have a ninety-nine-percent approval rating!"

He hauls us into the living room next, where Miss Faye—I reckon it's her—is sitting by the fireplace. Which, believe it or not, is burning in the late end of June. Somehow the room still doesn't feel too all over warm.

Miss Faye bounces up to greet us. I'm surprised how much younger she looks than Tee Barlow, maybe only in her thirties.

"Old goat must've robbed him a cradle," Certain Certain whispers to me.

Faye Barlow is little and pretty, with a large bosom, bouncy brown hair, and a space between her two front teeth.

"I call her my *gap-ed toothed woman,*" Tee Barlow says. "Straight out of Chaucer. You know how *saucy* they are, praise the Lord." He gives her a little swat on the tailbone.

Missus Barlow—Faye—smiles up at him, but I can tell she's embarrassed. She takes my hand. Her fingers are cold and small and soft.

"I'm so glad you've come," she says. She hugs me around the middle and puts her small mouth up close to my ear, whispering:

"Don't believe one word this man tells you."

CHAPTER

≫ TWENTY-NINE ≪

We look at each other a second or two, then Miss Faye lets me go, scurrying off to what I figure must be the kitchen. We can hear her in there slinging plates around.

"Isn't she great?" Tee Barlow says. "Let's eat."

We pile into the dining room, which has a table so long I figure you need a cell phone to ask somebody to pass the okra.

My eyes jump back and forth between the Barlows. Watching Miss Faye on the sly, I can't tell anything from her face. *What could she have meant?*

The tomato soup is good. The barbecue shrimp with sharp cheese and bacon, even better. The soup helps cut the cold of this room. Why is it so drafty in here? You would figure a hurricane couldn't get through those stones.

After supper Miss Faye clears away the key lime pie, and we talk about SEC football awhile. Miss Wanda Joy gives Tee Barlow a little nod.

"Is it time? Should we tell him?" he says.

"*Past* time," Miss Wanda Joy says.

"All right."

Tee Barlow gets up and disappears into the back of the house. He comes back a minute later and plops a roll of paper down in the middle of the table. Everybody helps uncurl it, setting coffee cups on the corners.

VANDERLOO PLANTATION, the paper reads. It's some kind of map, crinkled and yellowy around the edges, and the ink is very faded. I lean over and study it close—there are little hills in green, and then I can see the blue of the river.

"This is a topographical map," Tee Barlow says. "It shows the contours of the land. We are *here.*" He puts a finger smudge on a tiny square at one side of the map, then trails his finger down from there till I can see he's leading us right to the water's edge. He stops on a skinny, dark stripe connecting one shore to the other.

"That's the trestle," he says, looking around at all of us. "We aren't allowed to use it anymore. There's nothing really wrong with it, but it's been declared unsafe because we haven't kept the permit up. Too expensive. It's controlled by the Army Corps of Engineers."

Certain Certain gives me a look.

"Tell them about the *plan*," Miss Wanda Joy says, leaning forward, impatient.

Tee Barlow pulls at his beard. "Here's what I've been thinking. How about we ferry the folks over from the old landing?" He thumps a spot on the map. "My Chris-Craft will hold sixteen if they don't mind standing. How many do you expect in all?"

"I think we should anticipate a large response," Miss Wanda Joy says. "It's better to plan for too many rather than too—"

"Let's say four hundred, hypothetically," Tee Barlow says.

Sugar Tom lets out a low whistle. "Is there seating enough for that many?"

"Under the stars, plenty," Tee says. "Under cover? I don't know. But we can work that out."

"I would imagine we will have at least that many, considering the historical significance," Miss Wanda Joy says, black eyes lighting up. "The fact that we are doing it at *all* . . ." She glances at me. "It's a priceless opportunity to reinvigorate our ministry."

"Getting back to the boat," Tee Barlow says. "Let's say twenty-five trips, so probably two hours to ferry them all."

"That long? We'll need to get an early start," Sugar Tom says. He touches the curves on the map, craggy hand shaking. "What is the terrain like? Is it steep?"

"We can go over there tomorrow, and I'll show you the site," Tee Barlow says.

"We also need to get busy with the posters, radio shows, talk to the news organizations," Miss Wanda Joy adds. She looks at Tee Barlow, face blazing. "But don't you have one more thing to show us?"

Tee Barlow's watery eyes rove around the table, lighting on Certain Certain, Sugar Tom, then finally me. He pulls the map off to the side and slaps an old newspaper clipping down in its place where I can read the headline:

DEVIL COMES TO ALABAMA?

CHAPTER

 THIRTY

DEVIL COMES TO ALABAMA?

**Bizarre Phenomenon Witnessed
at Vanderloo Plantation
Multitudes Flee Terrifying Apparition**

MAY 16, 1934. VANDERLOO, ALABAMA.

A most extraordinary phenomenon made its appearance Tuesday evening, witnessed by hundreds of shocked onlookers attending the Calgary Holiness Church With Signs Following camp meeting. Witnesses say a frightening apparition made its arrival on the fourth day of the meeting, apparently accosting one of the clergymen in attendance as he was ministering to his flock.

The service was taking place near the remains of the Jacob James Vanderloo Plantation, an antebellum ruin and landing station on the Tennessee River, once infamous as the hub for the thriving slave trade in northwest Alabama. The plantation is now the gathering site for the church's annual Pilgrimage for Christ.

Accounts by eyewitnesses vary as to the exact nature of the phenomenon, though it was generally agreed by onlookers to be of a "diabolical origin."

"I was sitting there with my family, attending the service, when a sudden noise came up in the woods," stated one shaken onlooker, a Mr. Everett A. Simms of Minor Hill, Tennessee. "It sounded something like the noise a washboard makes, hard and raspy." The sound was followed by a tremendous cry, "almost like a scream," Simms went on. "But an unearthly scream, not like anything I have ever heard before."

Mr. Johnson R. McCready of Coalwater was near where the noise originated. "I was not fifty yards away from a stand of cottonwoods, where the noise seemed to be coming from," McCready declared. "I'm not ashamed to say, I was badly frightened. It was an awful mewling sound—some might call it a bobcat, which has been known to scream like the scream of a woman. But this was no earthly bobcat. Not as loud as the screaming was and the way it was shaking the trees."

Indeed, the trees were reported to have bent and shaken quite violently in the vicinity from whence the ghastly sound was emanating. Whole trees, pines and cottonwoods and even a sturdy oak or two, were "twitching with a fury that I hope never to witness again," stated McCready. "Trunks as big around as a man's leg, whipping and tossing, just like some monstrous giant had got hold of them, rattling them just as if they were nothing but turnips."

It was reported that a general panic ensued as the phenomenon or apparition appeared to approach the camp meeting. Terrified worshippers leapt to their feet and dashed about in an unruly melee, uncertain as to where to flee the approaching menace. Though witnesses were in complete accord as to the danger of the situation, they were uniformly unable to make a coherent description of what was actually seen.

"It all happened so fast," Miss Dodie Myrick of Leighton was heard to say. "Everyone began screaming and running. We did not know what to do. I never saw it. However, I could tell it was coming closer and closer. We all could. It had to be the work of Satan."

"It was the devil," McCready agreed. "Let there be no doubt about that. I won't ever go back to that place again. I feel it is accursed."

What exactly occurred next in the midst of the disordered chaos is sketchy, although all witnesses testified to the disappearance of the unfortunate pastor, Reverend O. T. Hallmark.

"It took Pastor Hallmark with it," Simms stated. "I saw him one moment, trying to comfort his flock, gather us together again. And then he was gone, quick as a whistle."

The helpless pastor was alleged to have been "dragged off into the underbrush," McCready declared. "I cannot say that I saw it with my own eyes, but that is the only thing that could have happened. We all saw him there, and then he was immediately gone. Some of us wanted to search, but there was such a panic."

No contact has been received from Pastor Hallmark, who remains missing. Witnesses state that there was a general retreat from the site of the meeting, with the apparition following close behind.

"Wooden chairs were flung about like toys, children were crying, folks screaming," Myrick stated. "There was a great sound of devastation behind us. We ran without looking back, in a complete terror."

"The meeting place, the whole camp, was smashed to bits," McCready affirmed.

His assessment was corroborated by an unrecorded number of additional campgoers, one of whom asked to remain anonymous. "It's the most God-fearful monstrosity I've ever experienced," declared the anonymous onlooker.

Other witnesses refused to be deposed regarding the incident, only stating they were still too frightened to speak with coherency.

"It's a day of judgment for us all," one man warned. "You knew just from the sound what it was. It didn't speak any words; I don't know if it rightly could. But that sound has me shook plumb to my core."

It is also unknown whether the site will ever again be utilized in the same fashion for future church functions.

An investigation was made by the Lauderdale County sheriff, William T. Pembrake, without much revealing the ultimate cause of the disturbance.

"My men and I crisscrossed the island and couldn't find a thing," Sheriff Pembrake asserted. "All efforts will be made to recover the missing man and determine just what went on out there."

As the investigation progresses, the *Tri-Cities Daily* will continue to report on the details of the search, as well as any further details as to the nature of the "terrifying" phenomenon.

━━━━━━━━━━━━━━━━━━━━━━━━━━

"Mercy," Certain Certain says. "Now you know why they call the property Devil Hill, Lightning."

Tee Barlow glares at him a little. Miss Wanda Joy settles back in her chair.

"Daddy King always said Pastor Hallmark was such a good

man," she says, eyes far away. "So many lives he touched—he will never be forgotten by those who knew him.

"He—he was my *grandfather*."

I stare at her, feeling my mouth clap shut.

"There has never been another service on that plantation," Tee Barlow says. "Not since that day. People stopped coming. The land was said to be cursed. Satan accomplished just exactly what he set out to accomplish, didn't he?" He looks at Miss Wanda Joy. "When you called with your proposition—what else could I say but yes? It would have been *his* dream. Pastor Hallmark's. To see his final mission fulfilled."

He turns to me. "Well, Little Texas? What do you think about all this?"

Before I can say anything, Miss Wanda Joy reaches over and touches my arm.

"You are going to preach on Devil Hill."

CHAPTER

≫ THIRTY-ONE ≪

"I made a mistake," Miss Wanda Joy says. "I've been holding you back, when clearly you are ready for this."

She makes a little smile that speaks to nobody else but me: *I never make mistakes.* And it says something else, too: *You asked for this.*

My mind is fluttering like swallows in a barn. Tee Barlow's newspaper clipping about the devil lays there looking up at me. I feel the blood in my face.

"It's so clear to me now," Miss Wanda Joy says, dark eyes burning. "The hand of the Lord has led us to this moment. It's time, Little Texas, for you to grow up."

I glance at Certain Certain. He closes his eyes and shakes his head. Miss Wanda Joy puts her napkin down and pushes her chair back so she can cross her legs.

"My father told a story," she says, "about a man who began preaching the gospel on a street corner in Andalusia, Alabama. One day he just opened his Bible and began to speak, letting the Holy Spirit flow through him. And for three long days not one person, not *one,* stopped to listen. That man stood all day long on that hot street corner witnessing to no one but the birds in the trees. In fact, he preached *three whole days* before a single soul showed up to receive the gospel. But soon thereafter came two, then three, then four. A handful. Ten. Thirty. Fifty. A *hundred.* Sheep to the shepherd. And upon the Rock, that man built a mighty ministry.

"Think about the size of his faith, Little Texas. He knew he was preaching to someone on those long, empty days. Someone who was listening. Someone who was working diligently in the background to answer his prayers. And that someone was *God.*"

"Praise His name," Tee Barlow says.

"But who was the man?" I say.

The lines come up on Miss Wanda Joy's forehead. She turns and jabs a long finger at the window in the direction of the island, voice suddenly trembling.

"I'll tell you who he was. *The very same man who was dragged off into those woods.* My grandfather. Lost, never to be found again. A man that *great,* that full of the Holy Spirit.

We owe him this, Little Texas. It's time. I haven't just been thinking about this since Meridian. I've been thinking about this *my whole life.*"

A fresh draft comes whispering through the room; the newspaper clipping rustles. Everybody is quiet, all looking at me.

I have a question, but I don't know how to ask it without getting her even more riled up. I put it to her as soft as I can.

"But . . . if Pastor Hallmark, a man that *godly* . . . if he wasn't able to . . . you know . . . what can *I* do?"

"That was over seventy years ago," Miss Wanda Joy says. "Who knows what truly happened that night? All we know is that my grandfather's flock turned on him and *ran. Christians,* and they ran like frightened dogs. Left him to do battle alone, and he was taken. This time I guarantee the children of the Lord will be victorious!"

"Amen!" Tee Barlow says, raising his fists like he's fixing to bust Lucifer right in the mouth.

"That's *enough,*" Faye Barlow says softly. She comes up behind my chair and puts her small hands on my shoulders. "You two are frightening him."

Sugar Tom coughs. "'And I was with you in weakness, and in fear, and in much trembling.' First Corinthians, chapter two, verse three."

"Amen," Tee Barlow says again, only quieter this time.

Everybody talks awhile longer, till Sugar Tom is fixing to drop off. Tee Barlow clears the newspaper clipping away.

138

"Well, it's getting late, and we have a big day tomorrow," he says. "Faye, why don't we show our guests up to their rooms?"

"I'll take Little Texas," Miss Faye says, hooking her arm in mine as we get up from the table. "I imagine you're tired from all that traveling."

Preach on Devil Hill.

"What? Oh. I'm all right," I say. "Thank you for the delicious supper."

We head up the wide staircase to the second floor. This is the biggest house I've ever been in and also the darkest. There are things that look like torches fastened to the walls, but which are really little electric bulbs made to look like flickering flames.

The place is overrun with plushy carpets and polished wood, heavy on the varnish. Vases, paintings, rugs on the walls with pictures of Bible scenes: Moses in the bulrushes, the two disciples on the Mount of Olives, Jesus riding His ass to town on Good Friday. Those kinds of things. A hundred percent better than the ones I've seen at gas stations, I'll tell you that.

Miss Faye takes my hand. When we're far enough away from the others, she tugs me into a side hallway. Puts her face close to mine.

"I don't know how much I should say," she says in a low voice. "But I don't want you to do this. What they're asking you to do."

I feel my heart speed up a little. "Why, Miss Faye?"

"Be careful. Not so loud." She whips her head around, looking back toward the light. The stairs creak, but the creaking goes away. She smiles. "And please don't call me Miss Faye. It makes me feel so *old*."

"Okay," I say, quieter. My heart is racing now. "But why did you tell me not to believe your husband?"

"It's Tee's personality." She presses closer, till I am breathing nothing but her scent. "It's so much stronger than mine. Even back at Ole Miss—Tee was my business instructor!—he always knew exactly what he wanted, and he *got* it. That's just his way. He's not a bad man. He's *not*. That's part of the problem, Little Texas—"

"Please call me Ronald Earl."

"All right, Ronald Earl." She laughs a little, showing her gap-toothed smile. "I mean—he has so much *faith.* Tee always believes everything will work out the way he wants it to. So he never considers the consequences of his actions for others. Am I making any sense, honey?"

"Some." It's hard to think about anything but the closeness of her body to mine. Her smell, her softness.

"When he wants something, it simply drives him," Faye says. "Anyone or anything that gets in the way of that, he just ignores or bluffs his way around it."

"You mean he lies?"

Her face pinches up. "Well. I don't know if I would out and out call it *lying.* I don't think he even knows he is doing it. He just gets so *fixated* on a thing, you know? And he'll say almost anything, do just about anything, to make it happen. It's just that this thing is not right, what they're asking you to do. It's dangerous."

I feel the skin on my own face tighten up. "So you think Satan is sitting over there on that island just waiting to drag me off?"

"Shhh. It's more a *feeling* I have. Tee—he thinks I'm a big fat pessimist, always seeing the rain in the rainbow. But that's not it. . . ."

She makes a little clutched-up sound in her throat and swallows hard before she can go on. "If you only *knew*," she says, "how long we have been living with his—his *obsession*."

"Which fits right in with Miss Wanda Joy."

Faye puts a finger to her mouth. "Let's walk while we talk."

This hall's the longest yet, lined with pictures of dead people with bow ties, flouncy dresses, slick hair, tall hats, starchy collars.

"Are all of them Vanderloos?" I say, to break up the mood.

"Yes," Faye says. "I wanted them out of here when we moved in, but Tee, of course, would not have one thing touched. 'It would detract from the authentic antebellum flavor,' he likes to say. As if he knows what he's talking about—he makes his money selling Aqua Glass hot tubs." She sighs. "I never intended on living here. It was all Tee's idea. But it's not this place so much. I love a lot of things about it, I really do. But over *there* . . ."

She waves her hand off toward the wall. I look, but there is nothing there but a picture of a man who appears to have been born before the invention of shampoo.

"What?" I say.

"Here they come." She grabs my hands and holds them together with her hands. *"Don't mention what we talked about."*

It's not till I look out the deep-set window in my room that I realize where Faye was pointing. Not at the wall, but across the water.

Devil Hill.

CHAPTER

⇒ THIRTY-TWO ⇐

My bedroom sits at the end of another long hall. The door is practically twice as tall as my head. If I propped it open, I could run straight down the hall right to my bed.

I drop my suitcase on the floor next to a dresser with a white bowl sitting on it. No TV. Out the window I can see double moons, one on the lake, the other shining through the limbs of a pin oak. Glisteny grass slopes all the way down to the water.

I'm not used to sleeping alone.

There's a tall cupboard in the corner with a bunch of long dresses inside. I sweep them back, and I'm surprised to find a little drum sitting behind them. I take the drum out and set it on my lap; it's big around as a dinner plate and has red trim and years of smudges. I thump it with my knuckle; it makes a good strong *k'dump* sound. *Who used to play it?*

I put the drum back and stretch out on top of the thick covers. The bed has four posts carved the way a honeysuckle vine will twist a dogwood trunk. It's piled with little square pillows stitched with Bible verses in thick red thread: ASK, AND IT SHALL BE GIVEN; CAST THY BREAD UPON THE WATERS; and DEATH, WHERE IS THY STING?

I kick my shoes off and watch the moon. I think how I know where we go after we die; the Bible spells it out plain. *But where is she?* Devil Hill rises across the water.

I get up and try to open the window, but it's locked. Through the glass I can hear crickets sawing and toadfrogs peeping. I force myself to look out at the blackest parts of the dark. No other lights for miles.

We are alone here.

I settle onto my knees in front of the bed and close my eyes.

"Dear heavenly Father, thank you for bringing us safely here. I ask that you watch over us in this house, and that you shower your anointing on the mission of our ministry. Please protect us as we go about your heavenly tasks, and especially watch over us in the night. Please look after the souls of the departed, especially Lucy, and clove her to your celestial bosom. Please send your heavenly angels to guide and watch over and protect Lucy's spirit and the loved ones she has left behind, and allow me the strength, the courage, and the understanding to learn what she means in my life. In the name of Jesus Christ I pray. Amen."

I cut out the light and lay there feeling the half-moon shining down on me. Then I get lost in a sleep so dark I might as well be on the bottom of the ocean.

⟫ THIRTY-THREE ⟪

Long about two in the morning, something gets me up with a start.

K'dump, k'dump, k'dump.

The room is all over cold, like a breeze is cutting across my bed. I glance at the window—it's still shut tight. I swing my legs around, feeling for the wood floor. The bed is up so high, I can't reach bottom without sliding over the side. The hardwood is cold to my toes.

I can hear them—footsteps creaking out in the hall, coming closer and closer to my door. A shiver wiggles up my back.

"Hello?" I say.

Nobody calls back, but the footsteps keep coming. Is something coming here just for me?

A big bang shakes the whole house, making my heart rattle. I don't see how in the world the others haven't woken up. But everything is quiet again outside my door. I wait, listening.

K'dump, k'dump, k'dump.

I walk from the bed toward the door.

K'dump, k'dump, k'dump.

Jesus Lord—the sound isn't coming from the hall, it's coming from the cupboard in my room. *It's the drum.* Something inside the cupboard is beating on that drum.

I rush to the bedroom door and wrench at the knob—it's slippery in my sweaty hands, and I have trouble turning it. The drum sound behind me gets louder and louder—I can't make myself turn around to see what's back there—the devil has come for me.

I slap around for the light switch, wanting to scream. *Where is it?* I scratch and bang on the door, wrenching the knob this way and that, yelling and hollering loud as I can. *Why is nobody hearing me?* I stop, sucking in air, and in the middle of all the drumming I hear it—a big creaking noise behind me. I turn around. . . .

The door to the cupboard is swinging open.

I yank the knob and give the bedroom door a big pull; it swings open to the hall, and a long slab of weak light slants into the room. The drum stops the moment the light touches the cupboard.

Dead silence. I dare to look behind me. Everything in the room—everything I can see in the light coming from the hall—looks like it did before. The long piece of light reaches clear over to the bed. I can see my shoes, my clothes hanging over the bedstead, the bedcovers jerked back. A pillow on the floor says BLOOD OF THE LAMB in bleeding red letters.

I grab up my pants and T-shirt and hightail it out into the hall, looking for Certain Certain's door. That's when I see it; something is at the end of the hall. It's white and bunchy looking, almost like—*it is*—it's a bedsheet hanging in the air.

But it's not draped over somebody's head like on Halloween; it's laying on something, covering up a shape only a couple of feet high. I stop, the clothes drop out of my hands. *This is not happening. It can't be happening.* But the shape is too solid. The sheet is draped over something rounded and low.

The white shape starts to move.

Sliding slow and straight up the hall toward me, a foot off the ground.

It's floating.

I beat the closest door I can find like a wild animal, hollering for Certain Certain. I beat on another one and another as the thing under the sheet gets closer and closer, cutting me off.

I make a sputtering sound and rush back into my room and slam the door shut.

No key and no way to lock the door. But what is a door to it? Nothing. Nothing at all.

I tear at the edges of the door with my fingers, feel the light switch at last, and turn it on.

Everything is just like it was. Not a single sound to be heard. Except my heart going like a piston.

I watch the crystal doorknob.

A scrabbling noise comes, moving down the sides of the door, fumbling and scratching.

The doorknob . . . it starts to turn. Clicks. *The door starts to open.*

I back away till I'm against the bed, grab the sheets behind me, and scrunch them up in my fingers.

I clamp my eyes and begin praying, praying harder than I've ever prayed before, stringing the words all out in a burst, "OhhelpmesweetblessedJesusGodmyLordprotectmeohsweet-JesusLordprotectmehelpmekeepmesafefromall—"

A new noise . . . I open my eyes just in time to see the bedroom door swing wide.

Its eyes tear into me. I can't believe it. I can't believe—

She's standing in front of me.

THIRTY-FOUR

Lucy in the blue dress, Lucy right down to her sneakers. Her hair is not flat like before; it looks all ripply, like wet ribbons.

She stands stock-still in the doorway, like she expects to be invited in.

I jerk up a lamp from the bedside table, accidentally click it on, flooding the room with light. I hold it back of my head, like a pitcher fixing to hurl a fastball.

Lucy's dress is smudged with long, muddy stripes. Her mouth is open, open so wide it makes her look like she's screaming. Only there is no sound. I can see her jaw shuddering like she's trying to close her mouth but can't.

I'm clutching the lamp so fierce, my whole arm is going numb.

Her skin has a wet sheen to it. Her fist is clenched like a walnut. She raises one thin arm and points it direct at me, her fist comes open, and she spreads her fingers wide. A little *tump* sound as something small and hard hits the floor.

Then the big, heavy door slams shut by itself, *bam,* so hard it rocks the frame in its casing.

My heart whumps inside my ribs. I sit down on the bed, still clutching the lamp, trying to pour my mind back inside my head.

How can I make it to the next minute . . . the rest of the night? I can't. I won't survive this.

Suddenly I hear feet tromping up the hall, regular sounds flood back in: voices, nighttime noises, the peeping bugs outdoors; the cake bowl has been lifted. I can't make my legs move, can't even call out. The knob gives a turn, and the door is wrenched open. Certain Certain's standing there.

"Hey, boy, what's going on in here? Heard all the . . ."

He spies the upraised lamp. Up the hall I see the other bedroom doors banging open. Miss Wanda Joy in a purple bathrobe, Tee Barlow in shorts and a sleeveless shirt, even Sugar Tom, barefoot in his silvery pajamas.

"Hey, Lightning, it's all right," Certain Certain says. "Put the lamp down." He comes into the room, walking slow. "Put it down, son. It's all right. We're all right here."

I let my arm drop, and the lamp falls to the floor with a woody crash.

The others are coming into the room now, stopping just inside the door, looking sleepy and afraid. I wrap the blankets around myself to cover up.

"What happened?" Certain Certain says, touching my arm. "Haints scare you out of your clothes? We found these sitting outside. . . ." He's holding my pants and shirt. Then his smile freezes when he sees my face up close.

"I'm—I'm okay," I say, quavering. "She—she was here again. Her. The girl. *Lucy.*"

Miss Wanda Joy comes over with Tee Barlow. Sugar Tom is rubbing his eyes with the heels of his hands.

"Why didn't you hear me?" I say. "Didn't you hear the racket up and down the hall? And the drumming—that's where it started, in the cupboard."

Miss Wanda Joy walks over and pulls the cupboard door open. "Drumming?"

"This room used to be Faye's aunt's when she was a girl," Tee Barlow says. "That's her things in there. Nobody has messed with those things in years."

Miss Wanda Joy gasps. She's pulling something out of the back of the cupboard—it's the drum, I can see the red trim.

It's smashed in. The top of the drum is all ripped up and caved in. Just like claws have been at it.

CHAPTER

⇒ THIRTY-FIVE ⇐

"I can't—I can't sleep here tonight," I whisper to Certain Certain. "Something's trying to get at me—please—I'll sleep on the floor in your room, anywhere."

He nods at me. "I'll see what we can do." He drops my clothes on the bed.

"I believe it might be better if Little Texas were moved to a different room, where he could sleep with someone," Miss Wanda Joy says, still holding the drum.

"No problem," Tee Barlow says.

Tee Barlow and the others leave the room, everybody

except Miss Wanda Joy. She sits down on the bed next to me, making it creak. Puts her big hand on my shoulder.

"Could it be I was wrong," she says, "thinking you were ready for this?"

"Ma'am?"

"This is just the beginning. Do you know what lengths Satan will go to to defeat the bearers of light?"

"But wait—if you had been here, you would've—"

"Were you *harmed* in any way? Or even touched?"

"But the drum—the drum—"

"Are you going to give Satan his victory without a fight?"

"No, ma'am, I—"

"Where would we be as Christians if we were to give up so easily?"

"You ought to know me better than that."

"You said you were ready to grow up." She shows just the barest traces of . . . a smile?

"I *am* ready. I've *been* ready. I just wasn't expecting—"

"What? You are in a spiritual *war,* and you didn't expect there to be skirmishes?"

"I don't know—I just never believed—I never believed in ghosts before."

"You have to see them for what they *are.* Satan's messengers want you to believe they are the spirits of the departed. That is the way they undermine your faith. *Faith* is your protection, Little Texas."

Certain Certain puts his head back in the doorway. "You coming?" he says to me.

I look at Miss Wanda Joy, feeling my jaw go hard. "Um. No, that's all right. I'm okay now. I'm going to stay right here. Nothing is going to root me out of this room."

"You sure, boy?"

"I'm sure. I'll be more ready next time."

"I'm only a couple of doors down. If'n you need me, just give out a holler."

I did. And you didn't come.

"I will," I say.

Miss Wanda Joy gets up to go. She puts the busted drum back in the cupboard and latches it shut. I follow her over to the doorway. The hall doesn't look any different as she makes her way back to her room.

I won't let her win. I won't.

But what *her* am I talking about?

I turn to head back to the bed.

"Ow!"

I look down—it's a little corner of brick about the size of a skipping stone, sharp under my foot. I pick it up, feeling its weight in my hand.

This is what she dropped.

I'm holding something she *held.* I turn it over and see words written in square letters the color of gold:

I LOVE YOU

CHAPTER

➤ **THIRTY-SIX** ❧

A cold, wormy feeling runs all through my back.

I drop to my knees.

Here is *proof.* Something they could see and hold. But I don't want to share this with anybody else. Not yet. It's too . . . *personal.* Something meant just for me.

So shaky and muzzle-headed, I crawl into bed, prop myself up with Bible pillows, and study it.

A ghost loves me?

A demon? A devil?

Those three words, *I love you,* tear into me and threaten

to blow me up. What am I feeling? I don't know. I don't know.

Does this piece of brick mean I'm not crazy?

Maybe sometimes crazy is a place where you can go and still come back from? Or what if it's all just a trick of Satan's, trying to fool me, draw me out, make me think she's . . .

Good?

I remember the claw marks on the revival tent. The noise outside the motor home. Could a girl like her, so *beautiful* and perfect . . . could she be evil?

I drop the piece of brick in the blankets and go digging through my suitcase for my copy of King James. Whenever I'm faced with a problem, I flip through the pages at random, poke my finger on a spot—eyes closed—and the words my finger strikes are the ones that hold the solution.

Close my eyes. Snatch the Book open. Set my finger down.

"Now therefore go to, proclaim in the ears of the people, saying, Whosoever is fearful and afraid, let him return and depart early from mount Gilead.

Judges, chapter seven, verse three.

Sugar Tom says *Gilead* means "hill of testimony." King David went to hide there, and Gilead was the home of Elijah, who brought fire down from the sky and ascended into heaven on a whirlwind. Am I supposed to witness? Give my testimony as to what is happening?

Or am I supposed to hide, fearful and afraid?

I leave the light burning and close my eyes. Every few seconds I open them and look at the cupboard. The door stays shut. The drum is still.

She loves me.

➤ THIRTY-SEVEN ⬅

Light is slanting across the water, turning the trees on the island golden. All the bad feelings from last night have leaked away. I may be crazy, but the world is still lovely and strange. In my hand is *Lucy's brick.*

The words are still there: I LOVE YOU.

A flash of cold joy explodes in my chest. I get dressed in a hurry and tuck the brick into my pocket.

"Afternoon," Certain Certain says when I get down to the kitchen. "Bogeyman keep you up? Don't worry, Miss Faye saved you something."

Faye bustles over, all smiles and smelling of flowers. She sets a plate of bacon and eggs in front of me. "Bad dreams?"

I shrug a little, fingering the brick piece.

"My man Lightning's got one powerful imagination when his head hits the pillow," Certain Certain says.

"Tee says something woke you in the middle of the night?" Faye says.

I take a sip of juice, stalling. "Yes'm. I thought I heard something, is all."

She snaps a dish towel at me, playing. "Please, call me Faye, I told you. This house *is* haunted, you know."

I drop my fork. Certain Certain looks up from his coffee, frowning.

"I should have mentioned it before. It was featured in one of those Kathryn Tucker Windham books. You know, *13 Alabama Ghosts and Jeffrey*? She came and did a story about our attic. Such a sweet little old thing. Gave me a recipe for butterfly biscuits."

"Do you believe in ghosts?" I say.

Faye smiles, making the skin around her eyes crinkle up, all sweet and friendly, plus sort of secret and mysterious. Like the two of us have this plan we're working together the others don't know about.

"Tee doesn't," she says. "Me? I like to keep an *open* mind." She passes behind my chair, gives my shoulders a little squeeze, then runs her hand along my arm as she heads back to the stove. It gives me a funny tingle.

"What's in the attic?" I say.

"Well—"

"Miss Wanda Joy and Sugar Tom are already down at the dock, waiting on you to drag your raggedy self out of bed," Certain Certain says loudly. "You ready to see the plantation?" He gives me a sideways look.

I push away from the table and Faye gives me a little pinch, says, *"Later."*

When we get outdoors, the sun is higher than I suspected and the water is jumping with tiny points of light. A breeze rattles the beech trees, and I can see a dog zigzagging his way down the hill on a scent.

Miss Wanda Joy's hair is trussed up in a yellow ribbon—a color I have never personally seen her wear.

"Tee will take us over in the pontoon boat," she says, smiling.

We clamber down the long slope to the water, the tall Johnson grass dragging against my jeans, throwing ladybugs into the air. The Barlows' dock points toward the island on the far side. From here Devil Hill looks like a foresty wedge of hillside that just happens to have a shoreline.

The boat is old and sits low in the water. It has a little piece of awning flapping on one end that you have to duck under.

"Oh, sumptuous day," Sugar Tom says, using me to help him get his balance as he steps aboard. His arms feel like pickup sticks with sleeves. "'He hath made every thing beautiful in his time.'"

"Amen," Tee Barlow says. "Everybody, please sit down."

The seats are damp, and the bottom of the boat smells of fish water. Miss Wanda Joy comes along first, then Faye, letting me help her with my fingers and giving me that look she gave me earlier over the breakfast table.

"Thank you, kind sir," she says, and gives me a kiss on the cheek. She takes my hand and clutches it the whole way, giving it friendly little pats. Nobody has ever touched me this much.

Tee cranks the boat and steers us into the channel through a cloud of blue engine smoke.

"Look yonder," he says.

In the near distance we can see the railroad trestle standing over us like a rusty crown spotted with bird mess. I smell the stink of the knocking engine.

Can ghosts float over water?

I'm surprised when we don't land at the first dock, but instead turn up the shore in the direction of the trestle, puttering away. The closer we get to the island, snatches of driftwood and river wash start jumbling the boat. A mud turtle flops off a log and puts his head up like a periscope.

"Fishing much good?" Certain Certain says.

"Channel cats as big as you want," Tee Barlow says. "I've taken out a sixty-pounder. They say divers up by the turbines have seen cats as long as a man, two hundred pounds or more. Put a smelt on a line, you can hardly drag it into the boat, praise His name." Tee Barlow holds up his fat hand to show us where he got finned years back. "The depth drops off quickly. You push out a little ways from shore, you are in deep, cold water."

"It's me, I'd be settin' up a trotline, shoot," Certain Certain says.

"There's a current," Tee Barlow says. "You can't see it, but it's there. Take a good strong swimmer to get back to the other side."

I look at the black water, shuddering a little. I have never been swimming all that much. I think I might could make it— but I wouldn't want to have to.

Every few seconds I sneak my hand into my pocket, feeling for the little piece of brick.

I watch a redbird sitting on a sassafras limb. It knows what is real, and that never changes. I don't. Not anymore.

On this big boat with five regular folks, I can only make believe I understand what we're doing here, *in this world.* Up to now I always thought I did. But nobody does. *Nobody.* It can all change in the blink of an eyelash. Leaving you undercut.

Unprotected.

All my prayers . . . nothing I know in the scriptures speaks to this. I reckon this is just what happens to people who see strange things. And I will still have to get up every day. Put on clothes. Preach. Eat supper. All the time knowing nothing is what it seems.

What if she comes again?

What if she doesn't?

CHAPTER

⇾THIRTY-EIGHT⇽

We're passing under the trestle now. So thick with woods at either end, looks like it grew right out of the forest. I can see the crossties above our heads, some of them missing, all of them dried out and weather-beat.

We come around a long headland where the island pokes a finger of hillside toward deeper water. Not a cloud in the sky. The air smells of pine trees and mown hay. The pontoon boat has to cut its way through big, floppy milfoil leaves to get us into shore.

"Good for bass," Tee Barlow says.

He noses the Chris-Craft into a square little dock where

165

we can hop out. We make our way up a twisty little path through some scrub rhododendron and dogwoods, and just as things start to level off, I see it for the very first time. The ruins of the old Vanderloo Plantation.

Lord.

⇒ THIRTY-NINE ⇐

"'And there shall be upon every high mountain, and upon every high hill, rivers and streams of waters in the day of the great slaughter, when the towers fall,'" Sugar Tom says. "Quite an imposing structure."

"They used to call it the Parthenon of Alabama," Tee Barlow says, hauling his belly up into his chest. "You can see why."

We hike up to a grassy clearing surrounded by oaks that have got to be a couple hundred years old. Some of the limbs are hanging so low, you could sit on them like benches. Between the trees stand a couple dozen tall pillars fixed in a rectangle, with the short side of the rectangle facing the water. The pillars taper at the top and are coated with gray mortar, but you can see a layer of bricks underneath. The brick is an orangey brown.

"Fired from native clay," Tee Barlow says. "Normally, columns like these would have been cut from granite. But there was none available. It certainly wasn't a matter of cost. Faye's ancestor spent $175,000, all told, to build Vanderloo, which was a bushelful of money for the time, just before the start of the Civil War."

"Soldiers ever occupy the place?" Certain Certain says.

"The Union used it as a field hospital," Tee Barlow says. "Confederates, as a lookout point. A Yankee officer was shot on the front steps."

The top of each column is decorated with sculptures that look like bunches of black corn on the cob. Here and there real plants grow out from the sides of the pillars, long and feathery.

"It was quite a house in its day, I imagine," Miss Wanda Joy says.

Only now there is no roof to hold up, nor walls, neither, and the foundation is nothing but grass.

"What are those?" I say, pointing. Stretched between the columns, about twenty foot off the ground, are some zigzaggy iron railings hanging in midair.

"That was the railing for the second floor," Tee Barlow says. "Gives you an idea how tall this place was, doesn't it?

Forty-five feet to the pilasters, three floors, with a big glass observatory on top."

We walk into the middle of the clearing. I scuff my foot around, come up with a couple of pieces of plank wood painted white.

"That's all that's left of the original camp meeting stage," Tee Barlow says. "Everything else was picked over for salvage lumber years ago."

"Satan," Certain Certain says, glancing my way. "Which way did he come from?"

"It was just beyond that stunted peach tree," Tee Barlow says, waving his arm toward the woods in the back. "Been left to grow up wild for decades."

"Who keeps this part cleared?" I say.

"We have a man who comes around two, three times a year and mows it with a Bush Hog. That's about it."

"I love the feel of this place," Miss Wanda Joy says at my elbow. "Imagine the witnessing that can be done in a setting like this."

We turn and look back the way we came for the first time, see the sweep of the lake, the fuzzy shoreline in the distance. I don't think I will be afraid here after dark.

"It's prettiest this time of day," Faye Barlow says. "I prefer the morning sun, don't you?"

"Now. The promotional details," Miss Wanda Joy says.

She pulls the Barlows off to the side with Sugar Tom, leaving me and Certain Certain to sweat in the middle of the old ruins. We sit on a hump of ground, propping our hands behind us.

"It's not so bad, is it?" I say. "Just a regular old place."

Certain Certain shakes his head. "Not so bad *now,* you mean. You wait till you get out here in the middle of the dark, noises in the woods, trees closing around you, columns looking like they might wind up on your *head.*"

I notice him thumbing his slave tag. "You know what went on out here, don't you, boy?" he goes on. "You think that kind of thing can't get down into the land, soak right into it like a poison?" He scuffs the ground with the heel of his boot. "This place feels dead."

"Are you saying you don't want me to do it?"

"Didn't say that."

"Then why are you trying to spook me?"

He plucks a stem of goldenrod and goes to chewing on it. "You doin' a bang-up job of that your own self."

We sit quiet awhile, watching Miss Wanda Joy wave her arms getting her points across. She's like a mosquito that has spied a vein.

"You don't believe me about last night, do you?" I say.

"Didn't say that, neither. I know real fear when I see it."

"But do you *believe* me? Do you believe me that it was *her*?" I slip my hand into my pocket, touching the brick. "She left something behind. Just like she did with the newspaper article."

I take out the piece of brick and hand it to him. Certain

170

Certain turns it over in the strong light. He hands it back to me.

"You want some more where that come from?" he says.

He stoops low and fishes around in the grass at the base of one of the pillars. "Here you go, Lightning."

He puts something hard and raspy in my hands. It's a little piece of brick. *The exact same shade.* It hits me so hard, I nearly gasp. *That's why her hair looked wet last night.*

Lucy's brick is from here. It's a piece of the old plantation.

CHAPTER

⇒ FORTY ⇐

"Did I ever tell you about my Pulaski angel?" Sugar Tom says.

We're eating a picnic of homemade dill pickles and pimento cheese sandwiches. Miss Wanda Joy and Tee Barlow aren't paying us any attention; they're too busy with the preparations. Faye hustles around keeping us filled with sweet tea and making odd faces at me. I can't help but think she is aching to tell me something.

"Maybelline Petty, from Pulaski, Tennessee. Giles County," Sugar Tom goes on. "Sweet as a picture and had a beautiful singing voice, too."

"Pulaski, home of the Ku Klux Klan," Certain Certain says. "They still hold their big parade up that way every year? What's it down to now, about eight folks?"

"My Pulaski angel wasn't caught up in any of that mess, praise Jesus," Sugar Tom says.

"When was this?" I say.

Sugar Tom takes a bite and chews thoughtfully. "Well, let's see . . . long about 1937—no, 1938. I was just about your age. She started showing up wherever I preached. Nobody thought twice about it—I kind of liked it, to tell you the Lord's own truth . . . she was that sweet."

"Was she your girlfriend?" I say, smiling.

Sugar Tom points a pickle at his temple. "Just listen. One day—long about Easter time—after the service, Maybelline came backstage, asking me to pray with her. Nobody else was there. She said she had a *secret,* and I was the only one she could tell. Well. I must admit, Ronald Earl, I was pleased. No, *proud.* Proud that such a girl would come to *me* to unburden herself. I was happy. *More* than happy to listen to her. She leaned in close—I can smell her dress to this day!—and she reached into her snap purse and took out this little pistol. Put it right against my chest."

"Lord," I say. "What did you do?"

"That's when she told me. Put her pink little bow of a mouth to my ear and *whispered* it. The gun still stuck in my ribs. She told me she had discovered I was the *Antichrist,* and

173

it was her mission as a born-again Christian to kill me in order to fulfill the biblical prophecy for the end-times. Make way for the Second Coming of our Lord and Savior."

"So what happened?"

"She pulled the trigger and shot me stone-cold *dead.*"

"What?"

"It's true. That little pistol went off—it sounded like a thunderclap in my ears—I felt the bullet go in, come out the other side. Maybelline threw the pistol down and ran. Then I died."

"No."

"Yes, sir, I did. For nine whole minutes. I could hear the world around me, see faces, hear people speaking, but I wasn't connected to any of it, Ronald Earl. It had no meaning for me anymore. I was dead."

"But—"

"That's when I had my *vision,*" Sugar Tom says.

"Oh Lord," Certain Certain says. He tosses the last of his sandwich in the bushes and walks over to help Miss Wanda Joy.

"Never mind him," Sugar Tom goes on. "I could see it, Ronald Earl. This short little fence—it couldn't have been more than twenty or thirty feet long. Just setting all by itself in this open, rolling country. Nothing but grassy little hills for miles in every direction. The loneliness! I can't tell you. That fence so downright tiny in the face of all those open spaces. No reason for it being there at all. Somebody had the nerve, no, the *faith* to build it. For what, I do not know. But there it stood. No road. No house or tree or even stone. Only grass and hills. It was South Dakota. That's where I had gone to, South Dakota. I knew it."

He takes a long drink of sweet tea, his neck moving.

"That's when I saw *Him*."

"Him?"

"*Him*. Our Lord and Redeemer. He started out on the horizon, just the ittiest bitty little dot, just a-wiggling this way and that. I took a set and watched Him come, what seemed like all day. It felt like it was hours afore I even knew He was a man. Then I commenced to feel afraid."

"Why?"

"Let me tell you something. There is a thing about living this life, Ronald Earl. You make mistakes. We all make mistakes. We try our best to walk in His footsteps, but we are so given to temptation, to fear. But I believe it's the things you *don't* do that get you wrapped around the axle. Are you understanding me?"

I shake my head.

"It's not that big of a thing to live a life without harming others," Sugar Tom says, eyes sad. "You just hang back, stay out of trouble. It's not that hard. But here is what is hard: doing what you know needs doing. Truly helping your fellow man. Loving thy neighbor as thyself is a *messy, hard* thing to do."

A red-tailed hawk lights on a sycamore at the edge of the woods. We watch it cleaning its feathers.

"You want to know why I was so afraid?" Sugar Tom says. "Because I knew He could see inside me. I knew He could see all the things I *didn't* do to help other people. All the ways I could have helped and didn't. That was it. I knew He would see that, and it raised the hackles on me, I'll tell you. It was my *shame,* Ronald Earl. That was what was at the bottom of my fear—I knew that He loved me. His love is unconditional. Complete. Perfect. But don't you see, that just makes it so difficult to be in His presence. We are not worthy, you understand me?"

I nod.

"The closer He got, the more I felt it—the total incompleteness of my *soul,* what I was lacking."

"But what'd He look like?" I say.

"Not like what you'd think," he says. "You know what the paintings are like, blue-eyed, long hair and a beard? His hair was short and curly, dark. Eyes very dark. Never saw eyes like that before. He *knew,* Ronald Earl. There was no bluffing Him, no deceiving Him. I felt like that fence. Do you know what I mean by that? There was no denying what I was. How alone I would be without Him. The only thing that was going to come out of my mouth was the Lord's own truth."

"Didn't He ever speak?"

"Indeed He did. He said this: 'Love.' That was it. Just 'Love.' Then He was gone. Ascended straight to heaven on clouds of glory. Amen."

Sugar Tom runs his fingers through his thin hair and

176

slumps back in his seat, eyes closed. A breeze from the lake plays over us.

"You said that girl shot you, you died," I say.

His eyes pop open. "My Pulaski angel."

"So what happened to her?"

He thinks about it. "They caught Maybelline at the Woolworth's in Nashville, Tennessee. Sitting at the counter drinking a cherry slush and reading a *McCall's* magazine."

"But you—"

"I came back. I still have the scar to show for it." He taps himself. "Right next to my breastbone."

"But—in your vision—what did Jesus mean? What did He mean when He said 'Love'?"

Sugar Tom smiles. "That's easy, Ronald Earl. *Love.* You understand? He meant it as a *verb.*"

CHAPTER

≫FORTY-ONE≪

Miss Wanda Joy hurries over.

"Tee just heard on NOAA weather radio that lightning has been reported less than ten miles away. We need to be heading back."

We pack up and walk down to the dock. As Tee Barlow eases the pontoon boat into the channel, the wind kicks up, slinging the top branches around, and shadows are filling the woods. Certain Certain is right—I don't ever want to be left alone on Devil Hill 'mongst those crumbling columns, with night and a storm coming on.

Back at the house Sugar Tom settles in for a nap. Tee

Barlow, Certain Certain, and Miss Wanda Joy set up shop in the dining room, sipping coffee and making plans while rain spatters the windows.

I head upstairs, but just as I'm hauling out my whittling, a knock comes. Faye is smiling in my doorway.

"Hi. I was wondering if you might be interested in seeing our attic? I want to bring some things down and hoped you wouldn't mind helping me."

The attic door is around back of the kitchen. The steps are steep. I'm surprised how bright it is when we step through the little door at the top. Big dormer windows, six to a side, jut out from the sloping ceiling. I take a look through one and can see the storm making the lake wrinkle.

"I sure wouldn't want to get caught up here in a tornado," Faye says.

"It feels safe enough," I say. All that stone and heavy wood. "Besides, I like being up so high. Watching the clouds scoot around. It makes me feel like we are sailing."

The attic is full of old furniture, boxes of clothes, Christmas decorations. Craggy old junk nobody could care a lick for, making me wonder is this an excuse for Faye Barlow to tell me something?

"This is where the ghost made its first appearance," Faye says, breaking into my thoughts like a mind reader. "Over by that door." She points at a little door set low in the wall. "That leads under the eaves."

"What did it look like?" I say.

Faye settles back on her rear, holding her knees. "Oh, I don't know. You've probably seen the pictures: a blob of light. An indistinct outline of a girl. That kind of thing."

"Did she say anything?"

"Oh, no. It was described as more of a momentary thing. My nephew was up here looking for the croquet set and saw her. He said the figure was just there a second or two, all in white, shimmering. Then she was gone."

"Faye." I kneel beside her, touching her on the elbow. "I get the feeling there's something you've been wanting to tell me?"

She cuts her eyes away and picks up a doll with hair made from pieces of cloth. She touches the doll to her mouth and turns to look at me again.

"I've been meaning to ask you, Little Texas . . . do you like being a preacher?"

I pull my arm back. "Sugar Tom says I was born to it."

"I believe you were." She brings the doll up again, almost kissing it this time. "But do you *like* it? Is it something you want to do for the rest of your life?"

"Well . . ."

"I'll never forget the first time I saw you . . . it was in Tupelo, Mississippi. Tee had taken me there to see the birthplace of Elvis. It's just this rickety little frame house, can you believe that? We happened on your revival completely by accident. My, but I was enthralled. The way you laid your hands on that old man, helping him to stand up from that chair . . ." She licks her lips. "It took my breath away. I think I kind of—well, fell in love that night. You truly have a gift."

Nobody has ever talked to me this way before.

"Thank you, I'm—"

Faye drops the rag doll and takes my face in her small hands.

"So you must know how much it means when I say this—I don't want you to preach on Sunday. Not on that island. I can't bear for anything to happen to you. I just *can't*."

She lets go of my face and puts her fingers up to her eyes. I place my hand on her shoulder on instinct.

"Faye—are you all right?"

She pulls her fingers down, eyes full.

"I'll—I'll be okay. You have to forgive me, Little Texas—"

"Please, just call me Ronald Earl."

"All right, Ronald Earl. Just please think about what I said. I wish I could tell you where this feeling is coming from, but all I know is it's getting worse and worse. I just can't—can't—please—just—just hold me."

Faye takes me in her arms, pressing her big bosom against me. I can feel her shaking. When she finally lets go, she sweeps her red eyes around the attic as if somebody was looking. I help her to stand.

"I'm so sorry about this," she says.

"It's all right," I say.

"I suppose we need to be heading on down now. There's nothing I really wanted from up here. Just the chance to talk in private."

We walk back to the stairs together. "Wait," Faye says as I put my hand on the doorknob. "Tee . . . he doesn't understand things like feelings. You know?"

She looks at me a long time, not speaking. Then she leans forward on her tippy toes and touches her lips to my jaw.

"Come on," she says, pulling the door open. "And please, not a word to Tee."

CHAPTER

⇒ FORTY-TWO ⇐

I let myself up to bed early. Will she come again?

What does she want from me?

Certain Certain pokes his head in to check on me. I tell him I'm all right.

The second he leaves, I wish he were still there. I don't like the shadows in the room. I try reading the scriptures by the lamplight to pass the time, but here's a secret most preachers won't tell you: a lot of the Good Book is kind of a grind. Did Paul have a girlfriend? Bet you five dollars he didn't. Bet you ten dollars he wished he had.

I set out my whittling things and work awhile, collecting

the shavings on my lap. A queen is not the hardest piece to do—not much different than a bishop—but I don't have another piece of ash this long, so I need to be—

A scratchy noise. It's coming from the ceiling.

I lay back, listening to the skittering, following it with my eyes.

There is a piece of scripture in a part of the Bible that nobody ever preaches from, on account of it's lustful and full of wicked thoughts about men and women in love. It's called the Song of Solomon. I've been reading it a bunch lately. Ever since—well, ever since my dreaming trouble started. Here is my favorite part, from canticle eight, verse six:

"Set me as a seal upon thine heart, as a seal upon thine arm: for love is strong as death."

I think about her, saying this verse over and over in my head. Then add one of my own:

Dear heavenly Father, please release Lucy from whatever force is keeping her bound up with evil. Take her to your heavenly bosom and comfort her and her loved ones. In the name of Jesus, whose love is strong as death, set her free. . . .

I pray the prayer for Lucy over and over, maybe a hundred times. Finally I'm slipping into a dream, feeling the blackness come.

But wait. *There's something in here with me.*

I put my hands out, reaching toward the blackness, just like I did before. I start pushing against it, pushing and ripping till I can see through to the light on the other side.

And she is there.

Gliding up to me, eyes shining, blue dress so flimsy I can practically see clean through it. Can see her shape, the curve of her small bosoms, her hips. Can I touch her right through that dress?

I put my hand out, feel the silky material—Lucy is barefoot now—my hand trails down, feels the smoothness of her arm, then her leg. And next thing I know, I pull her to me. I'm holding her. It's heaven. *Heaven.* Holding her sweet, beautiful—

The blackness comes again, and she is ripped away from me. And Lucy is running now.

I start to run after her. I can see her blue dress flying up ahead. Something is chasing her. I see it as nothing big, a dark shape at first. As I get closer, I can see its back is humped over, and it has ropy muscles like the branches of a big oak. Its skin is a scuddy red color, like blood mixed with dirt.

It's catching up to her.

I can't let it catch her, I *can't.* It will take her straight down to hell. I put on a burst, get up close, and fling myself at the thing's shoulders. I grab ahold of it, wrap my arms round its neck, lugging against it, my feet off the ground, making it carry my weight. Its skin is pus-sticky, and hot steam is coming off its giant bald head. Its ears are nothing but holes. It stinks like rotting meat.

It's too big, too strong. It keeps chasing, still gaining on Lucy. Reaching out its claws for her.

I start screaming the prayer. "In the name of Jesus, set her free. Set her free. Set her free. . . ."

I spring up hard in bed, my whole body gone cold, breath coming ragged. I can still feel the creature's shoulders, can still see the look of terror on Lucy's face as it tore into her flesh . . . *so real.*

The bedroom door—it's open.

The lamps flicker in the hall.

Something bumps my arm.

Lucy. Sitting right next to me in bed. Staring at me with eyes like powdered glass. The door slaps shut.

⟫FORTY-THREE⟪

I half scream and throw myself out of bed. Scuttle to the door backward on my hands and heels. I get up and get my hand on the crystal doorknob, twisting it back and forth.

I'm locked in.

My whittling knife is on the floor; it must've still been on my lap when I fell asleep. I snatch it up and hold it out in front of me, pointing the blade at her. She sits on the edge of the bed, so high up her sneakers are dangling. If she makes one move, if she starts toward me, I—

Something creaks behind me. The big door is swinging

open again, and the long hallway beckons like an escape hatch to another world. I start for it—

"Stay."

I wheel around looking at Lucy. Still sitting there on the bed, but her mouth is open. *Did she really just . . . ?*

"Wait."

I straighten up a little from my crouch, but my heart hasn't slowed down a lick. I'm standing there in nothing but my drawers. I've still got the whittling knife out in front of me, thumb on the fat part of the blade.

"Come on," she says. "Put that stupid thing away."

My hand tightens on the knife.

"I didn't come here to hurt you. Please put it away."

I hesitate, considering. The door is still open. I can still leave in a hurry if I need to. I fold the knife up, stick it in the waistband of my drawers. Show her my empty hands.

The smallest little grin pulls up both sides of Lucy's lips.

"Did you really think you could hurt me with that?" she says.

A ghost. I'm talking to a ghost. "I can't—I can't believe this," I say. "Any of it. I can't even believe I'm talking to you."

"Okay, then don't. But it won't change the fact I'm sitting right here on your bed. What's your name?"

"What? They call me Little Tex—"

"What's your *name*?" she says again. "Your real name."

"Oh. *Oh.* Ronald Earl Pettway." My voice is so quiet, I wonder if she can even hear it.

"Oh man. That's too bad," Lucy says. "Ronald Earl Pettway. It sounds like somebody who would shoot his uncle at a picnic. But I'll get used to it. How old are you, Ronald Earl?"

"Me? I'm sixteen this month—but . . ."

I'm the one should be asking questions.

"Wow, six*teeeeeen,*" Lucy says, drawing it out like it's a magic number or something. *Is she making fun of me?* It's hard looking into her eyes, talking like this—they are too . . . *shattered* is the only word I can think of.

"Well, how old are you?" I say.

I'm sorry the minute the words are out of my mouth. Lucy looks up in the air, eyes flicking all around. Searching. Like she's trying to remember. *Remember who she used to be.*

She looks straight at me. "It's not important."

"Are you—are you a ghost?"

She shows that little grin that's almost not a grin. "You're not afraid of me, are you, Ronald Earl?"

"I don't—I don't know what you are."

She leans to one side on her hand, like she's getting comfortable.

"Hasn't anybody ever told you there's no such thing as ghosts?"

I put my weight on my back foot, the one closest to the door.

"Oh. So you're a devil. Like in the Bible."

"Hey, you're shivering. Why don't you come over here and get dressed?"

She glances at my clothes hanging on the chair and pats the bed.

"That's all right," I say.

"Afraid I might bite?"

I watch her, still not really sure I'm believing any of this. A girl. In my bedroom. A *dead* girl.

"You didn't answer my question," I say.

"You didn't ask one. You said, 'So you're a devil.' Maybe I am. Does that bother you?"

"How could you not know what you are?"

Lucy sighs. "Believe it or not, you don't instantly get all the answers over here."

"After—after you're . . ."

"Dead?" Lucy says. "Okay. Might as well get it out of your system. You want to know what it's like, don't you?"

Her eyes make it hard to think. I finally manage to nod.

"All right," Lucy says. "You know all those TV shows, the ones where somebody pretends to be talking to spirits in the afterlife?"

"Yes. Me and Certain Certain were just watching an episode of *Crossing Over* where—"

"That's bullshit. . . ."

I wait, looking at her.

"Does swearing bother you?" Lucy says. "I'm sorry."

"I don't know—I don't know if we should be talking like this. Seeing how you're a devil."

"Because only devils curse?"

"No. I reckon plenty of folks curse."

She smiles again. "Won't the *Lord* protect you?"

"Don't make fun. It's not right. It's just—why would a ghost need to swear?"

"Hell, I don't know." She smiles a big smile. It looks real this time. "I'm sorry. I'm teasing you, okay? What else would you like to know?"

I think about ways I could ask it, decide there aren't any good ones.

"How come—why do you move so funny sometimes? And your voice—"

"Because it's so *hard*, Ronald Earl."

"What is?"

She moves her head, jerking it side to side like she's studying the room. "Being *here.* This place. You can't imagine. I don't know—I don't know if I can explain it."

"Try."

She looks at me awhile. "Have you ever—when you were a little kid—did you ever crawl up inside some place that was really tight? Where you could barely move?"

"I guess so. Certain Certain has this place up above the truck cab where he sleeps—it's not so bad, but behind it there's this tiny little space for storage. When I was little, I loved climbing in that space. I had to make myself as little as I could, squeeze myself in where I couldn't move a lick. Then we'd fly on down the highway, me balled up in there—"

"That's what it's like," Lucy says. "Being here. Except it's not just the feeling of being cramped into a space—it's like you're cramped into a *world*. A whole world that is nothing but small, cramped-up places. Slow. Everything is so *slow*. It's hard to—to make anything work. Do you understand?"

"Is that why you couldn't speak before? At the motel? And the drive-in theater? Last night?"

"Exactly! I wanted to talk to you so bad. . . ."

"So how can you now? What happened?"

"You. You did it."

⟶ FORTY-FOUR ⟵

"You set me free," Lucy says.

I feel my skin go all over with gooseflesh, and back away from her.

"Are you talking about my *prayer*?" I say. "Where I asked Jesus to set you free? How could you know about that?"

"I was there."

"Inside my head?"

"Yep. I'm there now. You talk about *cramped*."

"That's not funny. Don't you make fun of me."

"Hey, I'm sorry. I don't know what you want me to say. I was just suddenly there, inside your dream. It wasn't something I had any control over. I didn't do it. *You* did it. You brought me here."

I realize my hand is on the knife again. I slide it away, but keep it close. I raise my voice, cocking my head toward the hall.

"Maybe you're just trying to trick me," I say.

Lucy smiles. "They can't hear you. Yell your head off if you like."

I already know it's true. I can feel what I felt before—like a mixing bowl has been set down over the room.

"Are you magic?" I say.

Lucy shifts to leaning on the other hand.

"Are you still hung up on that devil thing?" she says.

"Bible says there will be signs and wonders. In Matthew. 'For there shall arise false Christs, and false prophets, and shall show great signs and wonders; insomuch that, if it were possible, they shall deceive the very elect.'"

Lucy looks mock-serious. "So which am I? A sign or a wonder?"

"Depends, I guess . . . on why you are here."

"You," she says. "I came because of you. I told you. You brought me here."

"How could I do that?"

"You don't have to know you are doing it. You just have to do it."

"But what did I do? I didn't do anything!"

Lucy's shattered eyes get bigger. "We all do *something*, Ronald Earl. You've been doing a lot of something lately."

194

No. No. She can't mean that. She can't know about that. She *can't.* How *bad* I really am. How *evil* I am becoming.

"What's wrong?" she says. "Come *on,* talk to me."

"What do you want?" I say quietly.

"Did you find it? What I left for you the last time?"

"The piece of brick you wrote on?"

Lucy's head flops up and down.

"That's why—that's why I'm here," she says. "I'm here for *you.* I'm here because I want to be here. I couldn't be here without you."

I swallow, feeling something in my chest. I make the mistake of looking straight into her face. When she's this still, it's hard to think someone is actually inside those eyes—inside whatever she is.

"Are you all right?" Lucy says.

"Not exactly," I say, hoping she doesn't notice my hands shaking.

"You're cold."

She levers her skinny arms like a puppet and slides stiffly off the bed. Her little shoes thump the oak floor. She stands there, hands at her sides, watching me. Now she looks like the girl I saw at the drive-in movie theater. Alive, but somehow not alive. My heart shinnies up my throat.

"Do you believe in me?" she says.

"I reckon I have to," I say, gulping the words.

"Then you have to believe in other things, too, Ronald Earl. You have to start *thinking.* Thinking with a new mind."

195

"All I've got's the old one."

She smiles. "Since you're a preacher and all, I didn't think you'd be—"

"Didn't think I'd be what?"

"Funny."

Lucy turns to the chair, reaches her hand out to my shirt—she puts her hand on it, then looks hard at her hand, like she doesn't remember how a person picks something up. Finally her thin fingers pinch together like a dying spider, and she lifts the shirt up. It takes her just as long to get the pants with the other hand.

"Here," she says, turning and holding them out to me.

"That's all right," I say.

"You don't have to be afraid. Please take them."

"No."

Her arms still standing straight out, she begins to glide toward me. *Glide.* Her feet—they aren't even touching the floor. But the worst is her legs. . . .

They're not moving.

I put my hand on the handle of the knife and back a couple of steps into the flickering light of the hall.

"That's enough," I say, trying to keep the fear out of my voice. "Don't come any closer."

She keeps coming. I jerk the door shut, stepping away from it. I wait a little while, watching the door. Finally I take hold of the knob. Jerk my hand away again. The doorknob is *wet.* I brush my hand on my drawers, feeling my Adam's

196

apple bob up and down. I touch the knob again, turning it with only the tips of my fingers. Give a gentle push, and the door swings open. . . .

A gush of mist rolls out from inside the room and a smell of damp. Lucy is sitting on the bed again, hands folded in her lap. My clothes are on the floor. She looks up at me, head snapping up so sudden I almost think I hear her backbone pop.

"I'm glad you didn't go," she says.

I pick up the clothes and pull them on. They feel clammy.

"I can't stay much longer," Lucy says, watching me. "When you left, I almost got pulled away. I'm . . . tired."

Something about the way she says it stings my heart. She doesn't look as scary sitting there with her feet dangling. She looks like a sad little girl.

I move toward the chair. Lucy tilts her head, curious. Lord, in this light—her eyes don't look like they have any pupils.

I sit down in the chair. She looks at me a long time. This is the closest we've been since I woke up with her sitting on the bed.

"So how did I set you free?" I say finally.

"Something was holding me," Lucy says slowly.

I remember the monster that was chasing her in my dream. "Who? The devil?"

"You. You were."

⇒FORTY-FIVE⇐

"I don't understand," I say.

Lucy shifts on the bed again, slouching.

"You had to believe," she says, "in me. At first you didn't. Not all the way. So I had to keep trying to come through until you did."

"So you can't come around unless I believe in you?"

"Yep. Something like that. The more you believe, the more you let me through. It's like you kind of *create* me."

"That's blasphemy. Only the Lord can create a person."

Lucy shakes her head. Shakes it so slow, I can barely tell what she's doing.

"No. I don't mean it like that," she says. "We're all creators. That's what we *do.* But what we create is our own reality." She lifts a weary arm and waves it around the room. "I couldn't *be,*" she says, "without your need. Your need made it possible for you to believe. You believed, so you set me free."

"What's my need, then?"

She struggles to smile. "Those dreams? The white room?"

She knows, I think. It's too much—too much to even think about. *I feel so—*

"Come on, don't be ashamed," Lucy says. "Please. Because we're here to help each other. Right? I have a need, too. They—they know I can't do it on my own."

My heart draws up.

"Can't do what? Who is 'they'?"

Lucy starts to speak, mouth going, but no sound comes out. She holds up her hands, takes the thumb and index finger of one hand and puts them round the wrist of the other. Like a bracelet.

"Them," she says, jaw clopping. She jiggles the fingers holding her wrist.

"A bracelet? Is that what you're trying to show me, Lucy?"

She bows her head. Bows it so low, you'd think she was bearing up under a heavy weight.

"Don't be thick," she says slowly. "You almost sent me away again. I don't know who they are. Not yet. That's what we're here to find out. They're showing me . . . they want me—they want *us*—to find them. Something is holding them here."

"Here at Vanderloo?"

"We have to work . . . together, you and me. Find out what is holding them and help break them free. We were brought together to do this, okay?"

"Why? Why . . . us?"

"I don't know all the reasons yet. Just the most important one."

"Which is?"

"Because I love you, Ronald Earl."

We sit there looking at each other. Lucy asks the question for me.

"How could I, right? That's what you're thinking. When I don't even know you? But I do. I've always known you. *Inside.*" She points at my chest, making me lean back a little. "I couldn't be here if I didn't. Not like . . . *this.*" She touches her arm. "You understand?"

"Solid?" I say, finally able to speak again. "You couldn't be *solid*?"

She smiles. "You've got a brain in there . . . after all. I . . . have to go."

"Wait," I say. "There are so many things I want to ask—"

"I'll come again. We'll start."

"But what about—what about the drum? Why did you do that? You scared me half to death."

The powdery eyes bore into me. "Ronald Earl. Don't be so afraid. There is no such thing . . . as death."

"But you . . ." I don't know how to say it.

"Me? Yeah. I pretty much died. That's not what I mean. Death is different from . . . dying. Death has no meaning. It's not *real*."

"But you gave me that article. About the boy with the burst appendix. You gave it to me at the drive-in theater. Now I know why. You were trying to tell me, weren't you? You were trying to tell me that's how you died."

Lucy looks at me, slumping a little more.

"But—you're in a better place now," I say. "Sitting beside our Lord. Waiting on the Judgment. Aren't you?"

Lucy shakes her head slowly, hitching and jerking. "You have to change. The way you think."

"But it's what I believe. It's the *truth*. The only truth there is. Anything else . . . puts your eternal soul in danger of the fires of hell."

"But I'm here now. And you have to believe . . . *bigger*. That's all. The truth is not that . . . *small*."

She reaches out to me. "Give me your hand."

I don't want to touch her, but I'm scared not to. I hold my hand up, trembling a little, and Lucy seizes at it so hard, my heart misses a beat. Her fingers are burning. She leans her head toward me, looks like she's trying to whisper.

"The drum. That wasn't *me*," she says.

The lightbulb in the lamp sputters and pops. I can't feel her hand anymore. Then the light flares up bright again; Lucy has vanished.

When I finally get up the grit to climb into the empty bed, the sheets are burning hot.

CHAPTER

⇒ FORTY-SIX ⇐

Back in bed, staring at the ceiling, I feel like I've been split right down the middle. Everything that was in me has been taken out. Then cold, clean water was rushed through all the scooped-out places.

It's like being born again. Only this time the old parts of me can't match up with the new. I don't know if I feel good or bad or crazy or all three. I *talked* with her.

"The truth is not that small."

But how can any truth be bigger than *His* truth? Isn't His the only one?

After a while the sun is coming off the lake. I lay here,

spread open, and it fills me up with light. She's real, and nobody will ever convince me otherwise.

On this very first day of my new life, I step out of bed, and the first thing I see is a big gold key laying right in the middle of the floor. It's heavy and cold in my palm, with a big loop on one end and teeth you fit in the lock on the other.

She must've left it for me. What does it fit into? "They want us to find them," that's what she said. "We have to work together." I slide it into my suitcase and zip it shut. Say my morning prayers, then head on down for breakfast.

Most of the others are gone by the time I get to the table. Faye Barlow is sitting there in jeans that come just past her knees, a yellow shirt, and a big floppy hat. She swirls milk into her coffee.

"Well, good morning, Ronald Earl," she says, face opening up when she sees who it is. She gives me a squeeze and a peck on the cheek that smells of orange juice. "I hope you slept well?"

"Mostly," I say, not wanting to lie.

I put my fingers on the brick piece in my pocket and eat while holding it.

"So what are your plans for the day?" Faye says.

"I'm thinking maybe I'll do a little exploring on the island."

She frowns.

"Is there anything wrong?" I say.

"Oh, I'm just a worrier. Ask my husband."

"What are you worried about?"

"Feelings. I get these feelings."

Faye comes over and drapes her arms around me from behind, locking her fingers in front of my throat. Her hands are wet. Settles her mouth on top of my head. I can feel the heat of her breath on my scalp.

"I've got a few things to do here, but I might join y'all later," she says into my hair. It feels funny being held this way. She turns me loose, and I slide my chair back.

"Be safe," Faye says.

Outside, the morning is warm, and close by the house there's a white oak full of blackbirds squawking back and forth. I walk toward the dock till I come to a little stand of cedars. It looks dark and cool in there. I step inside it, where I can't be seen, and finger Lucy's brick and close my eyes.

"Lucy?" I call out.

Nothing but a bobwhite singing in the distance. I open my eyes, and a long ways off I can see that same red-tailed hawk making a big turn over the sunny water. Devil Hill has a little bit of mist around its belly.

"Lucy?" I say again. "Are you there? Please say something if you are there."

Maybe ghosts can't come out in the daylight? "There's no such thing as ghosts," she said. I put the brick away and head down to the boat.

Tee Barlow is riding herd on three men loading something made of dark, polished wood onto the pontoon boat.

"The pulpit from the Bethel Presbyterian Church," he says. "I had to put a deposit on it. It goes back right after the service."

"Where's everybody else?"

"Gone to town. You want to come over with us?"

We motor over to the island, and Tee Barlow's helpers start getting the pulpit stood up at one end of the clearing. There is definitely a different feel to this morning. I decide to scout around. Maybe there's something left from the last time they had services here? I follow the edge of the woods till I come to a place where the older trees thin out. I look at it closer; it's the head of an old trail that runs off into the forest. I decide to follow it.

"Don't go too far," Tee Barlow calls. "The woods are full of woolyboogers." He laughs and smiles.

The trail is carpeted in pine straw and sprinkled with saplings. It's been a long time since anybody came this way regular. It runs parallel to the shore for a ways; I can see blue water glinting through the trees. Once I'm out of sight, I settle on my knees in a quiet place and bow my head.

"Dear Lord Jesus Christ, please let me know what I am to do about this vision that has been sent to me. If Lucy is a devil, please send her away. But if she is something else, and she needs my help, please grant me your power and your love so that I might help her. Amen." I settle back on my tailbone and haul out the brick again, cupping it in both hands.

"Lucy? Are you there?"

I wait, eyes closed, then something snaps close by. I jerk around.

A red-tailed fox is sitting in the middle of the trail looking at me, tail perked up in the air. I get to my feet and take a couple of steps toward it. He lifts his head and starts down the trail ahead of me. I follow along behind, watching the plumy tail bouncing up and down.

We walk like that a long ways, coming at last to a place where the trail narrows, choked with poison oak and tall purple milkweed. I push my way through, feeling very far from anything and downright alone. The sun is higher, but the woods are thicker, damping the light.

The fox just keeps trotting along, leading me. We come up another long curve, and up ahead the trail widens into a clearing, the forest floor dotted green and yellow where the sun peeps through. The place has a special feeling. "The kind of a place where the Lord lives" is how Sugar Tom would say it.

The fox sits down on his haunches right at the edge of the open place. He turns and looks back at me. Do foxes have rabies? I walk a little closer; the fox takes a quick, springy leap across a fallen sycamore, and he's gone in the underbrush.

"Shoot."

"Ronald Earl?"

I spin around, heart pounding. Faye Barlow is standing there. How in heaven did she get here?

"Don't you go any farther," she says, coming toward me, face darkening up.

"Why?"

"I was afraid you might stumble onto this place. I got to worrying so much about it back at the house, I had to come right over. You need to go back to the landing."

"I saw a red-tailed fox—it was almost like he led me here."

"Just come on now, the others will be waiting."

She takes my hand and we start back.

"What didn't you want me to see in that clearing?" I say after a while.

Faye stops and hugs me to her. Her body is soft and warm. She smells of vanilla extract. She pulls her face back and stares deep into my eyes, mouth just inches away.

"That place . . . it seems all right now, a beautiful day like this," she says. "But it's not a good place to go. Especially for you."

"It has something to do with the devil, doesn't it?" I say. "From that old revival service?"

Faye looks like she almost starts to laugh, then catches herself.

"Let me show you something."

She leads me a little ways off the trail, being careful to keep us out of the stickers. We come to where a big, old shagbark hickory has fallen, letting a lot of sunbeams through.

"Look here." Faye points at a bunch of red flowers hanging at the end of some long, drooping stems. "See this part that's curled up?"

I look closer. "They're pretty," I say, putting my hand out to touch one. She grabs my fingers away.

"This is a pitcher plant," she says. "A killer, Ronald Earl. A carnivore. A *meat eater*. Their insides are slippery, so the insects can't climb out. They say canebrake pitcher plants are only found farther down south, but here they are, on Devil Hill. Why do you think that is?"

"I—I don't know much about plants."

Faye straightens up from the flowers and takes both my hands in hers. Puts my fingers to her lips. I can feel the words slipping out of her mouth.

"It's natural to be attracted to a place like this," she says. "So alive and beautiful. It's hard to imagine there could be anything dangerous here. *Evil.* Just like the pitcher plant, that's the power of the attraction."

"What's in that clearing, Faye?"

She pulls my hands down. "Not here. I can't talk about it here. Let's go back."

"Why?"

"Because . . . *it listens.*"

⇒FORTY-SEVEN⇐

Back at the plantation Faye looks at me.

"I want you to come help me with something, Ronald Earl." She looks over at her husband and calls across the clearing, "Tee, can I borrow our star for a little bit?"

We walk together down to the landing. I start to climb aboard the pontoon boat, but she pulls me another way. There is a canoe sitting there in the milfoil. Faye climbs in ahead of me; I watch the canoe wiggle and tip under her weight, feeling a lump in my throat.

"I don't know," I say. "I've never much been in little boats. And I'm not much of a swimmer."

"We'll be perfectly safe," she says. "I promise you."

She sits down at one end, leaving me to come behind her. I step on the first skinny little seat and feel the canoe rocking under me. I sit down, my ankles wiggling.

"Now shove us off, please," Faye says. "Just the paddle."

I reach out with the paddle and push at the shoreline, and we slip away from the bank. Faye takes the other paddle and starts pulling hard at the water. "There's a little bit of a current here once we get out in the channel."

I dig my paddle in. The lake pulls harder at my arms than I expected, but after a few strokes I start to get the hang of it.

"Hey, this is kind of fun," I say.

We slide with the current beneath the trestle. Looking up, I can see the bottom of the trestle and the big iron legs coming down to the concrete piers. I glance back at the island, and the columns of the ruined plantation look like something from a painting.

"It's something, isn't it?" Faye Barlow says. She bites down on the words.

Back at the house, I wonder if I should show her the key I found. But she heads straight to the kitchen, all business, and we get to working on an Italian dish called manicotti. Faye has me stir up some eggs and milk, then shows me how to pour the thin batter into a frying pan.

"When they're done, you spread them with the cheese mixture and roll them up into tubes and pour the sauce over the top," she says. "You'll love it, I promise."

"I've never done much cooking," I say. "We mostly just eat out."

"That's too bad. It helps me to think. So, you know what I'm thinking about right now?"

I shake my head.

"I'm thinking about putting you into my little car and driving you right straight on out of here. Hiding you away somewhere up in Memphis or Nashville."

I look at her till batter drips down my arm from the spoon.

"I'm dead serious, Ronald Earl," she says. "You just don't know what you're getting yourself into. That place. You can't preach there. They won't tell you. So I'll tell you."

"What are you scared is going to happen?"

Faye puts a dish towel over her shoulder and dumps more spice and onions in the sauce, stirring them together till everything's rich and red as blood.

"You have to understand," she says. "The island—it was my *special* place. It always has been, ever since I used to visit my aunt here. It has always been a place I could go to get away for a few hours by myself. Watch birds, collect plants, draw."

She takes a deep breath and stops stirring. We watch the pot bubble.

"Okay. Okay. Whew. I have never told anyone about this, not even Tee. It was just about this time of year when it happened. I remember because the evening primroses were out, and I wanted to collect some to press. So I took the canoe over there one afternoon when Tee was on a buying trip in Atlanta. Everything was so beautiful! I followed that same trail you found this morning until I came to the clearing.

"Then, late in the day, without any warning, the sky turned pitch-*black,* and a lightning storm came up. I was afraid to take the canoe back. So I had to wait it out.

"There was no way to see except for the flashes of the storm. But I had never been afraid on my island. Not *ever* . . . I went into the clearing looking for a big tree to shelter under—I know you aren't supposed to do that—but I must have stayed there half the night, wet and miserable. Finally the storm passed. Then . . ."

Her eyes well up with tears.

"Are you all right?" I say.

"Something was *there,* Ronald Earl. Something was there in that clearing with me. Something so frightening and *evil*—"

"What did it look like?"

Faye stifles a sob. "I—I don't *know,* that's just it! I never really saw it. It was so dark, and it happened so *quickly.* It came at me! Came at me from behind and pushed me down in the leaves! I couldn't *move*! I couldn't—couldn't get away."

"Was it a man?"

"I thought—I thought at first it was . . . until I felt its *skin.* So slick and cold in the rain—like a *snake.* Some kind of *animal,* but it wasn't any animal. Because it spoke . . ."

"What did it say?"

"I couldn't understand it! It wasn't like any language I've ever known. It was . . . screaming at me—screaming and grunting and making this awful—this awful rattle in its throat. It did things to me, Ronald Earl. Things—I have never been able to tell anyone what it did. Not even Tee. *It did things to me. . . .*"

She sets the spoon down and begins to weep. I take her by the arm.

"Please," she says, very quiet. "Please just hold me a moment."

She takes me in her arms and squeezes me so hard, I can barely draw breath. I get hugged by folks all the time, I'm used to it. But I've never been clung to like this. She cries a very long time. All you can hear in that kitchen is her weeping and the bubbling of the sauce pot.

"You don't know—you don't know how much it means to me, you coming here like this," she says at last, whispering into my ear. "But I'm so *afraid* for you."

She's quiet a little while, just breathing. Then I feel her mouth against my neck. Her lips are wet and cool. Faye looks up at me, eyes swoled up and red, and gives me a tiny little smile. Kisses my cheek, then kisses it again. Then she puts her mouth on my mouth. Kisses me *hard.*

Oh my Lord. I am all funny and kind of sick inside. I begin to pull away, but she pulls me to her even stronger, keeps kissing, pressing hard with her wet mouth.

"I love you. I love you. I've always loved you."

214

Faye's hot tongue is working against my lips, like it's trying to find a way in. I keep my mouth clenched tight shut, wrenching my head side to side. But my struggling just makes her press harder, and then my mouth opens, and her tongue is there, pushing against my tongue, moving all over. Down below—I can feel it happening, feel the change coming, just like it happens in my dreams. Swelling against the front of her apron. Faye puts one of her hands there, touching me, feeling me get bigger. So dirty, so downright filthy and wrong—

It's not right. This is not right. Let go! Let go! Let go!

Finally she lets go, and I jerk away from her. I stand there, my hands covering my front, as Faye slowly slides down the edge of the cupboard till she's sitting on the floor. She puts her face in her hands.

"I'm sorry. Oh my God, I'm so sorry," she says. "Please forgive me. I'm—I'm just so lonely sometimes. It's like something *knew*—something knew what I needed, and it used me. It used me. It took *hold* of me. You have to forgive me. Say you will. Please."

I step back, still watching her, and swipe the back of my hand across my mouth. I feel sick and wobbly. I keep backing all the way into the living room. My leg brushes the couch, and I slump down against it.

Faye is whimpering in the kitchen.

Finally I can hear the scraping of the wooden spoon, the metal oven door opening and closing. Dishes being set out.

A little while later Sugar Tom comes into the kitchen with Certain Certain. "Why, that smells positively delicious," he says, easing into a chair. "What is it?"

"Manicotti," Faye says, quiet. She gives me a pleading look and swipes at her eyes with the dish towel. "Would you like a taste?"

She carries the wooden spoon to Sugar Tom, holding one hand underneath it for drips.

"Mmmm, I haven't tasted anything like that in *years,*" Sugar Tom says, smacking his lips and closing his eyes.

Faye brings a lick over for Certain Certain. "Is that garlic in there?" he says, smiling his raggedy smile.

"Only two cloves," Faye says.

"Look out, now."

"So . . . so how are things coming?" Faye says.

"Got a dozen men lined up. More than enough," Certain Certain says.

"Where's—"

"Miss Wanda Joy? She's still stuck in town. Making phone calls, visiting folks, getting the news stories ready. That woman is flat on *fire.* Stayed up half the night working on the press release. Seven papers this Saturday, if she can manage it. And believe me, she can. Gonna be a sizable congregation on Sunday, she has any say."

Faye doesn't say anything, just goes back to stirring. Certain Certain comes into the living room. "What you been up to, Lightning?"

216

"I've been showing him around some," Faye cuts in, standing in the doorway. "Now if you all will scoot, I'll get the rest of the things ready, and we'll have an early dinner." She glances at me, pressing her lips like she's in pain.

I look out the big front window. The sun is lower, turning Devil Hill blood-red.

CHAPTER

⇒ FORTY-EIGHT ⇐

The manicotti is delicious, just like Faye promised.

But really all I can taste is the taste of *her*. Her mouth, her *tongue*. I'm so ashamed. Her sidling up against me. All the feelings . . . how foul I must be to have that inside me. I can feel it like a sickness.

"Are you sure you're getting enough to eat?" Faye says over my shoulder.

She ladles more sauce over the rolled-up manicotti shells on my plate. My stomach hurts. I can't eat. She doesn't touch me the way she has been doing.

Maybe—is this why Lucy came to me? Because it *knows*.

Whatever is over on that island attacked Faye. It knows what is inside my soul. How black it is. How weak I am.

"Lust not after her beauty in thine heart; neither let her take thee with her eyelids."

It knows it can get to me, just like it got to Faye.

"This is going to be our largest service *ever,*" Miss Wanda Joy says. Her face is glowing; this is the kind of thing she does best, run around organizing a big production. "I've got articles lined up in papers all the way to West Memphis, Arkansas," she says.

She goes on about how unprecedented and spectacular it's all going to be, hardly stopping to breathe.

After supper Certain Certain finds a TV in the den. We watch a show about passenger pigeons. How back in the 1800s there used to be billions of them. So many the flocks could run one mile wide by three hundred miles long. Took days for them to pass by. Then somebody figured out they were a cheap source of meat to feed the slaves. Hunters killed the last flock in 1896.

"You ain't said much this evening, Lightning," Certain Certain says. "Didn't eat much, neither. You thinking 'bout the service?"

I shake my head. "I was wanting to ask you something. Do you think—do you think somebody could go to hell for . . ." I don't know what to call it. This thing that I've done.

"Spit it out, boy."

"Well. Don't worry about it. It's nothing."

"Nothing ain't something liable to send you to hell. What is it?"

I bite my lip and glance at the living room behind me. "Say if—say if this *girl,* she came up to you and . . . well, she . . . started something."

Certain Certain leans forward in his chair. "Something like what?"

"You know."

"Oh. *Ohhh.* Now I get you, doctor. Why, you planning on rubbing up against some gal sometime soon?"

"No, what if . . . what if I *already—*"

Faye comes in bringing us dishes of homemade peach ice cream. She hands me mine and plunks down next to me, watching me stir it around, pretending to eat.

"The History Channel," she says brightly. "Can't you two do any better than that?"

She goes to jabbing buttons on the clicker. Now we're watching a movie called *Sixteen Candles* instead. It's full of awful stuff—drinking, swearing, underwear. Right in the middle of the movie, Faye hooks her pinky finger around my thumb on the sly. I feel sick down in the very bottom of my stomach. *It's going to happen again, it's going to happen—*

I excuse myself and head to my room, insides knotted like rope. I grab my Bible and sit on the bed, force myself to read through the Old Testament books Nahum, Habakkuk, Zephaniah, and Haggai right in a row.

Nothing works. I want to see her, Lucy. I want to see her

so bad, I could chew glass. But maybe I shouldn't. I'm so scared she'll know. Somehow she'll *know* what happened between Faye and me. What will she think? Will she even talk to me again? Do I want her to?

I pull off my shoes, but I keep everything else on. Say my prayers and climb into bed. I tell myself I'll just stay awake, see her when she comes. Then I change my mind and pull the cord on the bedside lamp. The room fills up with dark—just a little stripe of yellow under the big hallway door. I cock my head to one side, waiting, and catch a single star skating across the big window. Before you know it, I'm gone to the world.

When I wake up, the light is on. Look all around, but the room is empty. There's a fly on my blanket—a big, fat summer fly. I watch its creepy black eyes, but it doesn't move. I reach my hand over, doing a trick Certain Certain showed me a long time ago—you cup your hand and sweep it across the fly, and the fly will wind up inside your fist.

I swing my hand quick, feel the fat, heavy fly smack into my palm. Then something closes over my wrist, clamping down so hard my fingers spread open and the fly scoots away. It's Lucy—standing beside the bed, holding my arm.

CHAPTER

⟩FORTY-NINE⟨

"You shouldn't have even touched it," she says. "That's what it *wants*. It wants you. Do you understand that?"

She's squeezing my wrist tighter and tighter, stronger than I figured she could.

"Let me go. Let me go, *please*," I say.

Lucy unclenches her fingers, and I scramble away to the chair, rubbing my wrist.

"Did I hurt you?" she says.

"It's just—you surprised me, that's all. Your hand—why's it so hot?"

"Sorry. I'll stick it in a bucket of ice water next time." She grins.

My heart is still going ninety to nothing. I can't get used to the way she comes and goes.

"What could a fly do?" I say.

"Maybe nothing. Maybe everything. You can't take chances like that. Anything that comes around you acting curious."

"Like you?"

"Present company excepted. We have to be careful, that's all. It wants you, too. The one that is holding them. It'll do anything it can to get to you."

"Including changing itself into a fly?"

"It wants all of us. Whoever it can get. Any way it can."

"Why?"

"How should I know?" Lucy looks away from me, almost like she's listening to somebody. "The ones it's holding—they're showing me—they're so *angry.* So much anger and fear. I think that's how it holds them."

"Who is 'them'? You were trying to tell me last time."

"That's what we need to find out. So we can set them free. But their huge anger—their *rage*—I think it makes them blind. Keeps them from moving on."

"Moving on *where*? Heaven? Because the Bible says—"

"Home," Lucy says. "They need to go home."

"You mean here—this isn't—"

She makes a disgusted sound.

"Don't be stupid. I'm not talking about a *place,* Ronald Earl. I'm talking about . . . *home.* You're always there. You just don't know it. This . . . world . . . is a distraction, okay? Everything about it. Everything that is . . . here. . . ." Her eyes flare in frustration. "When you're in the middle of it . . . what you call *life* . . . you think that's all there is. There can't be anything else. Anything . . . better."

"But there is?"

"Oh yeah. *Home.*"

"So what's it like there?"

"I don't know if it's right . . . showing you. But maybe I will sometime." She grins. "If I feel like you can handle it."

"It's that *bad*?"

"That *good,* goofball. Good can fry your circuits, too. You of all people ought to know that. What does it say in the Bible about looking on the face of God?"

"Okay. But if that's our home, and it's so great, why do we come here in the first place? To the earth, I mean."

"Ha." Lucy shakes her head. "Like I'm some kind of *teacher.* I don't know half what I need to know. Not one-*tenth.* That's one of the reasons it's important to be . . . *here.*"

She lifts her arms, making me know she means the world. *My world.*

"To learn?" I say. "We come here to learn?"

"*Grow.* We're supposed to grow. There are so many

things . . . you can't do here. Everything's so hard. Doing things the hard way kinda helps us grow . . . *faster*."

"So when we get done . . . *growing* . . . we go back *home*?"

"Bingo. Only there is no going back. You're just there. All the time. You *know* you're there. That's what *they* need to know. The ones it's holding."

"So why don't you just tell them?"

"Doesn't work that way. They can't see it, know what I mean? They're like an old-timey TV station—they can broadcast, but they can't receive."

"We're talking *dead* folks here, right? Are they spirits? Are they . . ."

"You mean, are they like me?" Lucy says. "Yeah, that's what you would think of them. They're dead."

"Well, how else would you think of them? Souls? Do they have bodies?"

She turns toward the window. No moon tonight. "Everything living has a body, Ronald Earl. Just not like what you would think."

"But you said they were dead."

"They are . . . it's just hard to think of them that way. Nothing living ever really dies. The *soul,* as you call it—that's what a person is. That's the real person, the *whole* person. This"—she tugs at the skin of her arm—"this is the part that's not real."

"So . . . the people we are trying to help are dead. Well,

they *passed on,* let's say. How can you be talking to them and not know who they are?"

"Who said I was talking to them?"

"Then how else do you communicate? How do you even figure they're in trouble?"

Lucy frowns. "Sheesh. Okay. They don't speak in words to me. Think of . . . pictures. They show me things—things that are kind of like pictures. Only . . . you are *inside* the pictures. Does that make sense?"

"I guess. Like the bracelets? They were showing you something that looked like bracelets."

"Yeah. Except the bracelets were *on me.* I could feel them. They're *heavy.* And they aren't bracelets."

"So what are they, then?"

"That's what I'm hoping to find out tonight, if you'll get a move on. Do you have the key I brought you?"

I unzip my suitcase and pull the old key out.

"Put it in your pocket, and let's get going."

"Where?"

"Come on."

I'm tying my shoes as fast as I can. "Okay, but you have to answer me this: Are we talking about *Satan*? Is that who we're fooling with here? Is that who is holding them?"

"It doesn't have a name, as far as I know."

She looks all around, agitated, like she's afraid of being overheard. For some reason Miss Wanda Joy's voice jumps up in my mind, quoting from Revelation: "'And on their heads were as it were crowns like gold, and their faces were as the faces of men.'" Only it's talking about locusts with scorpion stingers from the bottomless pit.

"What are you waiting on?" Lucy says. "Let's *go*."

She moves away from the bed, all arms and legs, awkward, then glides across the room to the door. My legs nearly turn to rubber just watching her.

"Can't you walk regular?" I say.

She looks over her shoulder at me with those eyes.

"What's wrong with the way I walk?"

"Never mind."

The door swings open by itself, and Lucy starts glide-walking up the hallway. We make our way through the quiet, dark house, me trailing behind.

We wind up in the kitchen. Lucy stops next to a skinny little door with a black doorknob. Seems she can see better in the dark than I can. She makes a funny jerking motion with her arm.

"I can't open this one," she says. "You try."

My eyes are just now starting to adjust. I put my hand on the knob and give it a turn.

"It's jammed," I say.

I set my knee against the frame and yank. The skinny door screeches open. A smell of raw dirt comes up in my face, and a big gush of cold air. Has to be the cellar.

"Look for the switch," Lucy says.

I hold on to the doorframe and feel around in the black.

Something brushes my hand, and I give it a tug and a light-bulb pops on, throwing a weak yellow glow down some rick-ety stairs.

"You want to go down *there*?" I say, feeling stupid for say-ing it.

Lucy gives me a poke in the back.

"That's what they're showing me. Get going."

"Ladies first," I say.

She just stares at me.

"Okay."

No handrail and the stairs are steep. The wood is so old, I can see the circle marks from the sawmill blade. I start down, hearing creaks and pops. There is definitely a smell of the un-derground. On one side is a scabby stone wall, cold to my fin-gers. On the other, a whole lot of nothing.

As we go down, I realize I'm caught between two strange and terrible worlds, and mine is getting smaller all the time.

At the bottom I step into a weak little spot of light.

"Whoa."

➤ FIFTY ⬿

So big and so old. There's an arched brick ceiling running off in several directions. The floor is nothing but dirt.

It's too easy to picture being tombed up down here. Lucy comes up behind me. I don't like the fact she's between me and the stairs.

"Why—why do you want me down here?" I say.

"That way."

Lucy points toward a looping string of bare lightbulbs running off down one section of archways.

I follow the lights—we pass a few old crates made of slats of wood, but they are empty, the tops busted in. I see scuff marks in the dirt where boots have come through, who knows how long ago. I come to a kind of intersection.

"Now what?"

Lucy points again—to another hall with a bricked arch over the top. Only there's no string of lights in this direction.

"That way?" I say, pointing.

Lucy nods hard. Prickles grow all over my back. I'm way down here with nobody, nobody else but *her,* whatever she is.

"Let me be your eyes," she says. She puts a warm hand on my shoulder, pushing just a little.

I walk a little ways down the dark hall, feeling the light shrinking. I move slower, with Lucy using my shoulder to steer.

"Why don't you go in front, seeing how we need to hurry?" I say.

"Nice try. I'll let you know if there's something there."

"Thanks a lot."

"You're welcome." I can hear the smile in her voice. Then she gives me another little push.

I go forward again as fast as I dare, afraid of tripping over something. But mostly just plain *afraid.* I start putting my hands out in front of me, thinking about spiders.

And worse.

"Will you be able to tell if it's coming?"

"Oh, we'll both know," Lucy says. "Keep going."

She's so close, I can feel the heat from her body against my back. I couldn't swallow if I wanted to.

"What if we get stuck down here?" I say.

"There," she says. "I can see it now. This is where they wanted us to come. They're showing me."

"What is it? I can't see a thing."

I feel my fingers bump something. It's cold and a little damp, like wood that's been underground a long time.

"That's the door," Lucy says.

"I can feel it." I run my fingers over the wood, feeling my heart up in my ears.

"Find the place for the key," Lucy says. "Lower, move your hand lower."

I gulp and move my hands all over it, knowing any second a centipede the size of a Slinky is going to creep over my fingers. Then I touch it, a big metal handle sunk in the wood, with a keyhole just below it.

"Found it!"

"Open it."

I dig out the heavy key. My hands are shaking; it takes two tries to fit it in the lock and turn it. The door clicks loud and sharp in the brick tunnel, making me flinch. I give the handle a shove, and it comes open easy with nary a creak.

A smell of rot creeps out of this room, like when you tump over a log in the forest.

Silhouetted against the far light, Lucy looks like she's floating above the dirt floor. She lets go of my shoulder and takes my arm.

"Go in," she says.

"Um, maybe we should go back and get a flashlight?"

"It's too late, Ronald Earl. It's already looking for us."

I feel my skin tighten, take one step inside the little room, and crack my head on something.

"Ow!"

I reach up, feeling the curve of a low arch against my scrabbling fingers.

"Sorry," Lucy says.

The room is really small; just enough space to close somebody in, swing the door shut, gone forever. Something moves between me and the light.

"Hey!"

My heart is hammering, but Lucy's still there.

"What?" she says.

"I was afraid you had . . . never mind."

"It's got to be here," Lucy says, suddenly all agitated. "We've got to find it. Keep looking."

"What am I looking for?"

"I—I don't know. They're trying to show me, but . . . I don't think they have a picture for it."

"Fine," I say. "I thought you were going to be my eyes?"

"All I can see is your butt."

"Real funny. Some ghost."

"Wait—I think maybe—they're showing me something different. Stairs. The stairs, coming down from the second floor, Ronald Earl. It's coming down. *Looking for us.*"

Sweet Jesus.

"Let's go!"

"No. We have to find it. It has to be here. Keep looking."

I squat down, feeling lower and lower on the far wall, skin crawling. Finally I come to cold dirt; it's damp and puffy, like maybe water seeps in here after a rain.

"Wait!"

There's something there; it's about the size of a suitcase, only more square. Rounded across the top. I run my fingers over it, feel pockmarked metal buckles and big leather straps flopped across the curved lid.

"It's—it's some kind of box!" I say.

"It's an old trunk," Lucy says.

"Let's go," I say, starting to pick it up.

"No—we only want what's inside. Open it. Hurry."

I get down on my knees now and start tugging furiously at the buckles, little wiggles of fear squirting over my back.

Finally I get the first strap loose, then the second. But still the trunk won't open.

I'm thinking about where it is right now. *The kitchen?*

I fumble to get a fingerhold and lift the lid. I get the tips of my fingers into the crack and hoist it up. I want more than anything not to have to stick my hands into this box.

"It's empty! No, hang on. . . ."

There's something flat on the bottom. I'm almost surprised when it comes out fairly easy. Then it flops open—I realize I've only got part of it, pages fanning in my fingers; it feels like a composition notebook.

"It's—it's stuck to the bottom!"

"Get it out."

"What if it tears?"

"*Get it out.* We don't have any more time."

I give a sharp tug, and the notebook tears loose, leaving part of its skin behind. I drop the trunk lid, *thunk;* you can hear it up and down the brick passage.

"Should I lock the door?" I say.

Lucy's already moving away from me, glide-walking. I turn the key in the lock, feeling it clunk, and hustle after her. I stick the notebook under my arm and follow her back toward the light.

Then just as I'm getting to the corner, out of the blackness of the brick tunnel, all the lights dink out.

We are in a tomb.

CHAPTER

⟾FIFTY-ONE⟸

The black is so dark, I can see flashes of my eyeballs when I blink.

"Lucy!" I hiss into the dark.

"Come on."

I touch the brick wall with my free hand, keeping my head low, and move as quick as I can toward her voice. I'm near about to panic when she takes my hand.

"Can you see?" I say.

"Shhh."

She gives my arm a tug, and I stumble after her, using the wall as a guide, heart kicking in my chest. We get to the corner and move out of the tunnel that led to the locked door. *We can't be far away now, can we?*

A sound comes from in front of us. *In front of us!*

Lucy yanks me back against the wall and claps a hot hand over my mouth. She squeezes my face hard. There's a kind of scratchy noise up ahead, like somebody running a screwdriver over the bricks.

Closer. Closer. Finally just past us, trailing away in some other part of the cellar.

I can't help it—I wrench away from her and start to move quick toward the hall where I think the stairs are, feeling any minute whatever is making the noise could be right at our backs.

"Come on," I hiss.

A cracking noise sounds just behind us, like stones crunching together. I'm half running now, fingers raking on the raspy bricks. I bark my shin on something and tumble down. Lucy hauls me to my feet. We're at the bottom of the stairs.

It's still behind us. I let go of Lucy's hand and scramble up the stairs on all fours as fast as I can, knocking my knees on the splintery wood till I slam into the door at the top. I nearly drop the book as I claw for the latch. I crank it hard, then tumble through into the kitchen. I roll onto my back and kick the cellar door shut and lay there gasping.

Alone.

FIFTY-TWO

"Lucy!"

I wait there breathing hard in the dimness—watching the door. Expecting the black knob to turn, something to come out, anything.

Where is she?

Nothing.

I jump to my feet and rush to the cellar door. It's jammed again. I put my weight against the frame, tugging and pulling, but it's like it's nailed shut this time. I beat on the door.

What has it done with her? If it's done anything to her, so help me *God,* I'll . . .

I drop to my knees and pray before the door, half silent, half in desperate whispers, for what seems forever, fighting my own terror. I get up, try the door, and it opens easily this time. I pull the light cord and call down the stairs, faint with fear for her.

I have to trust that she got away. I have to.

Please, God.

The composition book is still where I dropped it when I fell through the doorway. I pick it up and clutch it to my stomach like something might try to wrestle it loose from me, then hurry upstairs. My room is empty. I shut the door, wishing I could lock it.

What's to stop it from coming back for me? But somehow the night doesn't have that feeling anymore. It's like whatever was chasing us has left the house. Left because it got Lucy?

Please let her be all right. Please, God, please.

I bring the book over to the lamp. Its outside is spotted and gray, covered with faded little leaf shapes. It stinks of mold and looks to be held together by pure mildew. I turn to the first page. . . .

A single name: Thaddeus Palmer. Probably the person who owned the book. *But why not Vanderloo?*

In a fever I turn through the pages—what can it tell us about what Lucy and I are supposed to do?

I begin to read. The first page has two columns under the heading "1854," marked "Births at Vanderloo" and "Deaths at

Vanderloo." There are lists of names below each one, some marked with checks. The names sound old-timey: Silvey, Miss Parsey, Peg, Liddy.

I flip through a bunch more pages—more numbers and dates and names for other years. It reminds me of the green ledger book Miss Wanda Joy uses to tote up the love offerings after each service. Like somebody keeping records for a business.

A business?

I drop the book like my hands have been scalded.

Slaves. These are the names of slaves.

CHAPTER

⇒FIFTY-THREE⇐

Next morning I look out at an overcast sky, the water dark and broiling around Devil Hill. More rain is coming. I wonder about Lucy.

I head downstairs and stash the composition book behind a cushion in the den before going in to breakfast. They are all talking about the service, trying to figure out what tasks can be done on a rainy day. I wait for a chance to show the book to Certain Certain in private.

"How'd it go last night, Lightning?" he says, grinning a little. "Didn't hear a peep out of you."

"It was fine," I say.

There is a reason they showed us this, I tell myself. *Focus on the composition book.*

I pull Certain Certain off into the den after we eat and hand him the notebook.

"I wanted you to take a look at this."

Certain Certain turns the notebook over and takes a long look at the pages. "Well, I'll be God—where'd you get this, boy?"

I've never been very good at lying. "Found it down in the basement."

"What you doing prowling around down there?"

"Just . . . exploring."

He touches his torn lip, considering. "It's a property ledger from the Vanderloo Plantation, 1854 to 1866. Valuable historic artifact. Plantation owners used 'em to keep records of their property."

"Their slaves."

"Same thing. *Chattels*—same as a cow or a wagon or a bale of cotton. Sometimes owners, they kept their books theirselves. Other times an overseer did it for them. Look here. . . ." He touches a place in the book where it says "Letty's child" under the birth column. "Girl child born March eighteenth. Then look on down here." He points under the column marked "Deaths." "Letty's child" appears again next to "June 11."

"So her baby died," I say.

Certain Certain nods. "Total loss to the owner. That's the

way they looked at it. Poor little thing. Measles, chicken pox, whooping cough, things like that killed folks off all the time. Pretty near every family had two or three children who never made it to their tenth birthday. Now, with slaves, well . . . it was even worse."

"Didn't anybody ever treat 'em decently?"

"Some did. Some did, yes. But when you're being treated like a horse, does it really make all that much difference? Barlows know you got this?"

"No, sir."

"Something like this ought to be in a museum. You want me to give it to them, keep you out of trouble?"

"No, I will," I say. "But can I look at it just a little while longer?"

"I reckon it's okay, long as you don't damage it. Go easy on that binding, Lightning."

Heavy drops start spitting against the big windows, so I spend time up in my room studying the ledger book for clues and thinking about Lucy.

A gullywasher kicks up later in the evening with scads of lightning. After supper me and Sugar Tom head up to his room, and he digs out his old chessboard and gives me a game while we listen to the thunder spanking the sky. Tonight I'm so distracted, he kills my rook with one of his pawns.

"What's bothering you, Ronald Earl?" Sugar Tom says. He moves his bishop from clear across the board, hemming my king in. "Checkmate."

I cough, waiting to say something, then figure I should just get to it. "What do you think about everything that's been going on? Do you think anything's liable to happen at the service?"

"Ronald Earl," he says, "when you've been in the ministry as long as I have, there is *nothing*—nothing, I'm telling you—on God's green earth that surprises me anymore. You have to remember, we are *targets*—we don't hide our light under a bushel basket, we let it shine. And Christians aren't the only ones who see our light, believe you me. The others are drawn to it, too."

"What others?"

"The fallen ones. Warriors of darkness. They see the light, and they can't keep away. Did I ever tell you about the time I sat up with Miss Gayola Thompson? In Birmingham Memorial Hospital? When she was having her female troubles?"

"No, sir."

"I had fallen asleep in my chair, and she woke me up, terrified something was in the room with us. Kept screaming it was in a corner up by the ceiling. I was barely awake, and the lighting was quite dim, but I thought I saw something there, too. Makes me go cold all over just thinking about it. *Eyes,* Ronald Earl. Several sets of *eyes* up in that corner of the ceiling. *Watching* her. I reckon that's what they do. Beset a person in a time of great weakness, hoping to wear down their faith. Turn them against the Lord in their despair."

"You think it was demons?"

"Devils. Demons. Whatever you want to call them. Something was there. You could *feel* it in the room. Only saw those eyes for a brief little moment, but I snatched up my Bible and read the book of Leviticus straight through out loud."

"Why Leviticus?"

Sugar Tom pulls at his big, hairy ear.

"Lot of strength in that book, Ronald Earl. I've found over the years there are occasions where it's not the message so much as the words themselves. Do you see the difference? There is a great power in words we can *see.* Concrete, solid words. *Tabernacle. Altar. Turtledove. Meat. Bullock. Blood.* Leviticus is full of them. It yanks you away from the bad things and pulls you right back down to the goodness of the earth."

He raises his arms up, fingers spread, eyes rolling back in his head. His voice gets so big, it fills the whole room.

"'And he brought the ram for the burnt offering: and Aaron and his sons laid their hands upon the head of the ram. And he killed it; and Moses sprinkled the blood upon the altar round about. And he cut the ram into pieces; and Moses burnt the head, and the pieces, and the fat.'"

"I see what you mean," I say.

"Power of the *Word*," Sugar Tom says. "It's the bedrock the church is built on. Ran those devils right out of that hospital room. Miss Gayola slept good and sound for the first time in days. Woke up ready to bounce her grandchildren on her lap. The Word is our *shield,* Ronald Earl. No matter *what* is waiting for us on that island, the Word is stronger."

244

I try to think of the best way to ask my next question, somehow smooth it out.

"Um. Then why do you think . . . when Pastor Hallmark got drug away . . . why couldn't he—"

"Why couldn't he stand up to the devil? I won't speak to the size of a man's faith. Only the Lord can answer that. But I know you'll be fine. I've seen it in you—that power. When it's flaming full bore, nothing can stand against it."

I say good night and head out feeling a little better. Miss Wanda Joy catches me coming out of the bathroom. She's wearing her purple bathrobe.

"I've been meaning to speak with you all day," she says. A lock of hair big around as a coffee cup is hanging loose on her forehead. I wonder what she does with all that hair, how she ever gets it dry. "I hope you're as excited as I am."

"Yes'm."

"Certain Certain has everything well in hand. We may have five hundred attendees at the service. I've tried my best to secure TV coverage, but they all tell me they have a policy against filming church services, unless I want to buy time on Sunday. But a fellow out of Atlanta—*Atlanta!*—is writing a story for the *Journal Constitution.* This is going to be the cornerstone in the next phase of our ministry, putting Little Texas and the Church of the Hand on a sound footing for years to come."

"Yes'm. I mean, that's good news."

"Is anything wrong? You seemed quiet at supper."

"Just tired, I guess."

"I don't see how. You've had your days free to rest. Aren't you sleeping well?"

"Mostly. At least after that first night."

"No more demons hanging around?" She smiles in a way that pulls down her eyebrows above her nose, making her look like somebody planning something wicked.

"No," I say, and I think that's the truth, strictly speaking.

"Well, good night and sleep well."

She goes on past me, then stops and turns around. "Have you selected a text for your sermon?"

The question catches me off guard. "Um—no, but I was thinking maybe something out of Leviticus."

"Leviticus?"

"Yes, ma'am."

"Well. That's an odd choice. All those verses about sacrifices. Quite a while since you cracked open the Old Testament, isn't it?"

"I guess so."

"But perhaps that's best. Considering."

"Considering what?"

"Oh, nothing."

She smiles and steps into the bathroom, pulling the door shut behind her. I can hear the lock turn and the shower water start up.

She wants something to happen, I think. *Bet she's even praying for it.*

CHAPTER

➤ FIFTY-FOUR ⬅

A lightning flash practically rips open the window. I can hear rain hammering the yard outside. Wonderful. Perfect match for my mood. The clock in the corner reads 2:04. I fall back on my pillow.

"Are you okay?"

My mouth goes dry. Lucy's in bed with me—only this time she's *under the covers.* Her leg is against my leg. The heat of her body fills the bed with warmth. I reach and turn on the lamp on the table.

"Do you have to do that?" I manage to say.

"It's just so much fun," Lucy says, smiling. "You're constantly ready to be freaked out, you know that, Ronald Earl?"

I'm in bed with a girl. She's still a *girl.* I look at her sideways. Her arms are on top of the covers. She has one of the little Bible pillows pulled up against her stomach. I can see enough of the words to know what they say. Mark, chapter fourteen, verse twenty-two. TAKE, EAT: THIS IS MY BODY.

"Did you look at it?" Lucy says.

"Huh?"

She's pointing at the Vanderloo property ledger.

"Oh," I say. "I've been looking at it all day. I figured out what it is. It's the slaves from the old Vanderloo Plantation, isn't it? The people we're supposed to help. That's what they've been trying to—*wait a minute.*"

"What?"

"Where did you go last night? I didn't know what happened to you! I fell into the kitchen, you were right behind me—"

"It was too close to you. I couldn't let it get you. I had to go somewhere else. Somewhere that would pull it away from you." Her hair is limp against the pillow.

"So where did you go?"

"Home."

"Shoot. You're not going to tell me, are you?"

"I just did."

"Oh, forget I said it. But what would that thing have done

if it had caught us down in the cellar? Can it hurt me? Can it hurt *you*?"

Lucy looks hard at me, her frosty eyes making me blink.

"Is there anything that can't be hurt?"

"I don't know. No, I don't guess so."

"Anything can be hurt, Ronald Earl. *Anything.*" She shifts around. I can feel her pressing against me under the covers. "But your body is nothing. *My* body is nothing. You understand?"

It sure doesn't feel like nothing.

"'Your body is the temple of the Holy Ghost,'" I say. "First Corinthians, chapter six, verse nineteen. It's just a vessel. Dust."

"Except it doesn't really hold anything," Lucy says. "What we are can't be held. Not by a body. We're too *big. You're* too big."

She brushes against me. *Her skin against my skin.* I can't help it. I don't care what she is. She feels like a girl. A hot, soft girl. It's starting. I can feel everything stirring. Just like in my dreams.

I sit up. Slide my legs around out of the covers, away from her. I can't let her see. *Can't let her feel.*

"What's wrong?" she says.

I've got my back to her, sitting there on the edge of the bed, head down.

"I can't—it's not you. I mean, it's *you,* but it's not you. It's me. I'm the problem. I don't know what's wrong with me. I don't. I'm sorry."

She lays a finger on my back, making me buck a little. I can almost hear her frowning.

"Shhhh. Don't talk like an idiot. There's nothing wrong with you. You're perfect."

"Perfect? Lord. I'm about the furthest thing from perfect you can get."

"I meant . . . perfect *for me*."

CHAPTER

⇒FIFTY-FIVE⇐

We don't talk for a little while. Another lightning bolt rips the night to shreds.

"You'll never show me what it's like, will you?" I say. "*Home.* What it's like when you go there."

"Maybe," Lucy says. "Maybe I can show you. We'll see."

She's running her fingers through my hair. It feels . . . *indescribable.* "Don't you ever miss your parents?" I say.

"No. God, you're so sweet and dumb. I'm still with them. Every day."

"How?"

"Well . . . let's see. When you're *home,* everything is right there in front of you, all the time. You never have to miss any-thing. It doesn't go away. It can never go away. You just reach out—it's there."

"So you can see your parents any time you want? Be with them?"

"Yeah. Something like that."

I sit up on my elbows, making her pull her hand away. "I don't get it."

Lucy sighs. "See, what you think is them—my parents—*that's not them.* That's only the tiniest little part of them. They are way bigger than that."

"Damnation."

Her lips turn down, eyes sad. "I'm sorry. I'm not trying to make you feel bad."

"Just wish I was smarter."

She grins. "It's not a smart thing or a dumb thing. Just telling you the way it is."

I lay back against the pillow again. "Have you got any brothers or sisters?"

She does that funny little searching thing with her eyes, rolling them up and to the right.

"You can't *remember*?" I say.

"Cut me some slack. I just don't think about him much. I have a brother named Vincent. He's a lot older than me. Went off to Christian college in Virginia when I was still a little kid. What about you?"

"It's just me. I'm kind of adopted. My original folks—I was an accident."

"There's no such thing as accidents, Ronald Earl. That's one of the first things you learn."

"When you're . . . *dead*?"

"I told you, there's no such thing as—"

"I know. I know. But did it hurt? When you died? What was it like?"

She sits there looking at me as if I should know the answer.

"It's not important," she says at last.

"It's important to *me*."

Lucy laughs and pushes me with her arm. "Well, of course it hurt. What do you think?"

"But I mean . . . is it . . . something to be scared of?"

"It depends on the person, I guess. I bet there are people who are scared of rabbits."

"I got bit by one once."

"There you go."

"Hey, I didn't say *I* was scared."

Lucy smiles. "I don't know, Ronald Earl. Bunnies. *Brrrr.*"

"You know what I'm talking about. The *experience.* Did you see lights? A tunnel? Any folks come to greet you?"

"Hmmm . . . let me see. Publishers Clearing House. That check really is quite big."

"Aw, come on, Lucy."

"It was . . . foggy, okay? The important part is after. When you're *home,* the important part isn't *me,* it's *us.*"

"So we all have to act the same, think with the same brain?"

"Nope. You're still *you.* Completely you. But we're all *connected.* Safe."

"So there's nothing to be afraid of?"

Lightning blasts outside the window again, making the outdoors move and jump.

"I didn't say that," Lucy says. "You're asking me things . . . I just don't know. Turn over."

She rubs my bare back, laying her fingers there so light it's the best thing I've ever felt. There has never been anything better than that. *Never.* I feel my eyes welling up. I'm so afraid to let her see me. Afraid to speak. Afraid of what she might hear in my voice.

Lucy slips out of the covers and sits next to me, pulling the blue dress up to her knees. Her legs look so white. She touches my arm. Her fingers are scorching—"hot as hellfire," Certain Certain would say. But I don't want her to move them. I don't care if they scorch my arm off.

"I thought . . ." I stop myself.

She looks at me, beautiful eyes a scary, milky blue. "Please. Please tell me."

Why can't I keep my mouth shut?

"I thought . . . *ghosts* . . . I thought they were supposed to be *cold.*"

254

Lucy looks away. "Is that what I am?"

I breathe slowly in and out.

"You're a girl. That's what you are to me."

Now the tears are starting up in my eyes for real—I growl low down in my throat and clench my jaw to stop them up.

"I did my best," I say. "Please. I did the best I could. To heal you, I mean. Same thing I've done all these years. I always *believed* I could do it. There was never any doubt in my mind. Because it wasn't me doing it, you know what I'm saying?"

"It's all right."

"But I know I'm nothing special. I never have been. The power wasn't *mine* to begin with. The power to heal. It was just . . . like something I was borrowing . . . no, something I was *given*. It was a gift. I was supposed to . . ." I cover my eyes with my fingers. "I was supposed to give it away. To other folks. You know?"

She squeezes my arm tighter. The storm booms outside, a rolling, cracking sound drownding me out. But I have to keep going, have to spit it all out at once.

"But to think . . . I was the one . . . I let you . . ."

"What?"

"Die. I let you *die*, Lucy. I'm so . . . I'm so . . ."

"I know," she says. "You don't have to say it."

She leans up against me, drapes her arms around my neck. I keep my hand over my eyes, crying into my fingers. My shoulders are shaking. I try not to make any noise. I try, but sometimes I do.

Sorry. I'm so sorry. I'm nothing. Nothing. Nothing.

The words run over and over in my head. Neither of us says anything for a good while. She lets me get it out, all of it. Finally I raise my head up and look over. She's looking straight into my eyes.

"You are not *nothing*," she says, touching my chin. "You've *never* been nothing. Even before you ever became Little Texas. You understand me?"

I just look at her, her face blurry and smeared through the tears; Lucy takes up a corner of the blanket and rubs my cheeks dry.

"If that's what happened, if a ghost is what I am . . . then it's all right," she says. "You have to know that. You were just doing what you . . . do. Right? It's okay."

"But . . . you'll never grow up, or get married. Become a *mother,* you know, any of those things."

I swipe at my eyes, feeling my throat crinkle.

"Yeah. That's true. That's true. But I figure it this way— it's kind of a *trade.* Because they need me. They need me here, to help them. They need *us.* Besides, I still get to love you, right?"

I think about that little piece of brick. "I don't see how . . . how you can say that, Lucy. Not after . . ."

She shakes her head, her eyes still locked on mine. "You don't understand, do you? *You believe so hard.* Even when you're wrong about something. You're pure, Ronald Earl. Pure light. Everybody's got some light, but yours . . . it's so bright, they see it all around you. *It* sees your light. That's what it wants, to take it away from you. It wants your light."

"Tell me, please, what am I supposed to do?"

Lucy smiles. "Get your clothes on."

I start putting them on, sniffing and feeling embarrassed. Nobody has ever seen me cry before. Not even Certain Certain.

"Are we going somewhere?" I say, still wiping my eyes.

"Outside. Get dressed. It's a good time to show you."

A shiver runs across my back. "What's so important you want me to see it in the middle of a lightning—"

"Where it lives," Lucy says.

➤FIFTY-SIX ≪

Lucy kicks off the bed and glide-walks across the room.

"I wish I could do that," I say.

"You can," Lucy says. "You just don't know that you can."

"But—"

"Come on."

As she moves up the hall, her dress ripples like she's traveling underwater.

"Hey, you're moving better," I say.

"It's the moisture in the air. It's—it's better for me when it's raining."

"Why?"

She turns to glare at me. "Just because a person can drive a car, it doesn't make them a mechanic."

"But you know way more than I will ever know."

She smiles a wicked smile. "Ever? You'll get there eventually. Who knows? Maybe tonight."

"Real funny. Will it be . . . dangerous? Like in the cellar?"

"I won't lie to you. It's not the smartest thing in the world to do. But it's safer when it's wet. We need to go before the heavy rain stops. It probably won't come in this kind of rain."

"Probably?"

We stop in the kitchen.

"Can we at least get a flashlight this time?" I say.

"Hurry."

I find an umbrella and a big, square flashlight on a shelf in the laundry room. The flashlight is the kind that runs on those heavy, square batteries. I click it on, but it's persnickety; from time to time I have to beat it against my leg to keep it burning.

"Best we can do, I guess."

I start for the front door, then swing the light around to see if Lucy is coming—

"Holy Jesus," I say, stepping back.

The beam passes right through her. Just as if Lucy is built of glass, solid but somehow clear. When I pull the light away, she's whole again.

"It's the contrast," Lucy says. "You can't see it so much with the lights on."

"But—you're *real*, I know you're real."

Lucy looks at me hard. Her voice turns deeper, more far-away than ever.

"Don't fool yourself, Ronald Earl. I have to slow down so much to be here. To be . . . solid. Don't get too used to me. Don't forget what I am. Do you think I can stay this way for good? I can't. I'm *holding* myself here. For *you.* Because they *need* you. *I* need you. But I am what I am. And there's nothing I can do about it. Don't ever forget that."

"But I can touch you. . . ."

"And I can touch *you.*"

The way she says it makes my heart wrench. "Let's go," Lucy says.

I follow shaky-legged, half expecting her to flow right through the big oak front door, but she waits for me to open it. Outside the eaves are gushing rain. I pop the umbrella open and hold it over our heads.

But Lucy scoots away down the steps and out into the yard, so fast it's hard to keep up. I can see slashes of rain splattering her arms and shoulders, the blue dress turning dark. The umbrella strains like a dog on a leash.

The sky blazes with fire, and thunder cracks overhead like a mountain sliding into the lake. I hunch my shoulders as Lucy drifts on ahead. She stops at the edge of the dock, skinny arms at her sides, waiting.

"You know how to run this thing?" she says, pointing at Tee Barlow's Chris-Craft.

260

"No way. Besides, I don't have the key."

A big push of wind nearly carries the umbrella off, and me with it. Instead of walking out on the dock, Lucy glides down to the bank.

"Help me find it."

"What are we looking for?" I say, watching her cut her head left and right.

Then I see what she's looking at, Faye Barlow's little canoe nosed up into the milfoil.

I look at the canoe, then out at the black, churning lake, hearing the rain fall. "I've only been in a canoe one time. What if we tump over? Or the canoe fills up with rain? We're liable to drown!"

"Get in. There isn't time. The storm will slack off soon." She gets up so close, I can smell the water on her skin. She puts her hands on my arm, drawing me to her.

"Please, Ronald Earl. I need you."

"Lord." I stand there a few more seconds watching her drip, then step in and start furiously untying the tether.

"Come on, then," I say. "Get in."

Lucy looks at me, eyes glowing, face wet. She's so close, it nearly stops my heart. She's got her hand on the edge of the canoe.

"No," she says. "I'd rather walk."

And she gives the canoe a big heave, shoving me backward, and I'm spinning out into the current, alone.

➤FIFTY-SEVEN ❦

"Lucy!"

The sight is something I will remember the rest of my life: Lucy's thin, pale legs, the wet material of her dress snapping in the wind, matchstick arms pumping, hair 'lectrified, as she crosses the lake. She's so *brave.* The most brave thing I have ever seen. But it's more than that.

Certain Certain says there is such a thing as something being bigger than big—it's nothing to do with physical size. For the first time I understand what he has been talking about. I can see it right there in Lucy's body, balancing all the beautiful strangeness of who she is in the way she steps.

I wish so much Certain Certain could be here to see this. I can't help but think of our Lord walking on water.

I throw the umbrella down and dig in with my paddle, stroking the way Faye Barlow showed me. Lightning slaps the world again, making the trees on Devil Hill look like burning skeletons. Rain starts to run in my eyes.

I can't see Lucy anymore.

Another flash hits and I can see the trestle—so big and strange and surprising I bang the canoe with the paddle. I pull through the pillowy black, thinking about that sunken town below me. Cracked roads, ramshackly houses sprouting river weeds. Maybe a *dog.* Some dog nobody remembered, scared to pieces, running through the overgrown yards, whimpering just before he got thrown under a million tons of dark water.

Shut up. Just paddle. Shut up. Shut up.

"Lucy!"

"Here," she calls out suddenly. "Over here!"

I swing the flashlight around and see a flash of blue further upstream than I figured. I stroke hard for it. Lucy is standing there with a pole in her hands, a *metal* pole, floating just above the wood of the dock, rain jumping around her small feet. She looks like an angel.

Lucy drops the pole and gives me a hand up. It feels so good to touch her again. My hair and clothes are sopping. I look at the umbrella, feeling ridiculous.

"Come on," Lucy says.

We climb Devil Hill to the clearing. Even with the flashlight, it's hard to see where we're going. There are the pillars of the old house, pale and colorless. The stage is draped in tarpaulins that show up blue in the flashlight. A leaf glues itself to my cheek.

"We need to hurry!" Lucy yells over the storm.

She heads for the trees, with me chasing behind. Lucy is taking me to the trail where Faye Barlow showed me the pitcher plants. It curls off into a black so deep, it eats the flashlight beam whole.

The footing is slick, and Lucy gets further and further ahead, till I lose sight of her around the bend. But finally I come to a place I recognize—there's the fallen sycamore where the fox left me, right at the edge of that deep yellow and green clearing Faye Barlow didn't want me to see.

Is this where it lives?

Lucy's standing in what looks to be a room carved entirely out of leaves and branches.

"This is where it is holding them," she says. "After you see it, don't hang around too long. We don't know when the rain might stop."

"What am I looking for?" I say.

"You'll know," Lucy says. "Hurry. It won't be safe if you don't."

I take a couple of nervous steps deeper into the clearing, spraying the flashlight beam around. I aim the light up. The branches are so thick overhead, it's almost like a roof.

264

A snaky little cold dances over my shoulders. This place feels like something has marked it for its own. *Claimed it.*

A few more steps into the clearing, and I feel it. I've become a trespasser.

I shine the light around, angle it out further.

There it is—right in the center of all that space—the biggest, most scabbedy old tree I've ever seen.

The base is at least six foot across and probably twenty foot around or more. The trunk is covered with curly rolls of bark like silvery paper and burls the size of punkins. The whole tree looks *twisted,* as if some giant hands have wrung it out like a dish towel. Long roots as big around as a man's waist shoot out from the base of the tree in all directions.

I turn and look back; Lucy is still there, standing in the same spot, arms at her sides, head cocked a little. The light passes through her again—I can see the flashlight beam clear up the trail.

The wind pushes through the giant tree, making the limbs move, heavy and creaky. I can hear the leaves beating against each other, and branches rubbing against branches.

Then I hear it. Metal knocking against metal in the wind. "There's something hanging up there," I say. I move a little closer.

"Far enough!" Lucy calls. "Hey! That's far enough. *Come back.* If you stay too long, it will know you are here."

But I have to see the tree up close. I have to.

The woods glisten and whisper. I shine the flashlight beam in front of me and creep forward.

"Please!" Lucy cries out. "Come back—it's not safe!"

When it happens, I don't know what to call it.

The closest thing I can compare it to is when you nearly fall out of a high tree—the way your lungs puff out and everything inside you comes rushing up under your heart. Because you know how close you came to dying. Right then, right there.

That's what comes over me—if you could multiply it times a hundred. Like the bottom has dropped out. Not just the bottom under my feet, but the bottom under my *life.* There is nothing supporting me. I'm hanging in midair, fixing to plummet straight down into everlasting fire and damnation.

"Let not the waterflood overflow me, neither let the deep swallow me up, and let not the pit shut her mouth upon me."

I drop the flashlight and double over in the leaves, clutching at my stomach. A wave of sickness barrels up my throat; I have to fight to keep from puking. And then I do puke, and it keeps coming and coming till there's nothing left inside me. Then my body keeps trying to puke, but nothing is there, and it hurts so much, but I can't make it stop.

Finally it does stop, and I fall over on my side in the wet leaves. I'm going to die. Right here. Right now. I'm not even sure that I care. Something grabs hold of my arm.

"Come on!"

But I'm still so sick, I can't move. I mumble something to

her. Then she's hauling me up. Dragging me to my feet, pulling me away from the tree.

I swear two or three times, but Lucy just jerks me toward the trail like I weigh no more than a sack full of leaves. I stumble after her, not able to think about anything but the pain.

Without the flashlight, I have to trust her to know where we are running. I'm getting whipsawed by branches, tripped by roots, then a branch catches me in the forehead. I put my hand to my face, and it comes back slick and warm.

"Keep going!" Lucy says. *"Hurry!"*

We stumble into the plantation clearing, then slip down the hill to the water.

"Get in," Lucy says. "Get in! Get in!"

She shoves me into the canoe and piles in behind me. Takes up a paddle and starts to stroke. "I'll help."

We slide away from the dock. I pick up a paddle and stroke hard as I can. Then it's all black, and I don't remember another thing till I'm back at the house.

CHAPTER

➤FIFTY-EIGHT≪

I'm up in my bedroom. Alone.

Am I in shock? My stomach feels like it's been turned inside out. My head is sloshing like a yolk in an egg. But my clothes are draped across a chair to dry, and I'm laying in bed holding a damp rag to the gash in my forehead.

Faye Barlow, she is right. There is something evil on that island. Something so evil it makes me sick about the world. Just like I get sick watching the news. Knowing we are sharing the Lord's earth with people who murder little girls at gas stations. Chop heads off in Iraq. Lock folks up in their basement to torture them. Evil you can't talk to, can't work your way around. It makes me sick and afraid.

The evil on the island is an evil that can come inside your mind anytime you get close enough to it.

And I don't know how to keep it out.

And I don't know what Lucy is. I might not ever know. But I know what she is to *me*. Whatever she is, it is good.

I pick up my little Bible computer and start punching buttons.

Turns out the word *love* appears 640 times. Nearly three times more than the word *hate.* It's in there more often than *salvation.* More than *redemption,* more than *resurrection* or *Savior* or even *Christ.*

Love is in the Bible nearly ten times as often as *hell.*

It's maybe the most important word. Is it the strongest? The one word that will truly last forever?

I lay there with the light on, watching the ceiling, feeling the old house breathing around me, hearing boards popping in the floors. I've got the door to the hallway open.

Am I in love with a ghost?

≫FIFTY-NINE≪

The Sunday service is tomorrow.

When I wake up, my mouth tastes like I've been using it to clean sidewalks. The cut on my forehead is throbbing and raw. Somebody raps on my door.

It's Certain Certain. "What happened to your head, boy?" he says. "Witches been snatching at you all night? Looks nasty."

I reach up and touch it. "Ran into something in the dark."

"You ain't been down in that cellar again, have you?"

"No, sir."

"Well, breakfast is ready, only you look a little green around the gills."

"I'm all right. Hey, I want to go with you to the island today," I say as we head downstairs. "There's something I want to show you."

"What you getting at, boy?"

"She's real," I say.

"The little blue dress gal? You still fussing with her?"

I stop on the stairs and turn to face him.

"I've *seen* her. I've *touched* her. She took me to the island last night."

Certain Certain grins his lopsided grin. "In that storm? You sure you don't need to go see a head doctor?"

"I don't care if you believe me. I don't care if you think I'm crazy. That doesn't make it any less *true.*"

Tee Barlow asks about the cut on my forehead.

"Lightning been somnambulizing in his sleep," Certain Certain says, winking at me. "Probably ran into a door."

"Thanks," I whisper to him when we sit down to breakfast.

Faye Barlow comes in holding a little green jar. Her eyes look sad.

"Ronald Earl, here's some calendula cream I can rub on your—"

"No, thank you, I'll be fine."

It hurts to cut her off this way, but I don't want her touching me ever again. I think too much about the touching she did. *We did.* Does Lucy know? Can she see everything I do?

271

"Y'all ready?" Certain Certain says.

The outdoors has been washed fresh, and the sun is already burning the last of the mist off the lake. As we walk down to the pontoon boat, I take in long pulls of the clean air, blowing it out like it's pulling the sickness out of me.

"Better get your business done now," Certain Certain says, grinning. He jerks his thumb at two plastic King Johnnies standing in one end of the boat.

"Leviticus, chapter twenty-six, verse thirty-one," Sugar Tom says. "'And I will make your cities waste, and bring your sanctuaries unto desolation, and I will not smell the savour of your sweet odours.'" He frowns when he doesn't see me smiling. "Is there anything wrong, Ronald Earl?"

"No, sir," I say, taking a seat upwind.

Nothing moves on the far shore. In the bright sunshine, what happened last night hardly seems possible. "Morning courage," Certain Certain calls it. He chats with Tee Barlow about the stage.

Sugar Tom sits next to me and lights a Marlboro. The paper crackles when he takes a drag.

"When you get to be my age, Ronald Earl, you're kind of on the edge of things. Do you understand what I mean?"

"Yes, sir. Well, I'm not sure, really."

Sugar Tom taps the ash over the side. "When you're this old, you're not in the middle of things anymore. You do a lot of watching from the sidelines. It's nature's way. Moving us off, making room for the young. Folks tend to forget about us, forget we're still fully here. But we are. We think, we observe. We see plenty of things most folks don't notice, all because we take the time to do so. We don't have any choice."

I watch the ashes swirl in the dark water, and think of Lucy. How any day she's liable to just not be there anymore. The thought floods me with a kind of anger.

"What are you getting at?" I say.

"I've seen her, too," Sugar Tom says.

I'm too surprised to speak.

"That little girl in the blue dress. I can't recollect, what was her name?"

"Lucy," I manage to say finally. "You've seen her?"

"Yes indeed. One morning I got up before everybody else, came out into the hall to use the bathroom, and there she was. Just as solid as a fence post."

"What . . . what did you do?"

"Nothing. She drifted right up the other end of the hall and vanished. Never made a sound."

"Did she . . . did she see you?"

"She didn't act like she did."

"When did it happen?"

Blue smoke rushes out of his nose. "The first morning we were here."

"What! Why didn't you tell me?"

"I didn't figure you needed to know, that's all."

I lean toward him, hoping my voice is covered up by the noise of the engine.

"Did you tell Certain Certain?"

"Why tell somebody about something who isn't going to believe it until it happens to him?"

"But—we do that practically every day," I say. "That's what we do. Get people to believe in the Lord even though they can't see Him."

Sugar Tom exhales. "Did you know a granddaddy longlegs will eat the meat out of a walnut?"

"No. Well, I never really thought about it."

"Well, they will. But if you want to watch them do it, it takes *time.* A whole lot of time and being very still. Most people can't do that. Stay still for a long time. You find you an old logging road, pick a spot to sit down under a walnut tree. It might take an hour. It might take two. Maybe more. But when you watch long enough, they will come, you will see them. Do you believe me?"

"About the spiders? Sure."

"Why?"

"I don't know. Because you told me. I believe you."

Sugar Tom nods at Certain Certain. "See, Ronald Earl, it's easy to believe things about spiders. Not so easy about other things. You have to be patient."

"Shoot."

"Now, don't get disappointed. I'm just telling you I did see her. I *know* I did. I believe you. That's what I'm trying to say. *I believe you.*"

I pat him on the shoulder. *Lord.* Feels like nothing but bones underneath there.

"Thanks," I say.

"For what?"

"For everything. Just—thanks."

CHAPTER

⇒ SIXTY ⇐

As we make our way up the hill, I notice some branches down here and there, but not much else to show for the big storm. The whole island smells washed clean over. Tee Barlow and Certain Certain and the other helpers get to hauling the King Johnnies up to the clearing, while I get Sugar Tom situated in the shade in a special folding chair all decked out with cushions and a little thing to hold a drink of cranberry juice, his favorite.

I'm impatient watching the men work, standing up the Johnnies and hauling wet tarps off the lumber. But I'm determined to wait till Certain Certain can come with me.

Finally he takes a break, coming over to get a drink in the shade.

"Whew," he says, mopping his face on his sleeve. "Folks got to have they baffrooms, I reckon. All right, Lightning, what you got in mind?"

"There's something I want to show you back up in the woods. It won't take long." I turn to Sugar Tom. "You going to be all right here? Is there anything you need?"

"I'm fine right here, Ronald Earl. Plenty for me to observe. Take in. Don't forget what I told you. About being still, I mean. And seeing."

"I won't. You sure you're not too hot?"

He takes my hands in his, clutches them to him a second. "I'm fine. You head on."

"All right." I look at Certain Certain.

"Lead on, McDuff," he says.

We hike a good ways up the trail without talking, then Certain Certain pulls up, breathing hard.

"Getting old?" I say.

He grimaces, making his tore-up lip look awful. "You feel old, too, you been slavin' with the rest of us. This gonna take much longer?"

"I don't think so."

But it's always further back than I realize. "Mercy." Certain Certain picks at a spiderweb tangling his ear after we've walked a good ways more. "These woods are full of haints. Can't you feel 'em, Lightning?"

"I thought the Bible teaches we're not supposed to believe in that stuff."

"Not the kind like you're thinking. I mean the *history*."

I can see the long bend in the trail now, picturing Lucy's dress flowing out in front of me as she disappeared.

"It's in that clearing up ahead."

There it is—the tree, just about as awesome in the daylight. I can see the rusty metal things now, dozens of them, sprouting from the branches like muddy Christmas ornaments.

Certain Certain huffs up behind me. "Boy, this better not be a wild-goose chase, or I'm liable to—oh my Lord. Oh my *Lord.*"

I wait for him to go on, but he's just looking. "What do you think?" I say.

"Oh my Lord. You know what this is, boy? Oh my dear sweet *Lord.*"

Certain Certain takes a few steps into the clearing, then a few more. He squats down facing the giant trunk.

"My Lord. I sure never expected to see one," he says at last. "Makes a man feel downright *small.* Reverent."

"But what is it?"

"Trouble tree," Certain Certain says quietly. "Goes back to the beginnings of slavery. The trouble tree was the place where slaves took all their troubles. A place all their own where nobody would mess with them. A place where they could gather, mostly in secret, late at night, lament all their sorrows."

278

I squat down next to him. "What would they do?"

"Folks have written about it. Mostly white folks who didn't understand, made fun. The slaves would form a circle around the tree, most likely. Sing to it. Songs of *lamentation.* Go up one at a time, stroke the bark, whisper their troubles to the tree. That was their way of letting them go. Like them kings in Africa. Trees meant a lot to them, boy. *Sacred.* Spirits lived in 'em. 'Specially ones like this big fella here, hundreds of years old. A tree like this has wisdom in it. Strength. *Protection.*"

I try to see it—all those people, torches set up around the clearing for light. Gathering in a circle to stroke the tree and sing to it.

"Doesn't sound too Christian," I say.

Certain Certain snorts. "Shoot, you see them things up yonder?"

He points at the rusty metal rings and chains hanging from the fat branches. Dozens and dozens of them, sunk so deep in the flesh of the tree it looks like they are part of the tree itself.

"Manacles. Leg irons. Collars. That look Christian to you, boy?"

"No, sir."

"Well, that's who made 'em, God-fearing Christians. Slaves most likely slung them things up there after emancipation come about. Part of their way of celebrating."

Manacles, I suddenly realize. *That's what Lucy has been talking about. I can't believe I called them bracelets.*

"You're saying the people who used those things on the slaves went to *church*?" I say.

"'Deed they did. Some plantation owners even brought their slaves with them. Sat them around a little balcony looking down on the rest of the congregation. I saw a little church like that down in Port Gibson, Mississippi. Other owners saw the whole church thing as a threat. See, can't be teaching what Jesus taught, they thinking, on account of that means all people are loved, important, *valued.* Which ends up meaning *equal.* So all people are meant to be *free.* See where that thinking is headed?"

I nod.

"But for a good many years, they kept their tribal customs. Place like this, sacred tree, I imagine they used this clearing once 'pon time for a ring dance."

"What's that?"

"Ritual where the slaves formed a ring, moved in a circle, some stepping forward, some stepping back. A lot of hand clapping, chanting, leaping. Sometimes going on for hours, folks taking each other's places when the first batch got tuckered out. Sooner or later they brought the ring dances indoors and mixed them in with their Christian worship. Called them *shouts.* White folks didn't understand worship that *active.* Called it heathen. Sound familiar?"

I've heard people say that about our church. People who don't understand the anointing of the Holy Spirit.

"What those white folks didn't know, this was how those

people felt God," Certain Certain goes on. "Today we know it was the Holy Ghost bubbling up inside them. Everybody feels the anointing the way they feel it. Dancing, speaking in tongues, praisin'. It's a personal thing. Outside folks, they still don't understand, do they, Lightning?"

We stand there looking at it all a good while. I can't help but think about Lucy, the way she looked at the edge of the clearing, how scared she sounded when—

"Huh, what's this?" Certain Certain bends over and picks up the orange flashlight I dropped. He clicks the switch, then has to smack it against his leg. "Still works. That's a good flashlight. Expensive. Why would somebody leave it out here?"

"I dropped it last night," I say.

"You *truly* came out here after dark, Lightning?"

"Yes, sir. In the storm."

"Good gravy train. All by yourself? Whatever did you do that for?"

"I told you, *she* brought me out here, Lucy—"

"She ain't here today, though, is she?"

"Have I ever lied to you?"

"Not that I recollect, no."

"She wanted me to see this place. And now I know why. The trouble tree—maybe it really *can* do what the slaves thought it could do."

"What's that?"

"*Absorb* things. From all those people that touched it. Think about it. A hundred years, maybe *two* hundred, of people pouring all their troubles straight into its insides. Like maybe something has built up in the tree over time. You're going to laugh at me—"

"No, I won't. Spit it out."

"I think . . . all that anger, pain, and *fear*—I think it somehow *changed* the tree. Turned it into something different. Something *evil*."

A wind comes off the lake, making the branches of the tree move, rattling its chains.

It's listening.

It goes on like that a little while, neither of us speaking. Certain Certain looks around, squinches his face up.

"Let me tell you something, boy," he says after the wind settles back down. "Old places like this, I do believe they can soak up some of the bad feeling out there. I truly do. What is a body without the soul of the Lord breathed into it? Dust. So where does that soul go to when the body goes back to dust? Got to be *somewhere,* waiting on the Judgment. That's nothing but pure *energy.* Energy got to go somewhere. Good and bad."

He throws a hot arm around my shoulders. "But the true power is all on our side. Leave it to the Lord. He'll take care of things. Always has, always will."

"But Lucy . . . she was standing right here. Just as solid as you. I touched her. She pulled me out of here when the tree . . . well, I don't know what happened, exactly. I got really sick. . . ."

"I don't know what you've been seeing," Certain Certain says. "I don't. But I've counted you a friend ever since you could, well . . . *count.* I can see how serious this is to you. Pray on it, boy—"

"But I have. . . ."

"Then pray some more. No such thing as stopping when it comes to prayer. Only *quitting.* Now"—he pats his stomach—"speaking of energy . . . you think you could lead me out of this jungle? I could sure stand me some kipper snacks. What you reckon Miss Faye packed in that cooler?"

As we make our way out of the clearing, the last thing I can hear is the clinking and clanking of those hateful pieces of iron hanging in the trouble tree. Like it's noticing us leaving.

I feel better when we can see the plantation, the bases of the tall pillars sprouting long-stemmed grass in the cracks under the mortar. It's so bright and sunny after being in the clearing, it lifts my heart a little. Especially with old Sugar Tom sitting there at the edge of the shade, gone to the world.

Certain Certain chuckles. I can tell he is feeling the lift, too. "Tell you what, Lightning, Miss Wanda Joy is *right.* I do believe that man could flat sleep through the final trumpet. What you say? Should we wake him up for dinner?"

Sugar Tom's head is draped over on his arm, eyes closed, feet spraddled in front of him, same as always. I can see the volunteer workers moving a couple of green four-by-fours up on the new stage, skin red, T-shirts wet.

"What you say there, old son," Certain Certain says, nudging at him. "You trying to set the record for Rip van Winklers? Think you might want to . . ."

He stops. Sugar Tom doesn't budge.

"Sugar Tom?" Certain Certain says, shaking him a little harder. Sugar Tom's head flops forward.

"Oh my Lord."

Certain Certain lets go of the flashlight and drops to his knees, lifts up Sugar Tom's craggy head, puts his big fingers against the old man's eyelids, trying to make them come open. I see everything like it's moving slower, and all so clear: little wispy white hairs playing around on Sugar Tom's head in the breeze; Certain Certain's eyes big, afraid; his voice sounding like he's behind a wall or something.

"Ronald Earl," he's saying.

It's the first time I ever remember him calling me that. It's like the walls of Jericho are plunging down around me all at once.

"No," I say. "Oh no."

No. Sugar Tom's *dead.*

⇒ SIXTY-ONE ⇐

It takes the EMTs nearly thirty minutes to get here from the closest volunteer fire department. Sugar Tom's alive, but we don't know what is wrong with him or how to help. Tee Barlow is afraid to try and take him across on the boat, so we keep him in the shade and use shirts and a piece of tarp to try to make him comfortable. Certain Certain damps his head with a wet cloth. Sugar Tom's eyes look afraid; he tries to say something, but the words come out garbled.

We watch while the emergency people get him trussed up on a long board, arms folded in front of him, head tucked in place with a thick strap on his forehead.

"They think it might be a stroke," I hear one of the men say to Certain Certain.

"What's a stroke?" I say, clenching my teeth to keep from tearing up.

The EMT man is bald and looks like he has a weight bench at home. He talks without looking at me, fiddling with something in his bag.

"The blood flow gets cut off to the brain, meaning the brain's not getting any oxygen," he says. "A lot depends on how long it's been going on. If you get to it fast enough . . ."

"Was it the heat?" I say. "A heatstroke?" I should have gotten him better shade or made sure he was drinking enough.

"Nah, it's probably just age," the EMT man says. "A thrombosis, embolism. Hypertension. Too early to say."

They fuss with a lot of tubes, get something poked into his arm for fluids, and I sit right down in the dirt. Certain Certain comes up to me.

"You okay, big man? Don't worry. He's a tough old skizzard."

My hands clench and unclench in the raw earth, squeezing tight as I can. That's when I notice it. The marks in the dirt around Sugar Tom's chair.

"Hey."

"What?" Certain Certain says. "What is it, boy?"

"The *ground*," I say, more and more distressed. "I put him over here on account of it was in the shade, and there was some nice soft grass here—but look at it. Look how it's torn up all around his chair."

"I see it. Maybe he was kicking, you know, kicking his legs out and—*Lord Jesus.*"

We both see it at the same time. The big tracks in the dirt circling all round Sugar Tom's chair. Tracks that look like two crescent moons turned in toward each other.

I draw in my breath. "It's a cloven hoof."

➤ SIXTY-TWO ⇐

The halls at the county hospital are long and green. The lights are harsh. I have to keep brushing my sleeve across my eyes.

Me and Certain Certain are sitting on plastic chairs that are connected together by two big pieces of shiny metal. Up the hall a ways Miss Wanda Joy is pacing back and forth, can't sit still a minute. She's got a cell phone stuck to her ear, talking a blue streak, probably to Tee Barlow.

"Now, you and I know, all kinda critters could have made those tracks," Certain Certain is saying. "Big old buck nosing out of the woods. Billy goat. Cow wandering around loose."

"On an *island*?" I say. "Besides, you ever see a goat or a deer or a cow *that* big? Those marks were wider than my *hand.* And how come those men and Tee Barlow didn't see it? It had to be circling and circling just about the whole time we were gone. And not one of them saw it?"

Certain Certain lets out a long blast of air like he's been holding it in.

"So what are we going to do about it?" I say. "Cancel the service?"

"I reckon it's up to Miss Wanda Joy." She's still on the phone, stomping her foot now, trying to make a point. "She's the head of this ministry."

"We have to tell her," I say.

Certain Certain's white eyebrows shoot up to the top of his head. "Boy, you think she is fired up *now,* you tell her Sugar Tom's been attacked by the devil. She's goin' be *twice* as determined to hold that service."

He's right.

A heavy lady in rubber gloves and a bunchy blue outfit walks by holding a bottle of something. Certain Certain waits for her to get past us.

"I'm not saying you shouldn't be afraid," he says. "Fear, it keeps you sharp. But don't let it run things. Maybe there is something bad on that island. But maybe this thing needs to happen because of that very reason. Pray about it, boy. That's all I can say. Lord wants *soldiers* in His name. So pray."

Miss Wanda Joy stops pacing. She snaps the phone shut

and puts it in her big purse. A man with red hair wearing a white coat and holding a clipboard comes up to her. We can't hear what they're saying, but I can see Miss Wanda Joy's shoulders sag. The man writes some things on the clipboard and pats her on the shoulder; you can see her flinch—she has never much liked being touched. The doctor heads off down another hallway, and Miss Wanda Joy starts walking toward us, face all pinched. We stand up.

"He's resting now," she says, running a finger under each eye. "They are taking him to Florence to do an MRI. See how much damage has been done. Then when he's up for it, they'll start his rehabilitation."

"Could we go talk to him?" Certain Certain says.

"He's sleeping. They said . . . it may be the entire right side of his body that is affected. He will probably have to—to relearn some things. His doctor believes it's going to be a long-term thing."

"I'm so sorry," Certain Certain says. We stand there feeling useless.

"In the meantime," Miss Wanda Joy says, sniffing, "we have a great *work* to do. The service will go forward as scheduled. I have to feel this is a sign of some kind—a message that the tribulation is near, because the forces are working so hard against us."

"Are you sure, ma'am?" I say. "We could put it off awhile till Sugar Tom—till he feels better."

She clutches at my hand, fastening on it so tight it almost

290

hurts. "No, Little Texas. This is our *mission.* This is what we have come here to achieve. It's what—it's what he would have wanted. Have you seen the ladies' room?"

"Well, I reckon it's decided, then," Certain Certain says when she heads off to find it.

"I guess so," I say.

"It's still up to you, you know. She can't do this without you."

He takes in a long breath with his whole body. For the first time he looks like an old man to me. "I'm going to ride up to Florence with him, make sure everything is okay."

He lays his big hands on my shoulders. "Look at me, Lightning. Now listen here. Whatever—whatever you think is out there on that island, we've got the real power on our side. You understand what I'm saying?"

"Yes."

"That said, I wouldn't feel right running off without leaving you any protection."

Certain Certain dips his hand into the collar of his shirt. He draws the slave tag out on its leather cord and pulls it over his head. He slips the cord around my head, letting it settle on my neck. It feels strange there, still warm from his skin.

"No, I can't . . . ," I say, taking the cord in my fingers, starting to pull it off. "I really shouldn't . . ."

"It would mean a lot to me to know you have it," he says, pulling my hands back down.

"But . . ."

"Hang on. Just hang on and listen to me a minute." We settle back down in our seats. "You know what hospitals make me think of?"

I shake my head.

"That time back in Corinth when I got shot. It felt like I was at the end of a very long road. At twenty-six years old! But it wasn't just the pain or the fact I was vain on my looks, a real *ladies'* man, and now I would never look good ever again. It was more than that. . . . I didn't know anything *else* life might have for me. Wasn't interested in nothing else but *myself,* you understand. But then one day something happened that changed everything."

"What was it?"

"Wish I could tell it like Sugar Tom . . . that I saw the Lord appear to me. Or a burst of light like Saul on the road to Damascus. But it was like this: I was laying there feeling sorry for myself, face aching like fire, pushing some Jell-O around on a plate, when a knock comes at the door. I was surprised. The doctors mostly just breezed in. I knew it couldn't be anybody I knew—most of my relatives, friends, they had washed their hands of me.

"It was my Uncle Fish, from Meridian. Remember I told you 'bout him? I hadn't seen him in maybe three, four years. In my family he was *that Jesus Man.*

"'You messed up, didn't you, son?' was the first thing Uncle Fish said. But he didn't try to lecture or nothing. Just said he had something he wanted to give me. I figured it was going to be a Bible, but instead he handed me that slave tag, said it had been in our family four or five generations at least. He couldn't recollect how many *greats* to put in front of my grandfather, it was so long ago.

"I didn't know one thing about history back then, how important it is. Didn't care to know, either. What did dead people mean to me? I was *alive.* 'I'll tell you what they mean,' Uncle Fish said. 'Man who wore that tag was part of the Underground Railroad, leading slaves to freedom up north. The man who wore that tag was friends with *Harriet Tubman.* One of her warriors in the battle to end slavery. A *Christian* man. But he refused to take that tag off. Was honored to wear it. Sleeping with moss for a pillow, drinking brackish water full of baby mosquitoes, dodging patrols with a price on his head . . . that tag was with him. Till he passed it along to his children. Then it was handed down over the years till it came to be in my hands. Now I'm passing it along to *you.*'

"Uncle Fish leans over, gives me a kiss on the head, and says, 'The good Lord Jesus filled that tag with *love* and *protection.* And I pray He does the same for you. Only thing is, a big responsibility comes with it. When it gets passed along, it gets passed along with the knowledge of what has gone into it. What it stands for. But most of all—*what you are going to stand for.* That is the power of this tag, boy.' That's the last time I ever saw my uncle.

"I woke up long into the middle of the night, heartsick, thinking about everything he said. All that's ever been done for me—done by people who didn't even love me! I wept like a little baby, clutching that slave tag for all I was worth. *Praying.* Praying like I never knew the meaning of the word before. The next morning was the first morning of my new life."

Certain Certain taps the tag on my chest. "You talk about that trouble tree absorbing things, Lightning. Well, this tag has absorbed some things, too. You pour enough love into something . . . You heard 'bout those men trying to turn lesser metals into gold? Alchemists. Well, this is stronger than that. Way stronger. Gold can melt. Gold can pass away. But *love*—love comes straight from *Him.* Most powerful force in the universe. Cancels out anything else."

He straightens up, looks up and down the hall, then bores right into my eyes again.

"That tag's been protecting my sorry tail a long, long time. Sometimes I think it's got its own *feelings* baked right into it, you listening? All the people who have worn it, touched it—all that love passed down. You believe that? I don't think it goes against His teachings. Else I would have gotten rid of it a long time ago. Like the Master says, you have love, what can stand against us?"

"But what'll you do without it?" I say, voice choking a little.

Certain Certain smiles, showing me his dead teeth. "Don't you worry 'bout that. I've been wearing it so long, it had to have absorbed itself right into my skin. I'll be all right.

Remember what I said, boy. Wrap your hand round that tag and *pray*. He'll hear you. Always does."

Riding back to the Barlows', as I think about Sugar Tom and those cloven hoofprints, I can feel the slave tag pressing warm against my skin.

⇒SIXTY-THREE⇐

I'm sitting in front of the window in my room, holding that rook I've been carving. The moon is sitting on the lake, making everything sparkle. I can just make out the outline of Devil Hill.

I twiddle the rook in my fingers. This chess set was supposed to be ready by Sugar Tom's birthday, but I couldn't get it done in time. . . .

My eyes water up. *Sugar Tom* . . . These people are the only family I know. What if I never get to talk to him again? I always thought I'd be there someday when he would nod off, dreaming about South Dakota for the last time. What if that's happening now?

"Damnation," I say out loud, squinching my eyes shut and flopping over on the bed.

"What's wrong?"

I know who it is without even turning around.

For the first time since the healing, Lucy's hair is thick and dry, her blue dress crisp and clean. Her eyes are morning glory blue, clear and shining. I want to rush over to her, but part of me is terrified my arms will just swing through the air.

"Come on, tell me. What's wrong?"

"I'm—a friend of mine is sick. They say he had a stroke, and they don't know if he'll ever get better."

She takes a couple of steps toward me. Her walk is perfect, natural, nothing herky-jerky about it. "A friend?"

"Sugar Tom," I say. "He's more like my grandfather, really. He had a stroke over at the plantation today."

Lucy comes closer. Her eyebrows go down like she's not understanding or maybe wants to ask a question.

"It—it attacked him over there," I say, standing up from the window. "There were tracks all around the chair. Cloven hoofs."

"You mean *hooves*," Lucy says.

She's an arm's length away, practically glowing, she looks so good. *So alive.*

"You look . . . different," I say.

"Different," she says.

"Yes."

She touches me on the cheek. "What's different is not how I look," she says. "What's different is how you see me."

But she's not looking right at my face. She's looking somewhere lower. She stretches out her arm toward me, puts two fingers on my collarbone, runs them down my skin, tracing the bones around my neck, moving so slow I can barely stand it. Touching me exactly the way I dreamed of touching her at the healing. *The healing.*

"Hey. Why did you get in the canoe with me?" I say straight into her ear, almost a whisper.

She sinks right down in front of me, wraps her skinny arms around my legs, crumpling her face against my knees, holding. Just holding.

I have never been held so hard by anybody. It's so different—so different from the way it felt when Faye grabbed me. It feels like every ounce of heat in her body is flowing straight into mine.

I put my arms around her neck and set my chin in her hair. I think I could stay this way all night, forever.

After a little while Lucy lets go and pulls me up with her till we're standing so close, we can barely breathe. It feels as if my heart is getting bigger and bigger inside my chest. Lucy leans against me, puts her soft mouth next to my ear.

"You idiot," she whispers. *"I got in the canoe because I love you."*

Certain Certain's slave tag is dangling between us. She takes it out of my shirt and holds it by the rawhide cord.

"Certain Certain gave it to me to wear," I say. "He thinks it might protect me from whatever's on the island."

"Ronald Earl, there's something I haven't told you."

"What?"

"My last name."

"Okay, what is it?"

She lets go of the slave tag and puts her fingers in her hair. She looks into my eyes.

"It's Palmer. Lucy *Palmer* . . . sound familiar?" She glances in the direction of the bedside table. I look over there, see the slave ledger.

A rush of electric cold races all over my body. I could practically throw off sparks.

I walk over and pick up the ledger and open it. There it is on the inside cover:

Thaddeus Palmer.

CHAPTER

➤ SIXTY-FOUR ◄

"Palmer," I say.

"Yeah. He's, like, my uncle or grandfather or something with a whole lot of *great*s attached to it."

I walk a couple of steps toward the window.

"He's—he was the overseer, Ronald Earl. At the old Vanderloo Plantation. Once upon a time."

"You mean . . ."

"Yeah. The guy with the whip. They are showing me he had a hand in the auctions, too."

I watch her face. "Why didn't you tell me?"

"I . . . didn't know it was *me* he was connected to. I didn't remember . . . didn't remember my *name.* Till they showed me just now. It felt like I was inside the book."

"So what does this mean?"

"Well, now I know there was someone . . . someone who was like the *catalyst,* you know? Do you know what that means?"

I smile. "I'm not a complete ignoramus. More about seventy-three percent."

"I'm sorry."

"You mean somebody who set off all the bad stuff."

Lucy nods and takes my hands. "Well—it was going on long before he ever came around. But another thing a catalyst can do is accelerate something. From what they're showing me, I think he's the one—my ancestor, Thaddeus Palmer—he made it possible for it to hold them. The pain he caused. The hatred and fear . . ."

"So you coming back, doing this for them—is it like making up for something he did?"

"How do I know? But I think it's an important part of it."

"But doesn't that . . . doesn't it make you *mad*? You're basically saying you died just so you could help fix something some long-ago relative did."

"If that's the way you want to look at it."

"I don't believe the Lord . . . I don't believe He would sacrifice your life like that."

"What about all that 'sins of the fathers' stuff, huh? I know a little about this Bible jazz, too. Curses that carry down through generations for something somebody else has done."

"Oh yeah?" I say. "How about Ezekiel, chapter eighteen, verse twenty? 'The son shall not bear the iniquity of the father.'"

Lucy rolls her eyes and ruffles my hair, laughing. "You're a real *freak,* you know that? How do you know what He thinks? How do you know He's even a *he?*"

"Everybody knows that."

"So you know every little thing about Him, huh?"

"Well . . . I used to think . . . well . . . no. But He wouldn't *kill* somebody for that."

"Even if it freed a lot of people? So they could go *home?*"

I remember something Certain Certain once told me: "Soul's a soul, Lightning. No matter what state the body's in."

Lucy takes my hand. "Look, maybe . . . maybe it was just my time, Ronald Earl, you know? He, She, whatever is up there . . . knew that, correct?"

"Sure. He knows the number of every little hair on your head. . . ."

"So maybe, knowing His plan for me, it was a good thing to do? Since it was going to happen anyway? Can I ask you something?"

"Anything. Ask me anything you want."

Lucy pinches her lips. "Are you afraid of dying, Ronald Earl?"

I wasn't expecting this. "Well—I pretty much think about it nearly every day. It's kind of like my *job* to think about it."

"Why?"

"To help people. Help them know what they are supposed to do with their lives. So they can have eternal life."

"Life is eternal," Lucy says. "Already."

"I'm coming to figure that out," I say, stroking her fingers. "Okay, to help them have a *good* eternal life, then. Protect them from—from things like whatever is on that island."

"You're dodging me," Lucy says, looking deep into my eyes. "Are you afraid of dying?"

I take my hand away. "Everybody is, aren't they? I don't guess I'm so much afraid of it as I am scared about . . . what happens, you know? The things we can't see, can't know as long as we are down here. Like, do we just slide into the dark, waiting on the Last Days?"

"When the dead in Christ shall rise?"

"Don't make fun of me. What if somebody's not good enough? What if . . ."

"They go to hell? Is that what you're worried about, Ronald Earl? There is no hell."

"How do you know?"

"Hell isn't a place. It's more like a *condition.* You understand?"

"I think so."

"God expects us to be merciful, right?"

"Sure."

"And He's perfect, right?"

"He'd have to be, or nothing would make sense."

"Okay, then His mercy must be perfect. It has to be, because He's perfect. So just think how much more perfect *His* mercy is than ours."

"But . . . if somebody does really bad things, evil things—"

"They're already there," Lucy says. "Already in hell. Nothing can be worse for a person like that than to live the life they are already living."

"Oh."

Lucy beams. "See, you understand."

"No, I just know the way people like you think."

"People like me?" she says, sitting on the bed. And I hear just how ridiculous that sounds when she says it.

"No, well . . . you know . . . people who don't go to church. People who don't believe the way they're supposed to believe."

Lucy's eyes twinkle. "*Supposed* to believe? Don't make me kick your ass. I told you before—you're bigger than that. Way bigger."

"I just wish I understood more, that's all," I say, feeling the red come up in my face.

"You've *always* understood," Lucy says. "Whether you believe it or not. That's why they picked you. That's why they brought us together."

"What do I understand, Lucy? I don't know anything

304

about what it's like for you. What it's like over *there*. When you're *home*. Can't you tell me?"

Lucy takes a long breath. "Okay. Okay. Have you ever almost died?"

"Well, I got struck by lightning once."

"That'll do." She pats the bed. "Come here. Sit next to me."

"You're not going to do anything weird, are you?"

"Compared to what?" she says, laughing.

"Not funny." But I come over and sit down. Lucy lays back crossways on the bed.

"Lie next to me," she says.

I scoot closer, feeling the heat she is giving off, like a living furnace.

"Closer."

I get up against her now, the whole side of my body tasting that heat through her dress. I'm wondering what she wants me to do, but mostly I'm just not caring, on account of I'm touching her. For me, she is everything and swallows up everything, and all the bad things go away in the swallowing.

"Now," she says. "Lay your head on my—on my chest."

She lays there looking at the ceiling, not at me. Waiting on me to do it. I scrunch up on my side, tight against her, but it's hard to do it this way.

"Put your arm under me," she says.

She lifts up enough to let me slide my arm under, and then she is holding me as I hold her. I ease my head over. Settle my head onto her chest. So slow, so gentle, I can feel each part of her. First the dress, then Lucy herself, in separate pieces.

"Shhh," she says, putting a finger to my mouth.

Now my ear is flat against her. I wait, but nothing happens. After a little while I look up at her.

"Okay, I don't think it's going to work this way," Lucy says. "We have to try something different."

"What?"

"Look, I don't want to scare you or anything but . . . it's not going to work unless it's skin to skin." She waits, looking at me.

"Okay," I say.

Lucy grabs the hem of her dress, starts skimming it up her body. I shouldn't look, but I do. Her legs are thin, but they're so smooth and perfect. The dress is past her knees now. . . .

"You want me to shut my eyes?" I say.

Lucy stops. "A little late, huh? You're so innocent, you know that? *In-no-cent.* But that's one of the reasons I love you."

She starts pulling again; her legs widen out, so soft and curved . . . then her underwear, then above her underwear, her belly button like a tiny scooped-out shadow. All the way to just under her bosoms. She stops again.

"They're called *breasts,* Ronald Earl. *B-r-e-a-s-t-s.* It won't kill you to say it."

"Lord, okay. *Breasts.*" *Can you read my mind?*

Lucy smiles. "Not all the time. Only when you *really* want me to."

She goes to skimming the dress again—and she doesn't have a bra, there's just the swell of her skin. She's not like that girl Genna at the rest stop. Lucy's breasts are . . . small.

"You can start breathing again," she says. "Now lay your head down like before."

I lay my head over again, my ear flat against her warm skin. So tight against her, the air goes out of my ear like a suction cup. I'm stuck to her chest. I can smell her skin. Can feel the wet corner of my mouth *right there.*

I don't know what she needs me to do—then I figure maybe it's just laying still and quiet so she can concentrate.

I can hear it—I can hear her heart. And it's beating so *fast.* I didn't know a heart could beat so fast. *Kadump, kadump, kadump.* Then . . .

"Oh Lord."

⇒SIXTY-FIVE⇐

Something is changing.

The side of my head, my ear, my cheek, my jaw, all these parts of me—they start to lose their feeling. They start feeling just the same as Lucy's soft, hot chest. They are all the same parts, mine and hers; there's nothing between them, on account of there *is* nothing between them—they are pieces of the same body.

"Ohhhhh."

My head—it starts to *sink* into her. She's letting herself go all soft, and my head is going down *into her,* I'm *sinking.*

Sinking straight into her, and I'm still, so still, afraid if I even twitch a muscle, I will ruin it.

I'm passing through, except I'm falling, there's nothing else but falling and falling and—

"Open your eyes," Lucy whispers.

First it's all over white, bright as looking into the middle of the sun, but somehow the brightness doesn't hurt my eyes. Things start to settle around me, take shape. I'm sitting in a garden on a little bench made out of black iron. Leaves are floating in the air all around me, leaves so pure green it makes me ache to look at them. I can see veins running all through them, like I'm looking at them under a magnifying glass.

And I can smell something like honeysuckle, only it's a hundred times, a million times, the smell of honeysuckle, but still, it's not overpowering. I could lay there breathing in that smell till the Judgment.

I can't see water, but I can hear it, dribbling and splashing like a song spilling over this place.

This place—I've fallen into Lucy's *heart.* And I know what she said about hell must be true, because it's true about heaven. It's not a place, either. *It's a gift you are given.*

Lucy sighs, and I can feel her sigh roll through me like a golden warm day. The garden disappears. I can't see anything, only black. Then there is a chain, monstrous heavy, links big around as my wrist.

The chain sets to wrapping itself around me, starting with my legs, then pinning my arms to my sides, crushing the air out of my chest. Then it comes up around my mouth and I can taste it, can taste the rusty metal as it covers my nose and last my eyes, all the while pulling tighter and tighter. I can't—I can't stand it anymore. I have to pull myself back. Get out of her. Back into the room, away from her.

Can't breathe.

The chain is still wrapped around me, those cold links. I fight, trying to tear the chain off. Too big, too heavy, I—I—I—

Lucy claps her hands in front of my eyes, one big slapping noise. I see her white blue eyes. I suck in a big breath and fall over on my back.

She has given me a taste of how it feels to be held like those people are being held. The agony they must have been suffering all these years . . . to be *separated* that way—I have no choice. I have to do it. Have to help them break free.

So they can go home *again.*

I lay there awhile, my breath coming in short, shaky gasps. Lucy puts her warm face on my chest, cooing to me till I start to feel myself calming down.

"Let me know when it's okay," she says, stroking my cheek. "Let me know. Because we need to talk. We have to make a plan."

CHAPTER

⇒ SIXTY-SIX ⇐

When I wake up there is a knock at my door. The last little bits
of a dream about Lucy melt away. The knock comes again.

My head clears, and I remember about Sugar Tom and the
plan I made with Lucy. My heart tightens. I haul on my pants
and go to the door.

"Well, good morning," Miss Wanda Joy says. "It's about
time."

Her eyes are dark, exhausted, but lit up all the same. She
is wearing a long black dress and holding a New Testament
with a blue cover.

"Today's the big day, Little Texas."

"Yes'm."

"Well, we have much to do, so please come along."

I pull on my shirt and shoes and follow her down. Miss Wanda Joy stops me on the stairs, takes out a pocket comb, licks the palm of her hand, and smooths my cowlick back. She has been doing this long as I can remember. She does it two or three times before she's satisfied. I notice her hands are trembling.

"Is everything all right?" I say. "You look tired."

"I'm fine. Everything is ready. After breakfast I want you to spend a quiet day indoors before the congregation arrives."

"Have you heard anything from Certain Certain about Sugar Tom?"

"No. And I don't expect to for a while. He has a long road ahead of him. We need to dedicate tonight's service to him."

I think long and hard before I ask my next question.

"Did Certain Certain tell you about what we saw in the dirt all around Sugar Tom's chair?"

"The cloven hooves? I know about that. What did you expect him to do?"

"Satan, you mean?"

"We're taking his sting away. Our faith is too strong, our mission too righteous. He knows that. All he can do now is childishly act up."

"What happened to Sugar Tom wasn't childish."

Miss Wanda Joy takes my face in her hands, eyes burning direct into mine. She doesn't say anything, just stares, squeezing harder and harder till I can feel a tear track down my cheek.

"Tonight we are going to fight one of the Lord's battles, Little Texas. Tonight we are His warriors. Should we put down our swords and leave the field to the enemy without a fight? Romans, chapter sixteen, verse twenty. 'And the God of peace shall bruise Satan under your feet shortly.'"

She lets my face go. I can still feel the imprint of her big fingers. She touches the cover of her little Bible to the tear on my cheek and scrapes it away.

"Let's go downstairs," she says. "They're waiting for us."

CHAPTER

➤ SIXTY-SEVEN ⮜

At the breakfast table Faye Barlow asks about Sugar Tom and looks at me with a secret hurt all over her face. I know what she really wants to say: *I warned you. Didn't I warn you?*

"With the Lord's help and our prayers, I'm sure Sugar Tom will make a complete recovery," Tee Barlow says. He has us bow our heads and says an extra-long grace.

"Well, thank you, Tee," Miss Wanda Joy says when we open our eyes again. "So how is the weather report?"

"Couldn't be better. High sixties to low seventies when the sermon is scheduled to begin. Not much humidity, a bit of a breeze coming off the lake. We won't need the tent."

Miss Wanda Joy has made out some notes for me, and I spend a little time pretending to go over them, then wander around the house, slipping into the den to watch TV when Faye Barlow is not around. The day creeps by but also moves too quick. It's not that it lasts so long, but that I can feel each drip of its passing.

I head back upstairs to read after lunch. Usually on the day of a service I spend a lot of time talking with Certain Certain and playing chess with Sugar Tom. It feels awful lonesome not having them around. But it's worse than that. Without them I feel like I'm going into battle without my armor. I pray our plan will work. *If it doesn't . . .*

Don't think like that.

I fall asleep late in the afternoon and dream of that same farmhouse that is all white on the inside, and I'm walking through it.

Black sludge starts streaming down the walls. It spills over my feet, starts climbing up my ankles, then my shins, getting deeper and deeper. I can't find the way back out. . . .

I force myself awake. It's still daylight, and somebody is tapping on the door. I sit at the little table with my book to look like I've been reading all along and tell the person to come in. It's Faye Barlow. I feel my jaw tighten.

"I've been feeling so guilty and sad, Ronald Earl," she says.

"Knowing things aren't right between us." She comes across the room holding a big plastic bag draped over one arm. It looks to be a suit of dark clothes. "I brought you something for the service." I guess I'm looking at her kind of nervous, because she turns around and says, "Don't worry. I'll hide my eyes while you try them on."

I slip into the suit. The pants are just right; nothing is bunched up or loose. It's the first time in years I've had a suit on that is truly my size.

"It fits perfect," I manage to say, holding my arms out to check the sleeves. "Thank you."

"You look *wonderful,*" Faye says, turning around. "So handsome. I want you to keep it." She fiddles with the shoulders, then knocks some lint off my back.

"Is it . . . Mr. Barlow's?"

She walks over to the chair but doesn't come any closer. "It belonged to a cousin of mine, a boy named Bradley. He moved here when his mother, my first cousin, was sick, and there was really nowhere else for him to go. He lived with us nearly a year. Such a beautiful singing voice!"

I can feel some pain in her voice, and I let her go on.

"He—Bradley—he had an accident over in Morgan County. A drunk driver. Bradley was in the passenger seat, and he—he was killed."

"Oh. Lord. I'm sorry," I say, feeling uncomfortable. All of a sudden the suit feels a little tight.

"It—it was just so sad. He was *such* a beautiful boy in so

many ways. I'll miss him always. The last time we ever decorated for Christmas, it was Bradley who did it."

I put my hand on the material, running my fingers across the neat stitching, trying not to think about it. That this was a suit worn by a person who is *dead.* I slip the coat off and lay it on the bed.

"Well," Faye says. "I just wanted you to have that."

"Thank you," I say.

"Tee said to remind you, he will be leaving about four o'clock."

"That early?"

"He's going to start ferrying people over at four-thirty. He wants you to be on the island to receive them as they come over."

"Wait—you said 'he.' Aren't you coming?"

Faye gives me a pleading look.

"I'm sorry, Little Texas—Ronald Earl—I've decided I can't be there. Not after dark. I would walk a hundred miles to hear you speak—anywhere but on that island."

"I understand."

"Please—please don't feel mad. And don't mind me. My husband—he's embarrassed enough as it is."

"It's all right. Thank you again for the—for the suit."

We eat an early dinner, and my heart feels like a pebbly stone is stuck behind it. And every time it beats against the stone, I can feel it, every little pit and pockmark.

I give my black shoes a quick shine, then say a long prayer

holding on to my Bible, kneeling in front of the bed, eyes shut. I read once that this is not how the early Christians prayed. They prayed standing up, looking up at heaven, with their hands in the air.

"They must have been an optimistic bunch," Sugar Tom has always liked to say. *Sugar Tom* . . .

I'm not putting myself up there with our Lord and Savior, but I can't help thinking—when Miss Wanda Joy comes to fetch me—how they found Jesus in the garden and led Him away. Him knowing all along what was coming.

We head down to the dock, with me toting the prayer box instead of Certain Certain. Miss Wanda Joy has on a long blue dress I've never seen before; she must have just gotten it in town. I'm surprised. She is smiling, eyes like bubbles of shiny ink.

"You ready?" Tee Barlow calls.

Miss Wanda Joy grins.

"'And the Lord said unto Satan, From whence comest thou? And Satan answered the Lord, and said, From going to and fro in the earth, and from walking up and down in it.'"

"Amen, sister," Tee Barlow says.

Three of the volunteers are waiting on us when we get down to the dock. We all shake hands. The men are quiet. They all have hairy arms and look strong. It makes me feel a little better knowing men like this will be there with us.

Tee Barlow waves us into the pontoon boat. It's a little strange being in a boat dressed in a suit. I have to stand up

318

the whole way to make sure I don't mess up my pants. We swing out into the water, and as the boat slowly passes under the skeleton of the trestle, I can feel the long shadows of the iron crosspieces ripple over my shoulders.

I touch the little piece of brick in my pocket.

Lucy—are you with me?

⇒ SIXTY-EIGHT ⇐

Tee Barlow steers the boat up to the dock on the far side, and the men scramble out. I help Miss Wanda Joy step out, and we meet several other volunteer folks on our walk up the hill. They clap me on the back, offering best wishes and prayers. Miss Wanda Joy swishes through them like a queen.

It's funny how this part of being a preacher is something I've never gotten used to, being amongst people telling you how great you are. I don't feel great. I feel . . . small. Not young. Just small.

The clearing is already clotted with hundreds of folding chairs lined up in ranks. On the far side of the columns is a tall metal tree full of lights that look like silvery pots of fire. The shadows of the pillars run almost to the water's edge.

Somebody has stretched a banner across the old second-story railing with letters at least two foot tall, done up in paint so red it reminds me of blood.

WELCOME
CHURCH OF THE HAND
REVIVAL MEETING
FEATURING THE
RENOWNED HEALER
and WARRIOR FOR
CHRIST
~ *Little Texas* ~

"Perfect," Miss Wanda Joy says to Tee Barlow.

"We aim to please," he says, swelling fit to bust. "Praise His name." He says something to the workers, then heads down the hill to start ferrying the congregation folks over.

I follow Miss Wanda Joy up on the stage. A little room has been fixed up there with raw pine lumber hung with green curtains so we can sit in private before the service. The stage is built of pressure-treated two-by-sixes, green and splintery, giving off a funny smell. I can see the sawdust in the grass.

I open the prayer box up, take out the King James, and spread it open to First Corinthians. With no Sugar Tom here, it'll be left to Miss Wanda Joy to get the crowd roused up, and she can't do it the way he can—so I know she'll lean extra heavy on the scriptures.

We sit down together in the dark of the little curtained room, looking at each other, and Miss Wanda Joy's foot goes to tapping.

"You know how special it would be if Daddy King could only be here to see you tonight?" she says, smiling. "This kind of service was his meat. I remember one time—it was during the riots in Birmingham—we set up the tent in Hoover, near the worst of where it was going on. I was just a girl then. A year removed from mother's heart attack. Lost, alone, still grieving, though I didn't even know what that was then. I *clung* to that man—he was so strong. You should have seen him standing there, jaw like a stone, turned to face that crowd. We didn't know what to expect—there was talk among some that they would come and set fire to the tent, burn us out."

She lifts her head and looks at me. "Those churches that were bombed—you simply don't know what it was like, Little Texas. The *atmosphere.* I heard a man beg Daddy King to cancel the service. He just stared at the man until he slunk away. And I knew—I *knew,* looking at that face—everything would be all right. He was that kind of man. Nobody would *dare* try anything with him around. And they didn't. And I have never worried about it since."

I wonder if this is her way of saying I'm not turning out to be the kind of man Daddy King was. Always testing, always pushing. Or maybe: *Here's your chance to show me.*

Through the curtain flap I spy the first load of worshippers pulling up at the dock. It looks like a good-sized party, most dressed in white or light colors, at least a dozen or more. *It is officially too late.* Fear or no fear, I can feel the hum starting up behind my eyes, can feel the white inside of my head start to build.

It takes a good while to get the tabernacle full. Tee Barlow makes the runs as fast as he can, but there are still more and more of them coming. From the hill I can see the Barlow pasture dotted all over with cars and folks streaming down to the dock. I like seeing them come. Maybe if we fill this place to brimming, that will be enough. What can it do to five hundred people?

The light is sinking now. I reach into my pocket to feel for Lucy's brick.

I stand up, horrified. These pants have long, bunchy pockets where things can fall out if you don't pay attention or cross your legs too much. I kneel down, looking all over this end of the stage. There is nowhere I can see that it might have fallen through.

"What's wrong?" Miss Wanda Joy says.

"Nothing. It's nothing," I say, going through my pockets again.

"Did you lose something? Your notes?"

"No!"

Where could I have dropped it? I swear I'll go over every inch of this ground if I have to. . . .

Every seat is already filled, and still they are coming. The congregation has bulged out around the edges of the old plantation house. At least 150 people are standing.

I see Tee Barlow tie off the pontoon boat and start up the hill. The only thing left of the daylight is a purple-orange glow on the horizon as the night settles on us. I look straight up, but I can't see the stars much, on account of the blazing lights.

Miss Wanda Joy quits tapping and gets to her feet. *"It's time."*

The crowd almost instantly settles down the minute she swoops around the curtain, eyeballs firing. She marches up to the pulpit, looks down at the words in the book. Scans the congregation.

"Welcome, welcome to all of you here today. I thank you so much for coming to our first revival meeting here at Vanderloo Plantation. I want to recognize Mr. Tee Barlow for everything he has done to make this happen."

She starts clapping, and the crowd does, too, kicking their feet on the back legs of the chairs in front of them. Tee stands and waves his arm, looking pretend shy.

"Little Texas!" someone hollers in the back.

"Bring on Little Texas!" A woman this time.

Miss Wanda Joy holds her arms up for quiet.

"Reading," she says, touching the tip of her finger to her tongue and flipping pages, "from First Corinthians. 'For Christ sent me not to baptize, but to preach the gospel: not with wisdom of words, lest the cross of Christ should be made of none effect.'"

She reads for a while longer, with the people getting more and more restless. "We come three hours!" I hear somebody say. Miss Wanda Joy finally snaps the book shut and looks up.

"And now, the person you've all been waiting for, the miracle of the healing age, the wonder born of the blood of the Lamb, *Little Texas*!"

A great rolling roar sweeps over the stage, exploding from more throats than I've ever spoke in front of before. Foot stomping, hand clapping, whistling, chair banging, shouting; I can feel it not just in my ears, but in my whole body. Like being dipped into a vat of pure liquid love.

It's time. My time.

CHAPTER

⇒ SIXTY-NINE ⇐

My eyes sweep the crowd, looking for any flash of blue. All I see are the people standing and clapping, cheering, banging the chairs in front of them.

I roll my head a couple of times, arms raising, just like they don't weigh a thing anymore, till I'm holding them up to heaven. Listening to the screams, I feel it starting in my chest, and it runs out to the tips of my arms like righteous electricity. My eyes close, and the Spirit begins to pour in.

Gradual as anything, they start to settle back down in their chairs, looking at me. Here and there an "Amen!" breaks out. I swing my head, watching them, catching an eye, seeing their faces change. They don't understand that I'm not in control of it. They don't understand there is no switch I can turn on or off.

"We love you, Little Texas!" somebody hollers.

I hear coughs, murmurs, people whispering questions to each other. I stand there, waiting for a word, waiting for some kind of sign. I close my eyes.

Please, dear Lord, help me.

"Tonight," I say, on account of I know I have to say something, but the word barely comes out of my mouth.

I cough to clear my throat and start again, eyes still closed, but voice a little bit louder.

"Tonight."

I watch the dark behind my eyelids. At first it's nothing but black, not a spot of white, but then—then I see it; I see a *name* floating against the black. A name glowing so white-hot a rip starts to open up in the blackness behind it, and the white begins to pour through.

"Tonight." A third time, feeling a little bit stronger, holding on to the sound of my voice. I focus on the name, bearing down, and the tear in the black gets wider and wider, till the white starts to flood out all over, filling my head with light.

"Tonight." Feeling the white burn its way through my chest, my arms, lifting them up. And the words begin to spill out of me to overflowing, loud and certain, building into that familiar, unstoppable rhythm. I open my eyes and—

"Tonight. I wonder how many of you can remember, *ah!*

How many can remember a man from the book of *Daniel, ah!* His name was *Shadrach, ah!* and he had two friends, *ah!* Meshach and Abed-nego, *ah!* and they refused, *ah!* I say they *refused, ah!* to fall down and worship the idols, *ah!* of old King Nebuchadnezzar, *ah!* And Nebuchadnezzar, *ah!* he had them *bound, ah!* by his strongest warriors, *ah!* and cast into the fiery *furnace, ah!* But when Nebuchadnezzar went to *open* the furnace, *ah!* Shadrach, Meshach, and Abed-nego, *ah!* they all came tumbling out from the fires, *ah!* Not one hair of their heads was singed, *ah!* And old King Nebuchadnezzar, *ah!* he fell to his *knees, ah!* and said, 'Blessed be the God of Shadrach'!"

The people are on their feet, clapping, raising their hands, cheering, praying, saying "Praise Jesus!" and "Amen, *amen*" over and over, screaming my name.

My hands are floating. My feet are moving. I'm scooting back and forth 'cross the stage with a bubbling, churning energy that nearly lifts me off the earth. I don't know what I'm saying now on this dark night in the middle of this old, burnt-out plantation on Devil Hill, but it's gushing out of me like a waterfall: cities on fire, plagues of flies and toadfrogs, rivers of blood.

I can feel my head tilting back as I speak, everything quiet in me even though I know they are making a racket, everything slowing down till I can 'most see every thought in the air around me, see my words streaming into their bodies, changing them, making them to love me. Me. This is what keeps me doing this, I realize, letting go like this, taking my most secret insides and turning them inside out for the entire world to see.

"Little Texas, Little Texas, Little Texas!"

And I know whatever is on this island, *it* can't do a thing, I know it doesn't *dare* to do a thing—I've swollen up a hundred times my usual size. I could step right out in the water and wade to the other side without hardly getting my knees wet. It wouldn't *dare*—it's too afraid of *me.* Too afraid of the gift I've been given by Him.

"Come *on,*" I want to say, beating my boulder-sized fists on my chest. "You want to mess with me, come *on.*"

And then—right at the biggest part of it, right when I think I could *grow* myself all the way to glory—that's when I see her.

She is standing right up front wearing yellow shorts and a checkered top and waving her arms over her curly head—a big woman, big-boned as Miss Wanda Joy—she screams out and falls to her knees, then comes down hard on all fours and begins to crawl around, thrashing her head side to side. Twisting her neck so hard you'd think she would twist her head right off. And she's saying something, her mouth chewing the air, fighting to get the words out.

"Abbeennddi! Jut! Abbeennddi! Jut!"

The congregation is in a fever, but some of the folks nearby the woman can see what is happening. They go down, pulling at her arms, holding her to keep her from hurting herself.

"Abbeennddi! Jut! Abbeennddi! Jut!"

Everybody is shouting now, with the woman's voice on top of all of the others. She is frothing at the mouth, bubbles of pinkish foam spilling over her lips.

"Abbeennddi! Jut! Abbeennddi! Jut!"

"Help her!" I say, coming forward on the stage, kneeling down. "Bring her up here! Help her to lay down."

They are grabbing at her, but she is flinging them back, slapping at their hands.

"Abbeennddi! Jut! Abbeennddi! Jut!"

"Hold her!" one of the men hollers.

People are crowding in so close, the ones at the front are starting to scream.

"Move back! Move back!"

"You're crushing us!"

Miss Wanda Joy is up now, shoving her way through to see how she can get things under control again.

"Please! Let me through, please! Let me through!"

But before she ever reaches the woman—

A sound hits my ears.

Monstrous, loud, off in the woods. A sound with so much belly in it, it makes my legs go weak—*angry.*

I can tell the congregation feels the sound, too. I see them all sag at the knees at the same time when the sound hits— the whole mass of people sinking just like a weight is pressing them down, driving their heads toward the ground.

"Abbeennddi! Jut! Abbeennddi! Jut!"

The men drop the woman and turn to face the sound. She lays there, wallowing and scratching. Then even she becomes still when the sound comes again, a big, long, honking blast. So hard-edged and powerful all the people flinch like they've been hit. And then just as sudden, it's quiet—that in-between kind of quiet that is so much harder than regular quiet, on account of what you know is coming. . . .

A tall hackberry—one of those kinds with long worms of raggedy bark on its trunk—it cracks. Splits and tears, just like it's being struck by a giant invisible axe. A fifty-foot tree shivered down the middle and starting to fall.

The hackberry tree leans, then comes crashing down with a tremendous *whump* that goes all through your bones.

The hooting sound comes again, shaking right through my guts, smashing us with noise, and another tree sets up to shivering and thrashing not far from the hackberry. Then another. And another—pieces of limbs and branches thick around as pythons begin to jump and dance. Something . . . something is pushing its way through.

CHAPTER

➤ SEVENTY ❦

The sound rolls on and on, like it's coming from the center of the island—a pin oak comes down next, then a white oak, then a black gum. More people are screaming now.

"Help me up!"

It's Miss Wanda Joy; I realize she's been screaming at me to help her up onto the stage, fighting her way through the squirming people. I get her big arm and haul back hard, but she's too heavy; I can only get her partway up, and she flops across the treated wood. I get her to her feet, and the hooting stops in that in-between place; but with people screaming, trees crashing down into the clearing, I can barely hear what she's saying. She waves her arms at the crowd.

"Please! Please! We need to stay calm! We have to be orderly about this!"

She might as well be whispering in a sawmill.

It's here.

A pillar starts swaying.

"Run!"

The whole congregation begins to move in a big pile—stumbling, cursing, kicking to get out, stepping on the hands and feet of other people, tumbling down the hill toward the pontoon boat.

The sound of their fear is so awful, it makes my heart ache. Another tree comes down, landing so close by it bumps me off my legs. I pick myself up and see Miss Wanda Joy on the grass below the stage, fighting two men who are pushing her toward the slope of the hill. I jump down from the stage and start toward her.

The first wave of people fleeing the clearing reach the pontoon boat, and I can see it shudder in the water, overloaded, as they pile aboard. Others in the water are clinging to the pontoons, dragging them under.

I don't see Tee Barlow anywhere, just a gang of men on the boat trying to get it cranked. In between the blasts of the sound, you can hear them cussing and fighting over the steering wheel.

I am running toward the water just like everybody else when a new sound behind me makes me turn around and stare. I see a folding chair jump twenty feet in the air all by itself. I stop dead-still on the slope. Another empty chair shoots up, higher than the first. Then another, and another and another—for just a second the big gang of people pushing and hollering stop to gawk and tremble.

"Come, Lord Jesus! Come, Lord Jesus!" a woman is saying over and over, her arms upraised.

Some of the last words in the Bible.

Icy prickles run up my back. Whatever it is, it's slowly coming closer and closer.

The sound starts up again, rolling across the water, filling up all that empty distance. I flash on the old town of Vanderloo, streets and buildings and light poles, two hundred feet down. Like it's calling to something down there.

Now folks are shoving each other out of the pontoon boat even as new ones try to climb in. Some start punching, people grabbing at each other when there's not enough room to swing.

People are tumbling into the water. Some are jumping in on purpose, swimming heavy as horses out toward the dark, deeper water. I clap my hands over my ears, trying to shut out the sound.

Miss Wanda Joy comes dodging out of a pile of folks, arms scratched, her hair bun snatched loose, locks all wild and witchy. She pulls me to her and crushes my face into her shoulder.

"Please," she's saying. "Please." Just that, over and over.

There's a little trickle of blood just under her left eye.

"Look at me!" I shout. "Look at *me.*"

"Please—what—what can we do, Little Texas? What can we do?"

"We've got to get the people off this island! We've got to do it *now.* They can't all go in the boat!"

I have never seen her cry before. Not once. "Why would He allow this? Please tell me why. *Why?*"

"No time for that!" I say.

I take her arm and run, half dragging her down toward the water, but away from the swarming dock. We hurry deeper into the shadows, beyond the reach of the lights. I take off my suit coat and wrap her in it, then touch at her cut with my shirttail. Tee Barlow is standing not ten feet away beside a log. His clothes are muddy, and grass is clinging to his white beard.

"Tee!" Miss Wanda Joy says. "What are we going to do?"

"It's the Judgment," Tee Barlow says. "That's what it is. 'Therefore the ungodly shall not stand in the judgment, nor sinners in the congregation of the righteous—'"

I grab hold of his shirt and yell into his face.

"Keep her here! Don't let her go near that dock!" I shove her into his arms.

"What are you . . . ?"

But I'm already gone, running slantways across the hill to where the people are struggling to get in the water. I'm trying to think clearly as my heart thuds. Sooner or later whatever is tearing up the tabernacle is going to come down this hill.

"Over here!" I holler. "Over here! This way, come this way!"

They just go on fighting and pulling at each other, struggling with the boat. Then a huge cracking sound comes from up on the hill. The chairs have stopped flinging themselves all over. The stage, the place where I was standing just moments ago, rears up in the middle, timbers rising up and up, wood splintering, screeching.

So much power.

The rented pulpit comes apart in one big, shivery scream of tearing, the sound of the busting wood mixed with the shrieking of the nails wrenching theirselves loose.

Something runs through the crowd fighting around the pontoon boat—the way a horse's skin will wiggle and crawl—and just like that, all the faces turn, the whole crowd turns to me.

"Little Texas! It's Little Texas!" some of them start screaming. "Go to him! Go to Little Texas!"

They start at a rush, pushing and shoving and screaming, all barreling down on me now.

"This way! This way!" I say again and again.

I take off running, hurrying fast as I can toward higher ground, away from the dock, but away from the clearing, too. They are all running after me crosswise over the slope, heading in the same direction I am heading.

Toward the old railroad trestle.

≫SEVENTY-ONE≪

Folks in Sunday clothes, big strong men, kids, old women, all tear catty-corner across the hill toward the spot where the big iron beams of the trestle are sunk deep into the hide of the island.

I reach Tee Barlow where he is huddling with Miss Wanda Joy down in the shadows.

"Come on!" I yell, pulling at his arm.

Tee Barlow is muttering, eyes blank as a painted wall.

" 'The fearful, and unbelieving, and the abominable, and murderers, and whoremongers, and sorcerers, and idolaters, and all liars—' "

I backhand him across the mouth. He shuts up, his eyes flutter. "Little Texas?"

"Come with me!" I say, this time to Miss Wanda Joy, tugging her away from him. They both start to run at last.

The sound gusts over our heads again, and there is a great, shuddering *WHOMP,* making the ground shimmy under our feet. One of the pillars has fallen.

Everybody runs hunched over like they're being showered with hail. The trestle's just a hundred yards down shore, but the closer we get, the thicker the pricker bushes and vines.

Another loud crash bangs in the clearing. *Keep running.*

There's just enough light pouring down from the lamps in the clearing to make out the iron frame of the trestle. In the last few feet the crowd rushes past us, scrambling up the concrete base.

I haul Miss Wanda Joy further up the hill to keep her from getting trampled. People flood onto the trestle, shoulder to shoulder, fighting and screaming at the bottleneck. The old iron strains with the weight, and the timbers moan.

Please, Lord. Please let it hold. Keep them safe.

The trestle starts to shake, jammed with squirming, tangled people. But they're moving forward, four and five abreast, stumbling, stepping on fingers.

A noise thunders behind us—for a while that's all I can hear, a huge, roaring anger.

Lucy's voice sounds in my head from last night when we were making the plan.

"The best thing to do is, you don't show it fear, Ronald Earl. You've got to be arrogant. Haughty, proud. A real spiritual badass. That's its weakness. Pride in its own power. If it comes, it'll be pissed off. Don't try to stop it. You can't. Not by yourself. Lead them to the trestle. I don't think it will cross the water. It will be the fastest way off the island."

Tee Barlow climbs up beside me and Miss Wanda Joy.

"Go with him!" I shout to her. I turn to Tee Barlow. "You've got to get her across! Don't you let go of her *one second.*"

"But you—Little Texas," Miss Wanda Joy whimpers, "what about—"

Another blast comes, this time much closer.

"Move."

I give Tee Barlow a shove in his big tailbone with my foot. He stumbles forward and throws a fat leg up on the trestle's cement base and turns to give Miss Wanda Joy a hand up.

I watch them clinging to each other, pushing their way into the mob on the first splintery cross tie. For just the smallest little second, I think about going with them. I won't lie. But she's depending on me to carry through with our plan. Set those folks on the island free. Send them *home.*

"You've got to draw it as far away from the tree as you can," Lucy said. *"You've got to use the people at the service—use them for bait."*

"I can't do that."

"You can and you will. It's the only way."

The last of the congregation are scrambling over the

concrete base now, clambering onto the trestle. I can't wait around here anymore. Either they will make it or they won't.

A scream makes me turn and look one last time. *Lord.* Someone just jumped or fell from the trestle, hitting the lake like a rifle shot. The roaring over our heads changes to a low, sickening growl. My heart clutches with fear.

Dear merciful, heavenly Father, please send your angels to guide, watch over, and protect whoever just fell in. Please help them all, I pray. But I start moving.

I cut uphill, streaking through the woods, fumbling branches away from my eyes. Heading right back toward the destruction in the clearing.

Get the flashlight.

I step out of the woods near where Sugar Tom had his stroke. The fallen column is at my feet in a jumble of plaster and chimbley rubble. I stoop to pick up the flashlight, then jump back into the forest.

Another scream from down below rips through the forest, and the hooting roar comes again. What will happen if that thing gets hold of the trestle and shakes it down before they can all get off?

"Once the people are safe on the other side, across the water, it's you and me we have to worry about, Ronald Earl. When it figures out where we are, what we're doing . . . it will come for us."

I keep the flashlight off and start up the path leading to the trouble tree.

CHAPTER

➤SEVENTY-TWO⬅

Have you ever done something you knew was supposed to be right, but nothing about it *felt* right? The deeper I get into the woods, the more I can feel it. Anger. Hate. *Fear.*

I have to switch the flashlight on when I'm about a quarter mile in. A branch snaps off in the woods a ways, and I spray the beam around. *Nothing.*

Being this afraid is like being squished down into a block of ice-cold cement. I feel the weight of my fear with every step.

I stumble along, heart drumming, into the inky black. I can't hear the sound anymore—did it get them? Tear the whole trestle down?

Is it coming for me?

I run faster, pushing my way through the oak and hickory saplings. Finally I get to the long bend where the red-tailed fox disappeared. I know Lucy is waiting for me. As I round the long curve, the far end of the flashlight beam suddenly dissolves.

A wind kicks up from off the lake, making the chains and leg irons in the branches clang together. A sound so lonely and dead and forgotten, it makes me want to kneel in the dirt and pull the ground up over me.

"Lucy!"

There's only the lonesome pieces of iron talking to each other. *Where is she?*

I smack the flashlight against my leg; the beam flickers and holds. I sweep it around the clearing. *There*—I see the trouble tree, its muscular roots running all over the ground, trunk cranked in that crazy twist, and I think about our plan again.

"It won't take long for it to figure out what we're doing," Lucy had said. *"We'll need to move swift to set them free. I'll wait for you by the tree."*

"I'll be there. I won't let you down," I told her.

We squeezed each other's fingers, and she was gone.

But now where is she? What is she going to—

"Jesus."

It's a one-word prayer.

CHAPTER

⇒SEVENTY-THREE⇐

What was that?

Something—something just darted across the flashlight beam. Hunched over, low to the ground, running in a funny way, like maybe it's hurt. Bony-looking. *A flash of bluish skin.*

I swing the light around. The woods are much closer than they were a second ago. Then—

The flashlight beam licks over something a few yards in front of me. Something blue and kind of see-through and shiny, with wet, glisteny yellow hair.

"Where were you?" I say, feeling all the air rush out of me. "It's down by the trestle—what are we—"

"Hurry," Lucy says. She comes toward me, and her fingers tighten on my arm like tongs. "Keep going. I'll tell you when to stop."

I edge forward, closer and closer to the tree, her almost helping me along. The wind moans through the branches, making the manacles rattle hard overhead. The closer I get to the trouble tree, the more the humped roots shooting out from the bottom almost seem to writhe and quiver.

"There," Lucy says. "That's where you need to go to set them free. There."

She's pointing at a place where two monstrous roots squirt out from the base of the tree, roots nearly as tall as my chest and big around as drainpipes. I swing the flashlight around. The beam passes through Lucy's middle.

I can feel her sweet, warm breath on my neck. I boost myself up on the root and swing my legs over, ease myself down. The two giant roots have grown together at one end, making the place between them into a little football-shaped depression with a carpet of leaves and spongy dirt. The skin of the tree feels hard and cold as limestone. Lucy comes closer, peering over at me.

Are we supposed to *kill* the tree? With what?

"What am I supposed to do now?" I hiss.

Lucy points. The twisting of the tree's hide has spread open a hole in its middle. Deep enough to see into its insides, like a natural little cave.

"Inside," Lucy says, eyes glowing. *"Look inside."*

I set my feet against one of the roots, trembling, and push myself up toward the opening. The flashlight is crooked on my finger. I haul myself up with my arms and poke the flashlight up, shining it in and—

Nothing.

Only the inside of a very old tree. I can see dark humps of tree flesh colored gray and brown running up the inside of the trunk.

"Reach inside," Lucy says. "You might have to stretch a little."

I lean over into the hole, reaching with my fingers. There *is* something there. Something flat and kind of square, with a cool, pebbly hide. I draw it out of the tree trunk and let out a little gasp.

"Did you find it?" Lucy says.

"It's *Sugar Tom's Bible,*" I say, swiveling around to face her, showing her the black King James Bible with the red gilt edges. "How? How did it get in there? I was just holding it up at the clear—"

"It's not Sugar Tom's," Lucy says.

I climb down from the trunk, heart jumping, and set the old Bible on top of the root. My back is against the tree now. I bring the flashlight around again. She's standing on the other side of the root.

"You mean it's . . . then this belongs to . . ."

"Pastor Hallmark," Lucy says in a voice that's not her voice.

❧ SEVENTY-FOUR ❧

I sit down hard in the little space between the roots. The flashlight slides out of my hand and drops between my legs, shining up under my chin. Lucy comes over and looks down at me.

"Don't you remember me, Little Texas?"

"Who . . . *who are you?*"

She touches herself in the chest. "Don't you know me? You have *always* known me."

I am cold. *So cold.*

"The book of Mark," she says. "I'm sure you're familiar

with it. Jesus asks a man full of devils who he is, and the man says—"

"'My name is Legion,'" I say, "'for we are many.'"

My eyes bunch up; her face smears like paint dripped in water.

She looks down, not saying anything.

"Don't forget what happened after that," I say quietly. "Jesus cast the devils out of that man and slung them into a herd of pigs. They ran over a bluff and killed theirselves."

"You want to give it a shot?"

"Where is she!"

She smiles and speaks in a different voice. *Lucy's voice.*

"But I'm *here,* Ronald Earl. I've always been here."

I feel my heart plunging. *No. No.*

"It was you," I say. "*You* who tore up the revival tent. You in the hallway that first night. You never went away. It was always you. You killed Pastor Hallmark. You—*you hurt Sugar Tom.* It was *you* the whole time. Pretending to be Lucy. And tonight—"

"You're smarter than you look."

"You used me," I say weakly, eyes burning. "Why? Why are you doing this? What do you want?"

The thing puts its hands on the root like it's fixing to climb over.

"I needed you, Little Texas."

"I won't—I won't do anything for you."

"But you already have. The service. I needed the service. To bring them all here."

"But they got away! You *didn't* get them. I *saw* them get away."

It touches a tongue to its lips. "I was hungry. I didn't need *them.* I needed what they could give me."

"Hungry?"

"I fed off them. Their fear. I can feed off fear. Any fear." The thing turns and spreads its fingers out against the trunk of the tree, looking up into its branches. "It makes me stronger."

"What about the slaves? Their spirits?"

It reaches over and strokes the trunk of the trouble tree. "They're *mine. Souls in amber.*"

"What do you want with them?"

"They keep me . . . in *being* . . . their hatred, fear, anger. You are what you eat, as they say."

I pick up the flashlight and rise up slow. Aim the beam at the thing and gasp. I remember a deer laying beside the road once. One of the deer's eyes was open, and the car lights were shining on it. *That's what its eyes look like now.*

Lucy.

"You have to let them go," I say. "All of them. They belong somewhere else. A better place."

"But I don't want to," the thing says. "I told you. They're *mine.* I will keep them."

I lunge at Pastor Hallmark's Bible on top of the root, clutch it tight to my chest, eyes shut hard.

"Dear heavenly Father, O Great Redeemer, please send your angels to protect—"

The Bible wrenches itself out of my arms.

Smashes against the trouble tree. Keeps on hitting itself against the tree, harder and harder. I swear I can hear nasty little grunts each time the Bible smacks the tree, till finally it drops into a filthy little pile of mushy paper at my feet.

I hear a hard, ragged breathing coming from the darkness all around me. *Anger.* Huge, ugly. Anger so thick it's more solid than the tree.

Pictures start to flood into my head: That rest stop where the kids made fun of my hair. Pictures of me taking hold of one of those kids, the biggest boy, getting my fists in his hair, driving his head straight into a brick wall. Doing it over and over, till his head is splattered into nothing but paste.

Then it's my parents in the pictures, and I'm taking a claw hammer to their faces. Hitting and hitting and hitting till they don't have faces anymore.

Kill them. Kill them all. Miss Wanda Joy. Certain Certain. Faye Barlow.

Smash their eyes back into their brains, tear off their skin, burn their bones to ash.

"Get out!" I scream. *"Get out of me!"*

I slump back against the root behind me. Open my eyes. The thing is still there, looking at me.

"Why?" I say, voice croaking. "Why are you doing this to me?"

It smiles, lips pulled back, showing black, sharp teeth.

"Because I love you."

A sickening shiver of disgust runs through my whole body.

"You can't love. You don't even know what it means."

The face that was Lucy's face twists into an animal snarl. "What's wrong, Ronald Earl? Don't I look beautiful to you anymore?"

I sink down to my knees, hands hooked together, pleading, starting to weep.

"Please. Please let me go."

It's the sound of my own voice that does it—the shame and the quiver in it that tells me just what the thing is doing now. If it can't suck me in through hate, it'll do it through fear and shame and pure loathing.

"No," I say, unloosing my fists and beating them against the ground. "*No.* You want me, you aren't getting me that way. I won't let you. You're *ugly,* you know that? That's what you are. *Dog ugly.*"

Lucy stands before me, shining and beautiful again. She plays with her hair, looking at it. "It's such a little thing, isn't it? Beauty is all you need, Ronald Earl. Beauty can make you do anything. Even free some slaves. I used it to pull you in.

But aren't you forgetting Second Peter, chapter two, verse nineteen? 'While they promise them liberty, they themselves are the servants of corruption: for of whom a man is overcome, of the same is he brought in bondage.' "

"That's not—that's not what it means. You know that's not what it means. You can't use the Word that way!"

The face changes again into a mocking, sickly smile. "But isn't that what you do, your kind? Twist it whatever way you need it to be? Why, you even get to decide who goes to heaven or hell."

"I hate you. I *hate you.*"

"But you said you *loved* me," it says, grinning.

So hard to think . . . I have to remember . . . I know I felt it. But did I ever say it out loud? Did I ever really tell her? Why is that so important to me now?

I close my eyes, and I can see her . . . feel myself touching her, looking into her powder blue eyes. I can hear her voice.

She's real, I tell myself. *She has to be real. She has to be. Has to be.* Has to be!

I get to my feet, bringing up my fists. "Let. Her. *Go.*"

"Who, darling?"

"I know she's real. And I *do* love her. I do."

The Lucy thing leans back. "Are you saying you love the *dead*?"

The beautiful face instantly turns the color of ash, then blacker than ash. Pieces of it start to crumble, flaking away like old paint. . . .

I want to cover my eyes. But that's just what it's after. *My fear.*

"No," I say. "*No.* Not the vessel! It's not the vessel I love. It's what's *inside.*"

"Then tell it to me. You say I don't know about love. Tell me something about it that I don't know."

I grit my teeth and don't say anything for a long time. Maybe I'm just trying to stay alive, hold things off as long as I can. But then it comes to me. The best answer. The *right* answer.

"I never knew it would be so hard."

SEVENTY-FIVE

Just like that, she—*it*—looks like the real Lucy again. She's holding out her arms to me.

"That's all right," she says. "Come here, baby. Won't you touch me? Come here and touch me like you did before. You know how bad you want to."

"Lucy never talked like that," I say, clenching my jaw. "What have you done with her?"

The thing touches the blue dress it's wearing, like she did before. *Lucy's blue dress.* Presses a hand over its heart. *Lucy's heart.*

"She's here," it says. "Lucy is with *me.* We are in here

together. We will always be . . . together. This is where she wants to be, with me. That's why she tricked you. Got you to come here. So you can be with both of us, Little Texas. And then we will all always be together."

"I don't—I don't believe you," I say. "She would never be a part of you. She's—she's . . . *good.*"

It pulls its arms back. "Is that the best you can do? Lucy is *good*? I'm supposed to be afraid of that?"

"What do you want from me?"

"Well, you *do* have a gift. You're absolutely *stuffed* with light—together . . . we could do so *much.* I can offer you many things, Ronald Earl. How about . . . say . . . *eternal life*?"

"Go to hell."

"I'm sure I would fit right in, if such a place existed. But I have to tell you, Little Texas, there is only *this* place." It flings Lucy's thin arms around. "This *world.* It's all that has ever existed. Or will exist. So how about it?"

"I don't believe you. You're evil."

It sighs. "This has been so much fun. But it's time we got on with it. Didn't I tell you? You're here to perform a *healing.*"

Drawing the word out, all sneering and slow.

"Heal what? Heal *you*?" I say. "I don't think anybody could do that. The Lord could, if He wanted. I'm not Him."

"Oh, let's pretend. That's what you've been doing all along, isn't it? Pretending to be the Lord."

"You shut your mouth."

"Oh. Listen to the big man. What are you going to do, *save* me? All right, you get to be the Lord. Right now. This is your last chance to play. *Heal them.*"

There's a skittery kind of noise somewhere in the dark; I pick up the flashlight and turn my head just in time to see something at the edge of the beam. It clambers across one of the roots on its fingernails and drops at my feet.

⇒SEVENTY-SIX⇐

I jump back, aiming the light. Whatever it is, it's all hunched over and gnarled up.

Oh my Lord.

It *is*—it's a little man with bluish skin and close-cropped hair. Muscles stringy and knotted, face all tendons and bones. Big, square teeth like a horse. His feet are bare. His back is crooked over so far, he's practically looking straight at the ground. But he's not. The little man is watching me.

We stand there studying each other, me in shock, him

quiet but coiled up, ready. He paces this way and that in the little space. Then without warning, he springs at me and fixes his teeth on my arm. I holler out, knocking him back with the flashlight. I can feel the flashlight hitting bone.

The blue man splays himself against the tree root, then lunges at me again, digging into my arm with his broken fingernails and hissing like a hognose snake. I beat at him furiously with the flashlight, smashing at his face, knocking him to the dirt. He lays still a minute, but I can see his chest rising and falling. Both of us wait like that, breathing hard.

Another little blue creature slips over the root. I jerk the flashlight around. It's a woman this time, with long, rabbity hair and eyes red as dogwood berries.

She comes at me with her teeth and fingernails, ripping a hole in my shirt and slashing at my chest. I smash her with the flashlight, sending her screeching. Another creature drops over the root. Another. Another. They're coming so fast, I can't think, can only smash at them with the light. *Can't let them get me. I can't.* I swing the flashlight again and again, but there are more and more of them.

Too many! They start getting their hands on me, biting, pulling, tearing with their nails. I swing for their skulls with the light, but they're pulling me down between the roots, pinning me to the earth. The light sprays around, wild. I see shattered teeth, crooked fingers, pus-colored eyes.

They're trying to speak, but it comes out in a spitting, screechy growl. The rasping sound of their fury hedges up around me as they close in further and further.

The mush that was Pastor Hallmark's Bible is under my back, grinding into my shoulder blades through my shirt.

But then the bluish people fall back, giving me room to breathe. I see its face over the big root again, looking down into the flashlight beam.

"'Get thee behind me, Satan,'" I manage to say.

It genuinely laughs this time.

"You really believe in him, don't you?" it says. "Almost more than the other one."

The little blue faces bob in and out of the light, square teeth gnashing, mouths shaking with pure rage. It waves at them.

"You think they're mine, but they're not. They're *yours*. Don't you recognize your own?"

My own.

Own. I nearly choke on the word. "Souls in amber," it called them.

The bluish people aren't devils or demons. This is what they've become in centuries of pain and misery.

The slaves of Vanderloo Plantation.

The rusty chains clank in the branches, telling me, *Yes, yes.*

The slaves begin to jostle and snap at each other, spreading their sharp fingers.

"See how energetic you make them?" it says. "That's good. I'm hungry. *I'm always hungry.*"

"I won't listen to any more of this," I say.

"That's all right," it says, waving an arm. "You see, they get hungry, too.

"Take him."

⇒SEVENTY-SEVEN⇐

They slam against me. Several clap their filthy hands over my face; my mouth is full of nasty fingers digging their way inside, clawing at my tongue. I bite down hard, making them scream.

Biting, clawing, hitting. Their nails sting like nettles on my arms, tearing at my sleeves, raking my skin. I scream the words out:

"'O Lord *God,* remember me.' . . . 'My times are in thy hand. . . .'"

They are raining blows on me now, cutting me to pieces. My shirt is wet with my blood.

I feel as if I'm sinking into the earth.

I'm sorry.

Sorry I didn't do better. Sorry I lost my faith. Sorry I failed to help them.

I'm sorry, Lucy.

I fight as hard as I know how, but I'm getting dizzy, starting to feel like I'm dropping away. *Is this what it feels like to die?*

Certain Certain's face swims up in my head. I'll never see him again, he'll never know what happened to me. But . . .

Wait. *Wait.*

Even as I'm getting swarmed under, even as they are tearing at my clothes, my flesh, I realize something. *They* are *mine. They're all of ours.* And I remember. I remember.

"Lucy!" I yell. "I'm ready! I'm ready! I know what you want! I'll do it! *I'll do it.*"

The blue people scream like they've been stabbed with an ice pick; their bodies slink away. I gulp in a huge breath, let it out again. It takes all the air I have just to speak. I shove myself up to a sitting position, spitting and coughing. Finally I'm able to stand, clutching at the big root for support.

Its voice is a snarl, impatient. "What is it? What do you want?"

I touch my cheek, feeling the claw marks there, the warm, wet blood. "Anything can be hurt," Lucy said once. I hang on to that picture of her. The true Lucy.

"I want . . . I want to be with you," I say, taking in long, gasping breaths. "I know that now. You're what I've always wanted."

It licks its lips and pulls me over the root as if I were a baby. Takes my bleeding hand and puts it on its breast.

"This is the real strength, isn't it, Ronald Earl? The strength of the body. The *flesh.* There is no such thing as sin. No such thing as evil. Only energy and what you do with it."

It starts to take me in its arms.

Think of that. Think of her body, I tell myself. *Think of nothing else. You have to think of nothing else. Think of the white room. Taking Lucy there . . .*

Make it flesh, *oh Lord . . . make it flesh. . . .*

I lean in close to its body, my fingers closing over the rawhide cord around my neck.

I jerk the cord loose and slam Certain Certain's slave tag into the thing's forehead.

"Heal her now, O God, I beseech thee!"

The thing shrieks in rage and pain. Instantly I feel a blazing heat sear my fingers, but I keep pushing and pushing till I can feel the slave tag charring its way into its flesh—I hold it there, flat against the thing's forehead, forcing it to scorch its way deeper and deeper into its skin.

My arm flares with a pain like I've never felt before, so fierce the inside of my head bursts with lights. But I keep pressing the slave tag harder and harder, wanting to drive my arm inside its head.

Lord, let me see this great fire . . . let it take all of me . . . take

*me out of the earth . . . make me a sanctuary . . . let me go over, I
pray thee, and take off its head. . . .*

I keep pushing harder and harder, the pain becoming an
impossible agony, the skin broiling off my hand, the muscles,
tendons starting to burn away.

The thing rocks backward, but I clutch even harder with
my free hand, shoving the bones of my fingers deeper and
deeper into its wound—it's screaming now, and I'm screaming, too, and our screams join somewhere in the branches of
the tree.

And let me die the death of the righteous. . . .

It stumbles back away from me and sits down hard. I fall
on top of it. My burning hand pulls free of the wound in its
head.

The thing groans and starts to lift itself up on its elbows,
tearing at the burning square of flame on its forehead—

I slam into it with all my weight, throwing my arms
around its body. Screaming the only words I have left. Those
old words from the Song of Solomon. The ones that freed
Lucy the first time.

"'LOVE IS STRONG AS DEATH'!

"'LOVE IS STRONG AS DEATH'!

"'LOVE IS STRONG AS DEATH'!"

I scream the words into its chest, again and again and
again. It rocks and struggles under me, trying to buck me off.
I keep screaming the words over and over.

"'LOVE IS STRONG AS DEATH'!

"'LOVE IS STRONG AS DEATH'!
"'LOVE IS STRONG AS DEATH'!"

I don't know how long I shout it. How many times. I don't know.

Its body bows up beneath me, back bending, skinny arms taut as ropes. It shakes all over, and a big gust of breath pours from its mouth, sounding like wind.

The thing makes a terrible rattling noise deep in its throat, and its body settles under me, easing itself down, down, down, till all the strength is gone out of it. And there is nothing left but weakness, then the weakness goes, too. It is still.

I slump to the ground, falling over on my side, weeping.

When I open my eyes, the flashlight is reflecting off the white bark of the trouble tree. I lift myself up on one hand and hold my burnt arm up to the light—it's *whole.* Some of the pain is still there, but even that is bleeding away.

I look. . . .

The small body in the leaves begins to shift and change.

I watch it happen, breathing shallow. Watch the anger, the fear in its face, drain away.

It's getting smaller.

The body sinks slowly, slowly into the leaf mold. As it sinks, a low sigh slips away on the wind. Then there is nothing but the leaves rattling in the branches of the trouble tree.

It's gone.

⇒ SEVENTY-EIGHT ⇐

A sound like a child's gasp makes me turn—my breath catches—the blue people are still there.

But they're so still now. Still and watchful. Not hunched over anymore. Bodies tall, straight, unbroken. Skin glistening. Quiet. They look like . . . *people.* I can hear them breathing.

One of them, it looks to be an older woman, peels off from the rest and goes up to the trouble tree. She touches the tree, stroking it with her fingers. Then slips like a dissolving blue smoke in the beam of the flashlight right up its trunk. Lost in the branches.

Another one follows. A man this time. He looks back at me, looks at all of us, and passes into the arms of the tree.

They all leave that way. Dark blue shapes touching the tree, then turning into a kind of powder, lifting up from the ground, till they are wafting away.

Free. Free.

Everything is gone. Everything except the wind and the tree and the night.

CHAPTER

SEVENTY-NINE

My hand still aches . . . I don't care. I might sit right here till the battery on the flashlight runs out.

"You," a voice says behind me.

I try to get to my feet, but I stagger and fall. Try again, and this time she's there to catch me. Her hot tears roll down my shirt.

"I'm so *sorry,* Ronald Earl . . . I'm so *sorry* . . . I didn't know! I didn't know . . . I couldn't. I couldn't warn you. I tried, but I couldn't. . . . It was like . . . it was like . . . oh please, please . . . keep holding me. . . ."

I don't care if she's made out of steam or sound or

something that doesn't even have a name. "You're here," I say, weeping into her hair, clinging to her, barely able to speak. "You're . . . you're really *here*." Again and again and again.

Lucy looks up at me, eyes gleaming.

"For a little while . . . I don't . . . don't have much left in me. You understand?"

"But . . . I . . . how . . ."

"We thought . . . we thought we had everything figured out, but it . . . it *knew*. . . . I thought I would be safe . . . after it left to go . . . to where you were . . . but it took me . . . it *took me, Ronald Earl* . . . took me the minute . . . I came . . . I came here to wait for you . . . like being held by a thousand . . . *arms* . . . but *you* . . . God, Ronald Earl . . . *you* . . ."

My words come out in pieces. "Certain Certain . . . I remembered . . . the slave tag . . . fear, hate . . . if that's what was . . . holding them . . . I figured *love* . . ."

"*Shhh, shhh . . .*" She pats my hair. "I know . . . I *know*."

It feels so good to be in her arms. Good beyond any good thing I've ever felt before. My breathing, my heart, it all begins to slow. And still we hold each other.

"They're okay now, aren't they?" I say. "The slaves? They went *home*! Did you see them? I *saw* them, Lucy! I saw them go."

"I know. Yeah, they're *home*. We did it. *You* did it."

"It felt . . . it felt so good! Seeing them go . . . knowing . . . nothing would ever . . . would ever *own* them again."

"But, Ronald Earl . . ."

"Lord, how I wish Certain Certain could have seen it! All those slaves . . . *free* . . . free."

Lucy pulls back to look in my face. "The blue people . . . they weren't the slaves of Vanderloo, Ronald Earl."

"But—I saw them! Lucy, I saw them *go* . . . they stroked the tree just like Certain Certain said, and then they went away . . . they're *free* now, free—"

"The slaves of Vanderloo were free a long time ago," she says. "We didn't free them. They didn't have to be freed. They did that themselves."

"But . . . I don't understand . . . what did we . . . *who*—"

"Those were the *owners.*"

⇒EIGHTY⇐

I stand there listening to the wind. Holding her. Feeling the truth trickle over me.

"The owners," Lucy says after a little while. "And people like Thaddeus Palmer. I didn't know myself until . . . until I was inside *with them.*"

"But . . . I thought . . . I thought they were . . ."

Lucy nods. "Oh, those were slaves you set free, all right. The owners and overseers and auctioneers . . . you see that now, don't you? *They were slaves, too.* The worst kind. They enslaved *themselves.* And now I know why they brought us here—me and you—to help them. At first I didn't understand that myself. But who better? I know, we didn't do it, we weren't alive back then . . . but we've benefited, right? From what our ancestors did? Even all these years later?"

I look at the big tree in awe. "Certain Certain . . . he told me . . . it's something we owe. All of us."

Lucy's looking, too. The night is quiet. I don't see anything there, but I think she does. Maybe she does.

"I have to go, Ronald Earl."

I feel her voice in the middle of my chest like a branch that can't unbend. I know before I can say anything that what she's saying is true. But I have to say it anyway.

"But you're coming with me, aren't you?"

Lucy looks at me, her lips tight. She holds her fist out, reaches it out to me.

"What?" I say.

I put my hand out. She drops something in it. I can tell just from feeling it that it's the little corner of brick I lost back at the plantation. I know the words are still there.

"No. Please. No. Don't leave me here alone. You can't. *Please,* Lucy. I can't stand it. I can't. *I have no one.*"

"I—Ronald Earl—it's not up to me. It's *killing me.* It's killing me, too. But I have . . . I have . . . it's a gift. I want to give it to you. Before . . . before I go."

"*No!* I just want you. I don't care about any gift. Just—"

She puts a finger up to my mouth. I can feel the heat coming off of it.

"Please," she says, looking into my eyes. "It's happening

faster than I thought. Hold *still*. I'm going. I'm going. This—
it's really hard. I have to put everything I have—all of it . . ."

She closes her eyes and becomes very still, very quiet.
Somewhere out on the lake there is a bird making a long, unbroken noise. Lucy comes closer. I drop my head a little. Our
lips touch. I shut my eyes and try to wrap my arms around
her, but my hands pass through. She's putting everything she
has into our kiss. *Making it real.*

I keep kissing her, feeling her mouth, her warm lips, and
tell myself every part of her is right there. Her lips have to
be enough. They have to be all of her. *They have to be.*

I want to melt inside her. Not just my face. My mind.
My spirit. Climb all the way in, go wherever she goes.
Finally she pulls back. It's over. She holds her head away
from me.

"That's it," Lucy says, her voice getting faint. "That's all of
it. We can't . . . we can't touch anymore."

My eyes flood with tears. I try to fight them back, but I
can't.

"You remember, you told me what we are . . . it's too big.
Too big to be held," I say. "You told me—"

Lucy nods her head. "Goodbye," she says. I don't know if I
really hear it, or just believe I hear it.

"I love you," I say. I hope she can hear me. "I love you. *I
love you.*"

She's moving away now, not gliding, but walking.

Stepping backward into the black of the woods. Watching me the whole time.

When she goes, it's not like the others. She keeps on pulling back, waving her small hand. I reach toward her, fingers shaking. She's gone.

Gone.

CHAPTER

⇛EIGHTY-ONE⇚

"Little Texas!"

The man's name is Danny. He knows me; turns out he was here before, when Sugar Tom took sick.

I'm still watching the island. Watching it move away. It's too much, so I watch Danny instead. I can't focus on what he is saying, though. I have to focus on the things that make sense. Things that are simple. Like the fact Danny has hair like a brush and a fire-colored beard.

He dabs at my cuts and wraps a band around my arm and pumps up that black squeezy thing. He puts something in my mouth, looks at my eyes with a little flashlight.

I don't care about my body right now. Whatever is wrong, let it heal itself.

The boat engine rumbles. Red lights are flashing all over the pasture, white lights swinging down the shore. I look at the old trestle.

"They had to fish some folks out of the lake," Danny says. "It's a miracle nobody died. But everybody made it out, far as we can tell."

Everybody made it out. Especially one in particular. She wears a blue dress, has skinny arms. Sometimes walks like a bird riding on a breeze.

The lights start blurring, washing the nighttime out. I hear men and women shouting, see them coming and going. They start to blur, too. That's okay. I can see. I can see.

➤EIGHTY-TWO☙

I won't talk to any of them, so the TV people surround Miss Wanda Joy instead.

The hot lights make her squint. I've never seen her look so rough, eyes wild, hair in strings. One of the hospital cleaning guys points, pretending he is flying on his mop. I'm too far gone to care. We aren't who they think we are.

Certain Certain says all kinds of news folks are clamoring to see Devil Hill, but Tee Barlow has forbidden anybody access.

"Just a matter of time before CNN, Fox News turn up," Certain Certain says when he comes to see me in my room.

His eyes are red and watery. He perches on the edge of the bed. "Somethin' like this is just right for the freak-show slot. You gonna be hot as a two-dollar pistol, Lightning. Ministries all over itchin' to hear you speak. Likely be a whole new wave of revival come out of this, praise His name. So maybe somethin' good can come out of that old plantation after all?"

I squeeze his big hand. His skin feels cold. "Thanks for getting me out of there," I say, meaning the emergency room.

Certain Certain frowns. "Look like you been in a seven-day axe fight, lost your axe on the first day. How you feeling?"

"I've been better," I say.

They have a drip needle stuck in the back of my hand. Plenty of cuts, bruises, bandages. Seven stitches over my eye. But everything's still attached, nothing broken. *Except my heart.*

"You ready to talk about it, just let me know," Certain Certain says.

I haven't told him about how I lost his slave tag, how it saved my life. *Maybe my soul.*

What can I believe now?

I've seen too much. Besides, I'm just not built to not believe. Maybe all I can do is believe in *more.*

"You have to believe bigger. . . . The truth is not that small."

Lucy said that.

Everything is getting soft, starting to dissolve. The fog of the drip needle is starting to kick in.

"How's . . . Sugar Tom?" I say.

Certain Certain leans forward, tipping his ear to me. "What's that?"

"S'gar Tom," I say, slurring the words.

"Old skizzard? Talking."

"He *is*?"

"Like a teenage gal with a new callin' plan. Woke up late this evening; first thing he did was ask about you and the service."

"Is he—is he all right? His side, arm . . ."

"I don't know could he shin a bear up a tree without a stick, but he's a tough old cracker. He'll be all right, I'm thinking. But of course that's up to the Big Man."

"Can I . . . can I go see him?"

Certain Certain grins, his mouth tugging his tore-up lip into a grimace. He pats my arm.

"We can think about that in the mornin', boy. You lay back and get you some rest."

"But . . ."

"Don't worry. I'll be right outside. They goin' be beating this door down any minute. I'm gonna cut me a hick'ry pole, run they asses straight back to Peachtree Street, they get too rambunctious."

As he's going, I raise up my hand and wave. He stops.

"What?"

"Thanks," I say. "Thanks f'everything."

"Shoot."

And he's gone. I dream of nothing. Nothing at all.

➤EIGHTY-THREE➤

The first face I see the next morning is Miss Wanda Joy's. She comes stepping in, light as a cat in house shoes, when they wheel out my breakfast tray. She's looking about 300 percent better than she was. Her eyes are shooting black fire again.

"Well, Little Texas," she says, plunking down in the chair. She'd never think to sit on the edge of the bed like Certain Certain. "We had quite a time of it, didn't we?"

Miss Wanda Joy never asks how a person is doing unless she purposefully remembers to. It's just not her way.

"Are you okay?" I say. I scratch at the back of my hand where the drip needle was. "I'm sorry I didn't talk to them last night. I just . . . I wasn't feeling up to it. No. Really, it just didn't feel right."

She brushes my words away with a wave of her hand.

"It couldn't have worked out better. You won't *believe* the opportunities that have come out of this. Much better even than if the service had gone off without a hitch.

"We'll do the big networks first. NBC, Fox, CBS, anyone who will have us. As a courtesy. But *then*"—her dark eyes go wet—"then they will have to start paying. Cable channels. Magazines. Don't worry, I didn't give them much last night. Daddy King always said, 'Sell the steak with the sizzle.' A *book.* Do you think you could write a book? Just write it in your own words. I could help with the grammar."

"I don't know if—"

"Of course, everything is going to be so much bigger now. Your name will be known all across the country. The *world,* Little Texas. Just think about that! Japan. England. Perhaps even China. In South Korea, Billy Graham had an audience of *one million* attend a single service! But that's Billy Graham. As you know, fame is fleeting. What happened on that island will be old news in *days.* Maybe *hours.* If you want the maximum return, you have to keep it going, keep it in front of the public eye. Fan the flames. Tee Barlow knows a thing or two about this. He's got the island shut down in the meantime. We've hired some men to—well, don't worry about that. We book your new dates for you before the ink is even dry on the media contracts. With everything building to another service on the island. The television coverage would be enormous. The *money*—"

"But what about souls? Souls saved."

"Oh, that goes without saying! Now, the first thing is, we have this CNN thing set for this afternoon at two o'clock. We need to get someone in here, someone good and fast. I want your hair done, clean you up some. The cuts—the cuts are good. Stitches, perfect, that will really show up well. But here's the careful thing—we don't have a lot of time to go over this, what you need to say. We have to be so careful. Not one word about what happened to you after you went back. Not one word. We are saving that. Everything else—there are too many witnesses. Too many people already telling their stories. But what you saw, what happened when you were *alone,* that's the core."

"I wasn't alone."

"What? Well, of course you weren't. The Lord was there with you. Of course He was. We have to guard those details, save them . . . we especially can't afford to let it all dribble out in dribs and drabs. Now, here is how you are going to get around that, not telling them. Because it's the most important thing they will—"

"I'm not going to do this anymore," I say.

⇝ EIGHTY-FOUR ⇜

"Mercy," Certain Certain says after Miss Wanda Joy has left. "I would give ten dollars to have seen that woman's eyes when you told her."

We're moving slowly up the hall, me in a wheelchair, him pushing. "I feel stupid in this thing," I say. "There's nothing wrong with me."

"You sure about this now, Lightning?" Certain Certain says. "You know she's going to be after you, don't you? She ain't gonna let it lay."

"I know. But that's just the way it is."

"No changing your mind?"

"No. I won't . . ."

I let the thought trail away. I don't want to talk about the island. I don't know if I ever will. It's where I lost her. Selfish, I know. But I'm feeling a little selfish these days.

Maybe by not talking about it, I can hold on to her longer? Feels like talking about Lucy might water it down, make everything drizzle away. And then I'll have nothing.

Folks are so good at taking the most amazing experiences ever and turning them into something ordinary. Already some people are claiming there was a tornado on Devil Hill. How nobody ever really saw anything after all.

"It's so easy to not believe. That's what we're coming to," Sugar Tom likes to say. "Folks who know everything and know nothing at all."

"So whatcha going to do if you don't preach anymore?" Certain Certain says. "Won't you miss it?"

I let the wheelchair wheels turn a few turns. "I don't know. Go to a regular school. Maybe see a football game."

"Who you going to stay with?"

A scary little cold shivers through me. Scary, but also exciting. Like maybe I get to decide. "I haven't thought it out that far. What about you? You going on with the ministry?"

Certain Certain takes in a long breath.

"I've never been one to hurt for ways to make money. But it's been a long, long time since I ever did anything else. Besides, I can't see leaving Sugar Tom. Who's he got, if we all split up?"

"That's the whole thing," I say. "We shouldn't have to. We're a family. Families don't break up just because somebody wants to do something different."

We're quiet, both of us knowing we're thinking about Miss Wanda Joy.

"She's the one who'd have to change," Certain Certain says. "And I just can't see that happening. And you not being an adult, boy . . . that's something you going to have to work around. In two years you could join the army or something. Till then, I don't know. . . ."

We arrive at door number 302, and Certain Certain stops pushing. He knocks on the door gently and steps inside, then comes right back out.

"They helping him take a baffroom break. But it won't take too long."

I climb out of the wheelchair and stand beside him. I hang my head, looking down at my hands a long time. *Her hand*—it fit just there. *Her mouth.* I bite my own lip, remembering. I have to work hard to keep everything in. I can feel it all building behind my eyes.

Certain Certain gives me a little pinch on the arm. "Hey, big man. It's all right. It's all right."

I'm surprised to see Sugar Tom sitting up in bed when they let us in his room. He makes a big sputtering noise and drops his fruit cup.

"Ron'ld Ur!" he slurs, talking out of one side of his mouth. He's so thin. . . . Sugar Tom's holding his right arm funny, propping himself up with the other. There are cheap magazines spread around on the covers. BONES OF ST. JOHN THE REVELATOR DISCOVERED IN ARKANSAS, one of them says.

"Somebody ought to take a comb to your hair, doctor," Certain Certain says.

Sugar Tom starts to laugh, but it turns into a cough.

"How you feeling?" I say, touching his wrist.

"Puny," Sugar Tom says. He says something I can't make out, so I get him to say it again, cocking my ear closer. "I said puny's better'n being in South Dakota," he says.

"Did you see it?" I say. "South Dakota, I mean."

Sugar Tom puts down his plastic spoon. "Su-surely did, Ron'ld Ur. Grass waving right in . . . front of me. And she was there. Right there."

"Who was there?"

"Old *Pu*-laski," Sugar Tom says, spitting the word out. "My Pu-laski angel."

"Serious?" Certain Certain says. "That crazy little gal? Put a big hole in you?"

"Mayb'line Petty. I saw her. Pure as the living word. No . . . no pistol."

I laugh a little, then the laugh hangs in my chest. *Put a big hole in you,* I think. *Somebody filled up mine.*

"Where's your sooco?" Sugar Tom says.

"He ain't understanding you, Skizzard," Certain Certain says. "Have to speak up more clearly."

Sugar Tom looks at me, face getting red. He shifts on the bed.

"*Sooco,* son. Your sooco. No minister ever lived s'posed to go around without a sooco on."

Oh. *Suit coat.*

I remember my dream, waking up that time in the motor home, thinking Sugar Tom's suit coat was the devil. And I laugh. Then I laugh some more, till it's hard to stop laughing, and it's all running through me inside the laugh. All the bad parts and the hard parts. But the good is mixed in there with it. *Lucy.* And the good is so much stronger than all the rest, it's like the bad is something you threw in a river, and the river carries it away.

⇒ ACKNOWLEDGMENTS ⇐

Thanks to my fabulous editor and friend at Knopf, Cecile Goyette, and her wonderful assistant, Katherine Harrison.

Thanks to my extraordinary agent and friend, Rosemary Stimola.

Thanks to five fantastic writers, Catherine Ryan Hyde, Sena Jeter Naslund, Laurie Faria Stolarz, Lisa McMann, and Mary Pearson, for their friendship and kind encouragement.

Thanks to a matchless teacher and friend, Becky McDowell, as well as her brilliant students at Huntsville High School and notrequiredreading.com.

Thanks to my friends Amy Stewart, Shay Atchison, and Terri Hull, librarians extraordinaire, and their amazing students at Holtville Middle School and Stanhope Elmore High School.

Thanks to all my great new friends at the Alabama Writers' Conclave, the Alabama Center for the Book, MySpace, Facebook, the Writing Away Retreats, Black Cat Books in Manitou Springs, Colorado, and Tammy Lynn's Book Basket in Wetumpka, Alabama.

And, as always, thanks to my family, Deborah, Zach, Alex, Chris, and Joe.

And a special thanks to Socks and Paco for making my desk an adventurous place to be!

➤ABOUT THE AUTHOR ⋘

R. A. Nelson lives in northern Alabama with his wife, Deborah, and their four sons. A senior technical writer at NASA's Marshall Space Flight Center, Nelson loves poetry, quantum physics, old movies, spelunking, history, travel, astronomy, archaeology, basketball, exploring, and just plain old walking in the woods. He made an exciting literary debut with his critically lauded and controversial *Teach Me,* followed by *Breathe My Name,* which *School Library Journal* hailed as "thoughtful, moody, and entirely thrilling."

Days of Little Texas grew out of Nelson's longtime fascination with the fervor and messianic showmanship of revival preachers. As for ghosts, while Nelson's never seen one, he wouldn't dismiss the possibility of their existence out of hand. It occurred to him that it might be interesting to see what would happen if evidence of the existence of ghosts was forced upon someone whose religion demanded disbelief. With this notion came a corresponding vision of a teenage preacher and a beautiful girl in a blue dress—characters who became *Days of Little Texas*'s Ronald Earl and Lucy Palmer.

Writing *Days of Little Texas* was a joy and a challenge for Nelson, who doesn't mind tackling subject matter that "scares" him, meaning pushes him creatively. As a kid, he was the one who was always coming up with ideas for things to do or try, with the varying support of his brothers and "wonderful oddball friends." He created airplanes that were launched from a giant slingshot made from old tires, explored caves and bear-walked through storm sewers, built tree houses and forts, dreamed about inventing a time-travel machine, and designed a celebrated Horror House every Halloween.

In his adult life, Nelson continues to delve into a plethora of passions, including travel to obscure and mysterious places both far afield and close to home. He feels that there are "at least ten million or so very important things" that he should know but has yet to discover. The stories he has yet to create will no doubt draw upon both his treasury of past experiences and these future discoveries.

Visit R. A. Nelson on the Web at www.ranelson1.com.